Roped In

Additional Karen Maxwell Mysteries

George Washington Stepped Here
Worth Its Weight in Old

Also by K.D. Hays

Toto's Tale (with Meg Weidman)

Books by Kate Dolan

A Certain Want of Reason
Avery's Treasure
Deceptive Behavior
Langley's Choice
Restitution
The Appearance of Impropriety

For more information, visit www.kdhays.com

Roped In

A Karen Maxwell Mystery

K. D. Hays

ISBN-13: 978-1517380786
ISBN-10: 1517380782

DEDICATION

This book is dedicated to Jim McCleary and all the
coaches, past and present, of the
Kangaroo Kids Precision Jump Rope Team.
Thanks for all you have done to promote the sport!

For more information about competitive jump rope
and the people who contributed to this book,
please read the Author's Notes at the end.
Thanks!

Calling the landlord is something I look forward to about as much as having a tooth pulled or standing in line to get a new driver's license photo. But it had to be done.

I flipped through the names in the contacts on my computer, trying to remember whether I had listed him under his last name, Hagland, or just "L" for landlord. Or possibly "I" for "incompetent landlord."

From the length of time he took to answer, I could just imagine him sitting there, staring at the caller ID while he decided whether DS Investigations paid him enough rent to make it worth the effort to pick up the receiver. Leroy Hagland owns a lot of buildings in Ellicott City, but our office was in one of the crummy ones, tucked down in a hollow away from the restored stone buildings of Main Street. Here "restoration" was no more than a slap of paint and an exit sign in the stairwell to pass the fire inspection. So he never failed to let us know that we were about the least important of his tenants.

"H'lo, Mrs. Maxwell," his voice finally grumbled into my ear.

Since I've been divorced for five years, I hate being called "Mrs." and he knows it, but I think he takes a perverse joy in getting it wrong, so I tried to swallow my annoyance and focus on the reason for my urgent call.

"I know Rodney asked you about an air perfuming system," I began.

"It's an air purifier," Rodney insisted in a high-pitched nasal whine that carried all the way from his Administrator's cubicle on the other side of the office.

"Whatever." I waved for him to be quiet, even though he couldn't see me. Then I turned back to the phone. "Rodney didn't authorize you to add the charge to our rent. He just asked how much it would cost."

"I said we wanted to explore the option," Rodney clarified needlessly.

"So you don't want me to install the system?" Hagland asked in his perpetually tired and annoyed voice.

"No," I said firmly, "we do not. A thousand dollars a month is just too much."

"You can't put a price on clean air," Rodney admonished.

"Dave can," I called over to Rodney's cubicle, reminding him that my brother was still the boss.

Our intern, Brittany, giggled as she walked over to the printer.

I turned back to the landlord on the phone, "If you have your contractor pick up the trash more than once a month, I think we'll find the air a lot easier to breathe even without the Stratosphere 3000 air purifying system."

"Whaddaya mean, once a month?" Hagland growled. "Your garbage is picked up every week."

I shook my head, though of course he couldn't see that. "Nope."

"The truck comes at night, so you don't see him."

"He may come at night, but he doesn't pick up any

trash. The dumpster hasn't been emptied since the week after Christmas." I thought I saw a fruitcake in there we could probably salvage for next year's office party.

"Well, that hasn't been a month."

"It's been a lot more than a week."

There was a scratching noise that I assume was the landlord rubbing the phone against the stubble on his chin, but he might also have been using the phone receiver to scrape mud off his shoes or something. Finally, his annoyed voice came back on. "I'll look into it."

"I don't want you to look into our dumpster. I want you to empty it."

"You know what I mean," he snarled with even more force than usual. Then he just hung up.

"You should have been nicer to him, Karen." Rodney said as he came out of his cubicle balancing a tall green teacup on a tiny saucer. "Now he'll probably raise our rent."

I sighed. "You're right."

That stopped him. The teacup wobbled in his slender hand. "Y-you agree with me?"

"Yeah." I nodded. "He raises the rate every January."

But not by much.

I'd been handling administrative stuff at my brother Dave's investigation firm for over five years before he hired Rodney, the self-proclaimed "Office Maximizer" to "help" me. I knew how to deal with our recalcitrant landlord. I really knew how to manage all the office business without Rodney's help. But since I'd decided that I wanted to do some of the investigation myself, I simply didn't have time to do all the administrative work anymore. Of course we had a college intern working for us, too. Brittany The Bright-Eyed Wondergirl came in for at least a couple of hours every day to make the place look prettier. I couldn't see that she was much use beyond that.

Okay, that wasn't fair. She was interested in investigation and had helped me out with a few things. But she spent most of her time mistyping reports and scribbling incoherent phone messages.

Rodney spent most of him time "improving" the office to maximize efficiency. Last month, he tried to reorganize the office according to the principles of feng shui, but gave up when Dave spent the "coins of prosperity" on a hotdog. Right now, he seemed to think we needed improved air. The only useful thing I could tell that he'd done so far was to maximize our caffeine intake by keeping our new cappuccino machine in top operating condition. He particularly liked cleaning the milk wand.

He liked using it, too, so he very frequently made cappuccino for me, whether I wanted him to or not. Usually I did want it though, so this improved our working relationship tremendously.

Of course, a tremendous improvement on mud is only a better grade of mud, isn't it? Anyway, I continue to handle most of the bills, which is why I noticed the increase in rent before Rodney had a chance to order his air system. But now that I had that straightened out, I had to hurry and get through the rest of the bills before it was time to leave for my assignment.

Twice a month, I was supposed to follow Mrs. Linore Burkstead to the "Haute Coiture" salon and watch outside while she had her hair done. Her husband was convinced that she was having an affair with her stylist, so he hired our firm to do surveillance. He only wanted to pay for about a couple of hours a month, however, so if his wife was having an affair any place other than in the stylist's chair, he wouldn't be likely to learn about it.

It doesn't make much sense, but, as Dave says, it doesn't have to. As long as they pay us.

Mrs. Burkstead's appointment was at 2:30, so I would leave the office on Thursdays at about 2:00. By the time I had finished watching the shampoo and styling and followed her home, it was time for me to leave to meet my son when he got off the school bus.

That meant I had to get things finished early on Thursdays, and this mess with the rent had really slowed me down. I started to make really good progress on the rest of the bills however. All I had left was—

"I can't read this word. Is Dave coming in at all today?" Brittany whined from her desk.

I looked up to see her spin her chair around in frustration. Well, the first time, it was frustration. Then I think she spun around a few more times just for fun. The chair squeaked in protest with each turn, and her streaky blonde hair flew out around her head in a golden arc.

"Check the schedule." I nodded toward the oversized dry erase board chart Rodney had set up so that we could tell at a glance where all our "key players" were.

"It's blank." She snorted indignantly.

Of course it was. I knew Dave would never fill in his schedule in advance. We were lucky if we could figure out where he'd been *after* he'd been there, let alone before. The only thing on the schedule for this week was my surveillance at the salon and Rodney's meeting with an office furniture salesman.

"Is he on night surveillance again?" she asked with a spin.

"I can't remember," I mumbled in reply, hoping she'd take the hint and leave me alone. Just two more bills. Two. But I'd already lost my place and typed in the amount of the previous bill backward.

The phone rang and I reached for it out of habit, too late realizing I should have left it for Brittany or Rodney to answer. "Good afternoon," I said as I tried to type in the correct number with my left hand.

"Hi," a young man's voice said with enthusiasm. "Can I talk to Nate?"

"He's not here anymore. He retired." I switched the phone to my left hand so I could type with my right.

"Oh, great. I know he'll enjoy that. So, then could I talk to the new person in charge of capital purchasing?"

I stifled a groan. This chatty guy was just another telemarketer who happened to have our old senior partner's name in his database. "I'm sorry," I said quickly. "He's not available."

"Would that be..." the salesman paused ever-so-slightly as he no doubt looked through his database "Dave Sarkesian?"

"Yes."

"Can I speak with him?"

"No." Typing with one hand, I had almost managed to finish another bill. But I was probably putting in the amount backward again, since I couldn't focus while I was talking on the phone. "If you have information to pitch," I advised, "send it in the mail. We'll look at it when we have the chance."

"But this is a special offer, only available for a limited time."

"It so happens that limited time is just what I have. And you're not getting it. Good—"

"But I know Dave will want to take advantage of this offer!"

"—bye." I tried to put the phone back on the base without looking, but I missed and stuck it in a potted plant instead.

It was 1:45. Just one bill left. I could certainly finish by the time I had to go.

"Karen?" Brittany's voice broke into my thoughts about the Federal Express bill I was holding. "Who's the client with the night surveillance every few months? I'll look up the file."

"What?" I said, confused. There was a reason I needed to check the amount on the bill. But now I'd forgotten what it was.

Or was it the gas credit card bill that I was supposed to double check? .

My glance strayed to the clock on my desk. 1:48.

Brittany spun in her chair again. I think she'd just realized she could do this without tipping the chair over and it fascinated her. "Was it Wrey Electric?" she asked.

I gritted my teeth. "Why don't you get out the file and *see* if it was Wrey Electric?"

The chair squeaked, but the clomp of Brittany's clogs across the uneven floorboards indicated that she had stopped spinning and gotten up to find the file.

1:49.

The phone rang again. Brittany wouldn't be able to answer it in time; she was leaning over a file cabinet. Rodney was making espresso. With a sigh, I turned away from the bills and picked up the phone.

"Good afternoon," I said unconvincingly.

"Hey, Karen, it's Doreen."

Doreen, our insurance agent, is used to the nondescript greeting we use to answer the phone as well as my often rushed and unfriendly tone of voice. She sounded as cheerful as ever. I started to wonder whether I might enjoy a job in the insurance industry.

"Hello, Doreen." I shuffled through my notes, trying to remember what I had last asked her to do. She had to be calling me back about something. I was always asking her to look up stuff in her databases for us.

"Remember when I said you'd owe me?" she asked.

I let the papers fall to the desk. This time she was calling to ask *me* a favor. And I had about 10 minutes to help her. "I remember," I said guardedly.

"I need you guys to check something out for me."

"Uh-huh." I grabbed a pad of paper.

"We've got a claim for snow damage to a sunroom."

"Uh-huh." I wrote down *Snow damage. Sunroom.* We hadn't had much snow this winter. In fact, I think it had only snowed once so far, just a few inches, but that was enough to close schools for two days. We are pretty wimpy about snow here in central Maryland.

"Well," she continued, "the homeowners claim that the glass ceiling caved from the pressure and everything in the room was ruined."

This seemed pretty straightforward. I'm sure one of her regular investigators could have handled it, but if this was how she wanted the favor repaid, I wasn't going to object. Maybe her regular investigators were too busy.

"Okay," I said tapping the pen against the paper as I glanced at the clock. "Give me the address."

"There's more." Doreen hesitated.

"Oh?" It was now 1:54.

"They claim that everything in the room was damaged."

"You said that already."

"Everything is some furniture, carpet, and a rare parrot that was supposedly worth over $15,000."

The paper ripped as I dug the point of the pen into it. "A live parrot?"

"Well, I think he's dead now."

"No, I mean, not a parrot statue or something."

Doreen sighed. "Yeah, it was a real parrot."

"So," I scribbled a little design on the corner of the paper as I determinedly avoided looking at the clock, "you need us to find out if the bird's really dead?"

"We know he's dead. We need you to find out if he was in the room when it collapsed."

"What?" I laughed a little and it came out as a sort of a snort. "Do you think he was out partying or something?"

Doreen laughed, too. "No, probably not. But the pictures our investigator took make it look like the sunroom hadn't been finished at the time of the collapse. We don't think there was much of anything in the room at the time, including the parrot."

"Alright. I'll see what we can find out. You'll fax me your investigator's report?"

"Yep."

"Okay. Sorry to rush you, but I've gotta run."

"Thanks, Karen. I knew we could count on you."

I looked at the phone for a moment after I hung up. *A parrot. We're investigating the death of a parrot.* I knew right then Dave would assign the case to me. It would bring in no money and garner no prestige whatsoever for the investigator or the firm. But it might help restore his confidence in me, which had probably sunk pretty low after I got fired in the middle of my last case. My last real case. I didn't count overseeing a shampoo every week as real investigative work. I was starting to wonder if Dave was ever going to assign me any more real cases or whether I would be stuck doing routine bills and copyediting activity reports for the rest of my working life while everyone else in the firm did the actual work.

1:58. Time to grab my coat.

"I'm off to watch Mrs. Burkstead," I called to Brittany. "See you tomorrow."

"See ya." She waved the folder she was leafing through, presumably still looking for clues to Dave's whereabouts.

As I reached over to grab my purse out of the desk drawer, the phone rang again.

Rodney was still in the kitchen.

Brittany was still standing by the file cabinet.

With a sigh, I grabbed the receiver. "Good afternoon," I said tersely.

"I'm trying to reach DS Investigations," a woman said in a brusque but not unfriendly cultured voice. "Do I have the right number?"

"You do," was all I said in response. We keep our phone greeting as vague as possible to avoid tipping off relatives and friends of clients who find our number by mistake. "How can I help you?" I tried not to make my voice sound as tense as I felt. I'd been hoping this was another telemarketer so I could hang up and run. But if the caller was a potential client, I wanted to talk to her to increase the likelihood that I might get the case, should there be one. If I turned the phone over to Brittany, we probably wouldn't even get a legible phone number for this woman.

"I need to hire an investigator," she said gravely.

I waited in vain for her to continue. "Yes?" I prompted.

"But it needs to be… oh, how can I put this?" Gentility seeped through her voice, and I could almost picture her sitting under an enormous fan on the porch of an antebellum mansion, even though her accent put her closer to upstate New York than anywhere in the South. "It needs to be discreet," she said at last. "I can't have someone in a trench coat walking around with a magnifying glass at practice."

I smothered a laugh. "Discretion is priority in this business, ma'am." I pictured Dave skulking around in a trench coat with a big magnifying glass and almost lost it. I didn't think the potential client would be real impressed to have me giggle in her ear.

"Well, I wanted to see what your investigators look like, but you don't have any pictures on your website."

"No, ma'am." I'm not sure why I kept using the deferential "ma'am," since the woman didn't sound much older than myself. I think I just did it to try to keep myself from laughing at her ignorance. Maybe she thought we should have a big billboard on Route 40 so that everyone would know what our investigators looked like, including people being investigated.

"I wanted to come by the office," she continued with a faint whine in her voice "but you have only a post office box listed. You are local, aren't you?"

"Our office is in Ellicott City. Ma'am." Okay, now I was overdoing the "ma'am" bit, and I needed to cut it out and get a grip on myself.

"Well, you should have more information out there," she insisted. "I need to see what your investigators look like before I hire one."

"I think," I said slowly, "that if you tell me what this all about, then I can tell you whether we think we can help you. We don't put our investigators pictures online because investigations tend to be more effective when people don't realize they're being investigated."

"Well, yes, I guess that makes sense. What is your starting retainer?"

"Uh, nine hundred." The caller's suddenly businesslike question surprised me for a minute, but I knew that our retainer was lower than a lot of investigation firms, so it should be a good selling point for us.

"Very good. And how long has the firm been licensed?"

"Eighteen years." Nate had been in business that long. Dave had been licensed for a little less than 10 years. And I'd only had my license for two years and had hardly ever really used it. But she asked about the firm, not each of the investigators.

"Good," she said, as if checking items off a list. "And you promise that you can be discreet?"

"Of course." We'd never mingled with nobility or the rich and famous, but we had done work for the old moneyed families in Maryland and knew some of them could be passionate about maintaining their privacy.

"Good," she murmured, and again I had the sense that she was going through a checklist. I wondered if she might be the personal assistant to a rich woman who needed us to find missing heirloom jewels or locate the beneficiary of a testator's unexpected bequest.

"I need to hire an investigator," she said, rather redundantly.

"Yes," I said, trying to be patient as my gaze strayed to the clock. I was going to have to flat-out run down to Main Street to make it to the salon on time. But it would be worth it if I was able to rope in a new client. With this woman's educated voice and concerns about discretion, I thought we might be looking at something substantial. Even if it was just a woman wishing to keep tabs on her husband, she might be a client with enough money to pay for a extensive investigation. So I didn't want to make her feel rushed.

"Why do you want to hire an investigator?" I asked gently.

"I need an investigator. Your best investigator," she said firmly. "To find out who broke my daughter's jump rope."

2

"Your daughter's… jump rope?" I could hardly bring myself to say the words. A broken jump rope. I'd thought the dead parrot was as low as I could get for one day. This woman had to be crackers. And I'd had such high hopes from the tone of her voice.

"Yes," the woman continued smoothly, "my daughter jumps on a competitive team, and someone sabotaged her rope during the regional competition."

They had jump rope teams? Jump rope competitions? Wasn't jump rope something little girls in pigtails did during recess? "Uh, I'm not sure I understand," I mumbled, with a glance at the clock. Should I take notes? Or try to get her off the phone? Over the years we'd learned the hard way that even if a client was willing to pay, sometimes a matter just wasn't worth investigating.

"My daughter is a member of the Jumptastics Jump Rope Team," the woman explained with obvious pride. "You've probably seen one of their shows—they perform all over Howard County."

"Um, no, I guess I haven't seen them." *Because they're probably on the little kids' playground at recess*, my mind screamed. Jump rope is something to *do*, not something to watch.

"Well, in any case," she continued "Hayley has a chance to make it to the world competition in South

14

Africa. That is, she had a chance. Until someone did this to her."

South Africa? Who would take their little girl to South Africa to jump rope? If nothing else, maybe I could talk some sense into this woman. "Um, look Mrs. …"

"Callaghan. I'm Gina Callaghan."

"Mrs. Callaghan, how old is your daughter?"

"Seventeen. Eighteen next month."

My jaw hit the edge of the phone receiver. Girls that age are getting ready to go to college. They do not wear pigtails and jump rope at recess. I wanted to make sure I heard her correctly. "So your daughter is in high school?"

"Yes, at Centennial. She's a senior. I'm not sure if she'll be able to continue competitive jumping in college, so this is her last chance."

The desperation and concern in her voice sounded genuine. And the mother in me made me relent. So maybe this made no sense. If Gina Callaghan was willing to pay to have the firm investigate a broken jump rope, I guess we could do it. Or at least consider doing it. We could meet her in person.

"Okay," I turned to my desk calendar "can you come in tomorrow morning?"

"Yes, I think I can clear room in my schedule. What time?"

"10:30." That would give me time to run through paperwork and talk to Dave about Doreen's parrot.

"And where is your office?"

"As you're coming up Main Street from the river, you go about four blocks, past the Mexican restaurant, and look for Merryman Street on your left."

"Yes"

"Then come down the hill. We're in a two story brown building on the left side. Number 12. Come around to the side of the house and ring the buzzer. We're on the second floor."

"Are you in a house?"

"Well, it used to be a house, and it still looks like a house—from the outside." From the inside, it looked kind of like a hunting lodge decorated by Martha Stewart, with the Dave's beloved antler coat rack by the door and "improvements" from Rodney like a tabletop fountain that he plugged in to cover the noise from the photocopier. But I figured Gina Callaghan could see this all for herself in the morning and decide whether she wanted DS Investigations to look into her allegation of sabotage. And we could decide whether we thought she was nuts.

My son Evan is nearly 10-years-old now, so I shouldn't have worried about him being at home by himself for a short time after school. But I did anyway. His sister Alicia, who is 12 and almost old enough to legally babysit, would not be home until later because she was staying after school for drama club. But Evan is a good kid, not the daredevil type, except when it snows and he tries to use a cookie sheet as a snowboard.

Fortunately for me, there was no snow today, though it was cold enough for it. The undersized trees lining the road into my townhouse development stuck their bare brown branches into a dull grey sky. The ground was a mass of dried mud, decorated with tufts of dormant grass and bits of leftover leaves. An ugly winter day. But a safe one, and today I was grateful for that. No snow to tempt Evan to see if the dog could pull his sled along tire tracks in the street. I didn't think he could get into too much trouble before I finished my surveillance of Mrs. Burkstead and came home.

I was wrong.

I arrived home to find a fire engine in front of the house and Evan standing on the sidewalk with my neighbor Amy and her daughter, a cute little blond cherub of about five. Evan looked huge next to her, with his scruffy coffee-brown hair sticking up in odd places and his shirt sleeves hanging too long because he has a habit of stretching them out and pulling his hands up inside them. It actually made sense for him to do that now, since he was standing outside without a coat in January. No one seemed worried, and this kept me surprisingly calm.

Well, the dog was worried and barking as if the firefighters standing around the yard were aliens who had come to transport all her dog food to another planet, but I was used to that.

One firefighter was talking into a radio while two others looked over at me with bemused grins.

Now I was definitely not worried. I was wondering if I should be angry. Obviously the firefighters had been called out on a less-than-dangerous mission. I hoped it wasn't a prank call.

"What's going on?" I asked as I stepped over a small cluster of free newspapers that I was too lazy to pick up and walked over to Evan and Amy.

Evan slouched as if he thought he could curl up and make himself invisible. "Nothing."

I waved toward the fire truck. "Nothing?"

"Well, I…" He dug the toe of his shoe into the mud and looked at Amy.

She looked right back and nodded, as if urging him

to tell the story.

"I wanted to make a waffle," Evan said to the mud.

I wondered where this was going. "We don't have a waffle iron."

"No," he finally looked up at me, his dark eyes pleading for leniency, "just one of those waffles you put in the toaster oven."

"Okay." I nodded for him to keep going.

"And, well, I forgot about it, I guess."

"Huh?"

"I turned on the toaster oven and went to, um…" He looked down again.

"Play video games?" I guessed. He was supposed to do his homework first.

He nodded.

"So it caught on fire?" I guessed again.

He nodded. "It looked like a volcano. And all the smoke alarms went off.

"And so you came outside and asked a neighbor to call 911?" I guessed for a third time.

"Er, I didn't really have…"

"I came over and got him," Amy explained, pushing her glasses back up to the bridge of her nose. "I heard the alarms and since your van wasn't out front, I figured you weren't home from work yet. So I made him come over to my house."

"Yeah," Evan added, "except I wanted to stay outside since you always tell us to meet on the sidewalk if we have a fire."

Suddenly I felt weak. There really *had* been an emergency, and if my quick-thinking neighbor hadn't been home watching, Evan might have been in serious danger. I grabbed Amy's arm. "Thank you," I said in a shaky voice.

"It was nothing," she said. We just happened to be outside watching because Nicole likes to be out when all the kids get off the school bus."

"But Evan could have been—"

"No," she reassured me quickly. "The firefighters said there was nothing burning when they checked out the house. It all stayed inside the toaster oven. No harm done."

"But what if you hadn't come over? What if he'd tried to put it out with water and—"

"I wouldn't do that, Mom," Evan insisted. "I know not to use water around electric things. We learn that in Scouts. Every year."

"You see?" Amy smiled. "It would have been okay."

I shook my head. It might not have been okay. It was just sheer luck that Evan wasn't hurt or killed. I should never have left him alone. "You are not allowed to use the toaster oven," I admonished Evan, waving a finger in his face just like a mom in a cartoon. "Ever!"

"But Mom…"

"Not ever, do you understand?"

With a look of hurt and disgust, he turned and ran off, disappearing around the hedges at the side of the house.

My hands were shaking, and my voice had come out all harsh and angry. But inside, I knew that shaking was due to fear, not anger. Well, yes it was anger. Anger at myself, not at him. He couldn't know that, of course. And by the time I'd realized it myself, he was gone with no chance for me to apologize.

I sighed and raked my hands through my hair, which is about as close as I get to combing it most days since it's so short. Then I remembered that Amy and her daughter were still standing there. I turned to her and attempted to smile and joke about it. "Well, that went well, don't you think? I've probably got him dying to turn on the toaster oven every chance he gets now."

She put a hand on my arm reassuringly. "Don't worry about it."

"It was my fault for leaving him alone."

"He has to learn to be alone sometime."

"But he's obviously not ready yet."

"Oh, I don't know. He handled himself very—"

"He almost burned down the house!" I interrupted hysterically. "And himself with it."

At the height of my motherly melodrama, I heard a man clear his throat behind me. A voice crackled on a radio nearby, and I remembered the firefighters. I turned to see if they were still enjoying the episode.

All of them except the man who had come up behind me were back on the truck. The one who was left, the guy in charge, I guess, had a serious expression, so if he thought the incident was funny, he was at least making an attempt to hide his amusement.

"We've searched the premises, and everything's secure, Ma'am," he said. "The best thing to do would have been to close the door on the toaster oven and wait for it to burn out. But since he was alone, calling us was the right choice."

"Er, thanks." I couldn't look him in the face. Even the firefighters knew I made a mistake leaving a nine-year-old alone.

"This is Unit Four," the firefighter drawled into his radio. "We are headed back to the station."

"Thank you," I said as he started to turn away.

He nodded in acknowledgment as he responded to something else on the radio. One of the guys on the truck waved. As the truck pulled away, the dog started up another frenzy of barking in the backyard. Thank heavens she was outside so nothing would have happened to—

But Evan had been inside. Did I care more about my dog than my own son? What kind of a mother—

Now I was overreacting again. Nothing happened. I needed to get a grip on myself.

I turned back to Amy, who was kneeling down next to her daughter, pointing to the back of the fire engine.

"Didn't get to see the ladder." The girl pouted from inside the fur-rimmed hood of her puffy winter coat, "And they didn't spray any water…"

Amy's round face lit with an indulgent smile as she pushed her glasses back up on her nose again and turned to me almost apologetically.

I forced myself to smile in return. "I need a Diet Coke. Want one?"

"No, thanks." She sighed. "I've gotta get dinner started. But can I get you to join me on a walk later?"

I hesitated. Just spending time with Amy did not automatically guarantee that I was going to reveal another example of how messed up my life had become. Yes, our walks did tend to evolve into discussions of my children's problems or ex-husband's inadequacies, but it didn't have to be that way. I could force her to reveal some defect in her husband. Or her adorable daughter. Or maybe she had a problem goldfish or something.

"Please?" she begged. "You know I'll make up some excuse to sit down in front of the TV if you don't go with me."

I mentally checked my schedule and didn't remember anything in particular that I had to do, so I caved."Sure, I'll go. Eight o'clock okay?"

"Yep, it's perfect."

Nicole tugged at her mom's blouse. "I go to bed at eight."

"That's why it's perfect," Amy answered, taking her hand.

"But I wanna go," the little girl insisted, jumping up and down.

Amy started to steer her daughter toward their house across the street. "See you later," she called to me.

"I wanna go!" Nicole repeated, still jumping even though her mother was pulling her forward.

"No, it will be past your bedtime," Amy answered.

"But I WANNA!" the girl screamed at a volume that seemed physically impossible from a body that size. I wondered if she was wearing a hidden microphone. She dug her heels firmly into the ground to prevent her mom from pulling her any further.

Amy was probably going to have to pick her up to get her home.

"Bye." I waved as I turned away quickly so that Amy to deal with this rebellion without an audience. Maybe her life wasn't as perfect as it seemed. Maybe I'd forgotten what it was like to live with a five-year-old.

Maybe my life wasn't as messed up as I thought.

Then a rush of panic flooded over me as I saw a white pickup truck turn the corner.

Maybe I'd forgotten that I'd invited my boyfriend Brian and his parents over for an early dinner.

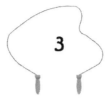

3

A welcoming hostess would have waited out on the lawn and walked up to greet her guests with a smile as they parked in front of the house.

I was not a welcoming hostess.

I raced inside as fast as I could and slammed the door behind me.

Was it Thursday already? I couldn't believe I had forgotten. They must have the wrong day. It had to be the wrong day.

After I looked frantically through the jumbled entries on the kitchen calendar, not even able to remember what week we were in, I finally made myself stop.

It didn't matter if they had the wrong day. They were here, and I had to do something about it.

Fast.

This would be my first time meeting his parents, and of course their first time seeing my house, so I had to make sure it wasn't a complete disaster.

From the tiny narrow foyer, I stepped into the almost-as-tiny kitchen. My gaze scanned the table and counters— an empty toaster waffle box, a sleeve of crackers, a can of spray cheese and a cup with cloudy liquid in the bottom. Not too bad, actually. Just the remnants of Evan's after school snack.

But I looked through the counter behind the sink

that opened into the next room, I cringed. My guests would be spending most of their time in the nebulous open space that serves as a living room, dining room and dog highway to the backyard. And it looked like a war zone. There was no time to deal with the brown streaks on the carpet by the sliding glass doors or the stacks of baby pictures waiting to be sorted into albums. But I had to clear off the dining room table or all six of us would be eating in a miniature kitchen that still smelled faintly like burnt waffles.

Unfortunately, since we don't eat there very often, the dining room table had become a depository for everything from school notices to folded laundry, not to mention the miscellaneous junk that I couldn't ever put away because it didn't really have an "away." The edges of the table were littered with a tube of superglue, a little bag of extra buttons from a new blouse, half a package of shoelaces, a book of poems given to me by Evan's teacher, and a half- eaten candy cane with fuzzy antlers and googly eyes. It all had to go.

I grabbed the afghan off the living room sofa, laid it on a chair, and pushed everything off the table onto the afghan. Then I wadded it all up together and stuffed it in the corner, behind a fake potted plant. Now that the junk was off the table, though, I could see how dusty it was. No time to get a dust cloth. The only loose fabric in sight was the afghan, and that was already gainfully employed.

My shirtsleeve? I was wearing a white blouse, so that would be pretty obvious.

Ding! The doorbell. Time's up!

I swiped the biggest swath of dust off with the tail of my blouse, tucked it into my pants, and headed back down the narrow foyer to the front door.

Evan's backpack was sitting right next to the door where he'd dropped it when he came in. The straps lay in front of the threshold, as if he'd laid a deliberate snare to trip up whoever came in the door next. I picked up the backpack, but the only place I had time to move it was into the already overcrowded coat closet. As I shoved the bag inside, the handle of the vacuum cleaner swung out to jab me in the leg. Pushing the vacuum handle back in with one hand, I quickly shut the door with the other hand, trapping my attacker inside as the hinges squealed in protest.

Then I turned to the front door, hoping I hadn't just wiped a big wad of dust across my face. I couldn't believe they were here already. I know we'd agreed on an early time so that they could get to a show later downtown, but it couldn't be more than 4:30.

What kind of person shows up for dinner at 4:30?

"Hello," I said as I pulled the door open, hoping I'd remembered to smile. I probably hadn't done it in time.

A big man filled the doorway—Brian's dad, presumably,—so I could see right away where Brian got his size. He was actually a little taller than Brian and though his hair was thinning and gray, he stood straight, with no stooping or other sign of age.

He wasn't frowning, exactly, but he wasn't smiling, either, and that made him look a little forbidding.

The petite woman at his side was easier to face. "Hello, Karen." Much smaller than either her husband or her son, Brian's mom shared her son's wide, open features, warm smile, and bright blue eyes that sparkled with a sense of mischief, as if any moment could turn into an occasion for laughter. Her smile made me feel a little less jumpy, but I found it a little disconcerting to have someone I had never met speak as if she knew me.

I felt I was at a disadvantage somehow.

I was, actually. She knew my name, and I just knew her as "Brian's mom," Mrs. Kieffer.

As I stepped back to allow them to come in, I hoped desperately that the bathrooms weren't too dirty or the dog hadn't left anything embarrassing by the patio door. Brian was the last one to come in, and as he did, he leaned in close, grazed my cheek with a kiss, and whispered "Sorry we're early. Dad gets real nervous about traffic getting into the city."

The sound of his rich voice, the tickle of warm breath against my ear and the strength of having him at my side made all the unease fade to insignificance. If I needed to live through moments like these to have this man in my life, it was worth it.

I would have given him a hug, but the last time I did, one of my earrings got tangled in his long hair and I didn't want to risk it. His dark wavy hair was tied back as usual, but loose tendrils escaped to curl around his face.

Besides, his parents might not approve of a hug in front of them.

What is it about being around parents that turns us into insecure children again?

Brian stepped over to his mom in the living room and took her coat. This raised a warning flag in my mind, but I wasn't sure why. I was hoping fervently that there weren't great huge balls of dog hair hanging on the legs of the coffee table.

"You have a lovely home, Karen," Mrs. Kieffer said. "Such an understated decor."

What did that mean? Did that mean she thought I had no decor? Well, she was right. My townhouse was still painted the original neutral tones given to it by the builder, with cheap nondescript vinyl flooring in the entry hall and kitchen and carpet that could be called the color of dry dirt throughout the rest. I tried to keep it fairly clean, but had never been ambitious enough to put up fancy window treatments or anything.

"Thank you," I said, deciding it had at least nominally been meant as a compliment.

The squeal of door hinges warned me that Brian was opening the coat closet to put his mom's coat inside.

"Wait," I lunged toward the closet, "why don't we—"

My voice was drowned out by the avalanche of bookbags, boots, umbrellas, badminton racquets and other closet debris that tumbled out onto Brian's feet.

I think I flushed down to the roots of my hair. "Sorry."

"S'okay." He grinned as he quickly tossed everything back inside. The vacuum cleaner handle shot out toward him, but he caught it and stuffed it back without missing a beat.

In the living room, Mrs. Kieffer cleared her throat. "Brian said you have two children?" She looked around as if expecting to see them climb out from under the sofa.

"Uh, yes." I hurried into the living room to join her. "Evan and Alicia. "There they are." I pointed to their portraits on the wall by the stairs. Evan in his soccer uniform, proudly clutching a ball, and Alicia in a pink tutu with a crown on her head. Okay, those pictures were a little old. Alicia had long since quit ballet and liked to wear black nail polish and big clomping heavy boots. And while Evan still loved soccer, he had lost the round cherubic face and wide spaced baby-teeth grin of his preschool years.

"They'll be joining us for dinner, I hope?" Mrs. Kieffer asked.

"Alicia will be late. She has play practice and doesn't get dropped off until about 5:30."

With a nervous glance, Mr. Kieffer stepped toward his wife, and said in a low voice, "We're not going to wait that long before we—"

She cut him off with a casual wave of her hand. "No, don't worry. Of course not."

He was going to say "before we eat."

They expected to eat at 5:00 probably. Right when I had suggested. But I had been thinking they would arrive at five and eat about 5:30 or 5:45. Their show didn't start until 8:00.

I glanced at the clock on the wall. It was 4:40. I could barely get a carryout pizza on the table before five. And Mrs. Kieffer didn't exactly look like the type to eat out of a cardboard box. She had a casual elegance, as if she wore clothing that had been personally designed for her and had spent her life posing for "candid" magazine photos. Like one of the Kennedys or something.

I wasn't going to serve macaroni and cheese or fish sticks to this woman.

Inviting them over on a weeknight had not been one of my better ideas. I'm sure when they met Brian's first wife, she had planned everything to the last detail. But even if she hadn't, I'd heard that Chloe was one of those talented people who could make anything out of nothing.

I was not.

"Would you like something to drink?" I asked, rather forlornly. I had planned to make two kinds of iced tea and this lemon punch that one of Brian's friends had made at the historic site where he volunteers on Saturdays. But of course, since I'd forgotten the dinner, I hadn't gone shopping, and I had no lemons or fancy teabags. I didn't have time to make the drinks even if I had the ingredients. I was sunk.

"Thank you. Anything without caffeine would be great," Mrs. Kieffer said.

"Would you care for something?" I asked Mr. Kieffer.

He shook his head.

"Hey, Dad," Brian said, "Karen has a border collie that looks just like our old dog, Shiloh."

"Oh, yeah?" His eyes brightened, and for the first time, he actually looked interested in being at my house.

"Yeah. She's out in the back." Brian waved toward the glass door that led out to the deck.

His dad stepped up to him and almost grinned. "Bet you want to keep her out there, too."

"Ah no, she's great. Go take a look."

As his parents walked toward the back of the living room, he turned to follow me into the kitchen. "I'll help you with the drinks," he offered.

"What did he mean about keeping my dog in the yard?"

"Nothing. Just an old joke." He opened a cabinet. "I'll get out glasses."

"Thanks." I peered into the refrigerator. "I don't suppose your mom likes Ice Blue Gatorade?"

He laughed. "No, probably not. But she loves water with a splash of lemon and orange juice, if you have that."

"That I probably do have." There was about an inch of orange juice left in the carton and a bottle of lemon juice on the door.

"I'll fix it. And you can give my dad a glass of milk," Brian suggested.

"But I didn't think he wanted anything."

"Mom will make him drink it before dinner. She says it helps prevent heartburn."

I picked up two of the glasses he'd taken out and held them up to the light to make sure they really looked clean. "So she knows my cooking will give him heartburn, huh?"

"Everything gives him heartburn."

"It's probably from all the milk." I handed him a glass for his mom and poured milk into the other one.

"Maybe." Brian grinned. "But I've never had the nerve to suggest it, and I'm sure dad hasn't either."

We had been speaking in low voices, but now I let mine drop to a whisper. "So does she rule the house?"

"Definitely," Brian whispered back. "Dad would not willingly drive all the way to Baltimore to see a musical about hairstylists. But Mom wanted to see it, so…"

I laughed as I put the milk back into the refrigerator. "And she's got you going along, too."

"Yeah. But at least I like musicals."

Just as I was starting to relax again, I saw the time on my watch. "Oh, rats."

"What?"

"Nothing." I peered at the refrigerator shelves desperately, as if I expected to find a fully cooked dinner hiding behind the tub of sour cream.

"Karen," there was a note of warning in Brian's voice. We had some problems with me not communicating very well, and I guess he figured I was headed down that road again.

Which was true.

"Okay." I shut the refrigerator and turned to face him. "I forgot that you were bringing your parents over tonight. I don't have anything ready for dinner. I haven't even been to the grocery store."

He grinned. "Yeah, I figured as much."

That made me a little mad. I was visibly upset and he found it amusing? "So," I demanded, "I look as flustered as I feel?"

"No, it's not that. But, it always smells like food in this house, whenever I come over for dinner."

If he was trying to reassure me, it wasn't working. "You mean my house smells like a restaurant?"

"No, like someone's been home cooking all day, like in a spaghetti commercial. But when we walked in just now it smelled like…"

"Wet dog?"

"Well, yeah, a little. But more like, I don't know, dried flowers or perfume or something."

"Potpourri," I murmured. "The fall fundraiser for the drama club."

"Okay, that's the smell."

I sighed. "I can't serve that for dinner, though."

"No…" He opened the cabinet with the pots and pans, and then quickly closed it as if he knew right away it didn't have what he needed.

"What are you looking for?"

He opened the cabinet with the canned food. "Do you have any carrots?"

"Yeah, but I keep them in the refrigerator."

"And some rice?"

"I think so."

"Then we're all set." He pulled out two cans and set them on the counter triumphantly. "My dad likes

Spam."

I looked suspiciously at the dusty can he was pointing to. "This must have been left from the previous owner of the house. I never buy Spam."

He picked up the can. "It says it's still good for a while yet."

"Let me see that." I reached for the unfamiliar rectangular can. "It says '16.' That's probably 1916."

He laughed. "Just fix the rice and grate some carrots for me and I'll do the rest."

"I'm not serving suspicious Spam to your parents."

"It's my dad's favorite dish."

"Spam and grated carrots? What, does he have bad teeth?"

"Mom calls it 'Hawaiian Haystack.' It's rice with diced Spam and cream of chicken soup and whatever else she happens to have around. I figured you probably had carrots. Pineapple is good, too, but I didn't see any."

"Nope, we're out."

"Grated cheese is good, too."

"I probably have some."

"And those crunchy Chinese noodles."

"You're out of luck, there. But I do have Fritos"

He nodded. "Hey, I've used them before."

"You make this a lot?"

"Every time they come over."

I guess I didn't look convinced because he came over and draped his arms over me in a big reassuring hug. "Relax, Karen," he said softly. "Everything will be okay."

And for that moment, at least, I could believe it. If I hadn't been keenly aware of his parents being in the next room needing to be fed, I think I could have just stayed in Brian's arms and forgotten about all the annoying things that had happened that day, or any other day for that matter.

But the dog barked outside. Mr. Kieffer made a comment, and that was the end of that moment. "We'd better get you all fed and off to the theatre," I murmured as I pulled away. It was gratifying to see that he looked as reluctant to let me go as I felt leaving his arms.

While I grated carrots and cheese, Brian fixed everything else and even managed to find Evan and talk him into setting the table. I still hadn't figured out why we had Spam in the cabinet—maybe I bought it for a canned food drive at school and then forgot to send it in. Anyway, it worked. Spam and all that other stuff. Brian's parents thought I'd planned it deliberately and even my kids liked it.

Mrs. Kieffer was an easy conversationalist, encouraging Brian to talk about his latest plans for his church youth group and when Alicia arrived, getting her to tell us about her roles in the drama club.

"Aren't you in any of his plays?" Mrs. Kieffer asked, looking from Alicia to her son.

"They're just for high school kids," Alicia answered a little wistfully. She shook a lock of chestnut brown hair out of her eyes with a dramatic toss of her head.

Mrs. Kieffer raised one eyebrow as she looked at Brian, (which is a very cool intimidating mother trick that I would love to learn someday). "Well, if that isn't the silliest rule I've ever heard."

"Mom," Brian explained, "we have to keep some things separate, just for the older kids."

His mother's gaze never wavered.

"But, you know," he continued, "Alicia has been

coming to the middle school youth group the last few weeks and some of them have talked about wanting to perform so maybe we can work something out."

That was as good as done and both females knew it. They exchanged a knowing glance, and Alicia looked appropriately grateful. This would be her reward for going to church each week.

Though I guess I've always believed in God, I had not been a real "church person" for most of my life. But Brian was, so for my New Year's resolution this year, I had vowed to make an effort to go every Sunday. The kids came with me, or at least they had so far on the weekends they hadn't been with their dad. It was a big church. Less formal than the ones I had been to as a kid, so that was good, but it was full of people who all seemed to know each other. Of course I didn't know any of them. I could handle it for an hour each week, but I couldn't quite see how Brian could want to spend so much time there with youth group, and the basketball league and Sunday School and all the other stuff he did. But then, I really had only known him a few months, and I'm sure he didn't know what made me do half the stuff I did, either.

We still had a lot to learn about each other.

I knew quite a bit about his hobbies, but almost nothing about his job as an engineer at some firm in Columbia.

He knew substantially more about my job, since we met while I was investigating a theft at the colonial house where he volunteered and he was one of the suspects.

"Brian told me you're interested in living history, too?" Mrs. Kieffer asked me when there was a lull in the conversation.

"Well," I pushed a little piece of diced Spam around on my plate as I tried to think of a diplomatic way to answer her question. "I, uh, have been learning a little bit about it." I had pretended to have an interest in history so I could go undercover as a volunteer at the site where Brian worked as a blacksmith on Saturdays. That was my first case, and since it ended, I hadn't been back, which said a lot about my true interest in history.

"Karen was at the 1776 House for work, actually," Brian explained. "She's a private investigator."

His voice rang with pride as he spoke. I was a little embarrassed at the way he almost bragged about my job and implied that it was much more impressive than it really was, but I was also flattered. And I realized that he must have told his mom about me back before he knew why I was at the 1776 House, back when he thought I was just another volunteer. So maybe he'd been interested in me just as long as I'd been interested in him. It was a reassuring thought.

But embarrassment was the unhappy emotion that won out, because suddenly Mr. Kieffer took an interest in the conversation. He leaned forward across the table, fixing me in his gaze. "An investigator, eh? Do you work with local police a lot, or do you find that they get in the way?"

"Most of them work pretty efficiently, so I can't say they get in the way." We seldom ever work on anything while the police are involved. People call us for things the police won't investigate.

"Uh, huh." He nodded. "And when there's been a murder, how long do they rope off the crime scene?"

I hated to disappoint him, but I had to shake my head. "I don't really know. Our firm doesn't get called on murder cases." That's something the police *will* investigate.

"Do you have a forensic specialist at your firm?"

"Well, no, because—"

His face fell as the realization struck that my job was not anything like the shows on TV. "Oh, I guess not if you don't investigate murders."

"We leave that for the police."

"But I'm sure you must work on some very interesting cases," Mrs. Kieffer interjected smoothly. "Remember all those wonderful stories Chloe used to tell about the children she taught? I'm sure Karen has a lot of great stories like those."

I appreciated the attempt to bolster my importance, but I really didn't want to talk about my job or be compared with Brian's deceased wife. My status as an actual investigator was pretty precarious, since I'd been fired from my second case and hadn't really had an opportunity to prove to my brother that I was capable of taking the lead in an investigation. I felt like talking about it would be sure to invite disaster of some sort. And I didn't exactly have a stash of amusing prepared stories ready to entertain people as Chloe apparently had.

"Most investigation work is done on a computer now," I explained. "So much more information is available online than there used to be."

"But you do go out in the field, obviously, or you wouldn't have been out at the 1776 House," Mrs. Kieffer observed.

"I do. On occasion."

"Oh, I'll bet you really have had some really interesting cases," she said with great enthusiasm. "But you probably can't talk about them, can you?"

"No, I can't," I said quickly, grateful that she'd

given me an easy out. "Client confidentiality."

And this was true of course, although I could give out some general information in a way that wouldn't violate confidentiality standards.

But I was incredibly grateful to Brian when he looked at his watch and suggested that it might be time for them to finish up and head out to the theatre. There was no way I was going to admit that I was about to spend the next few weeks investigating the death of a parrot and a broken jump rope.

4

The short drive to the office the next morning didn't give my cell phone enough time to fully recharge, but at least it had enough power to turn on. So while I searched in vain for a parking place, my ears were assailed with the piercing tune Evan had selected to alert me that I had new text messages. I was sure he listened to every choice my phone offered and then picked the one he thought would annoy me most.

Of course, it would have been worse if he had picked the annoying tone because he thought it was the one I'd *like* the most. Did he think my taste in music was that awful?

The tone repeated again. I definitely needed to figure out how to program the thing for myself. I couldn't be dependent on my children forever.

Parking had become more difficult to find in Ellicott City during the five years I'd been working in Dave's office. Main Street, with its eclectic collection of shops and restaurants, had been a nightmare for years, but now the side streets were often jammed, too, even the unfashionable ones like Merryman Street. Each week it seemed like I had to park further and further away from the office.

Fuming about the time I'd wasted did not put me in a good mood when I finally found a spot three blocks away from the office. And to get to the sidewalk, I had to climb over an enormous pile of boxes filled with paper, cans and other stuff set out next to the curb for recycling. I stepped on a loose water bottle, and it slid out from under my foot so that I collapsed into a pile of yogurt containers. Fortunately, they had been rinsed out so I wasn't covered with sour milk or raspberry goo.

It seemed that the trash wasn't getting picked up here, either. Or to be precise the recycling, which is a cleaner version of trash. If you have to fall into a pile of something on the edge of the road, recycling is about the best you can hope for.

Not that I really appreciated my good fortune as I walked down the hill to the office. Before long I started thinking about the Friday staff meeting. We probably couldn't avoid it any longer.

"Nine-thirty in the conference room," Rodney announced as I was hanging up my coat on the antlers.

"Conference room?" I tried not to groan aloud. The headquarters of DS Investigations consisted of a large open space with an office carved out of the corner for Dave, a cubicle in the adjacent corner for Rodney, a tiny kitchen, a bathroom, and a former coat closet which I sometimes used as my own office when I needed to practice my contortionist skills or escape from the rest of the staff. The open space in the middle held the receptionist's desk where I usually sat, a copier, a smaller desk for Brittany, printers, and filing cabinets which Rodney had rearranged several times since Dave hired him a couple of months ago. There was no conference "room." But Rodney had decided that we could create a temporary one by bringing our own desk chairs into a cluster in front of the photocopier. We just had to make sure that Dave wasn't sitting close enough to it to set his coffee cup down on the sorter tray, because machines lubricated with lumps of undissolved coffee creamer don't function at their peak.

I'd hoped he'd given up this idea, but then, Rodney was not one to give up easily. He'd decided that we needed to have staff meetings every Friday morning to recap the week and set the schedule for the next week. Dave liked the idea—in theory—the way he likes all of Rodney's ideas until he actually has to live with one of them. So far we had managed to come up with excuses to avoid the staff meeting, but this time we'd forgotten all about it and now I feared it was too late.

"We have a meeting at 9:30," I informed Brittany when she strolled in a few minutes later, her face red from the January air.

"Okay." Her platform clogs sounded heavily on the bare wood floor as she clopped over to her small desk and slung her backpack underneath it. Then she turned back to face me. "Why?"

"It's our weekly staff meeting. Where we meet."

Her forehead wrinkled in confusion. "I don't get it. We meet every time we're at work together."

"This is so we can tell each other about what we're working on." I couldn't believe I was justifying Rodney's idiotic idea.

"I can just text everyone and tell them what I'm working on," she explained as she dug her cellphone out of her hip pocket. "And then I don't have to move my chair."

"The exercise will do us all good," I said as I headed to the kitchen for coffee. The only thing more inefficient than a staff meeting would be a staff texting session.

Fortunately, Dave didn't arrive until after 10 and we

had a meeting with Gina Callaghan set for 10:30 so by the time Dave got settled into his chair with his package of hot fudge Pop-Tarts and blonde coffee, Rodney only had a short time to hold us captive.

I started the meeting by describing the cases closed that week and listing the ongoing surveillance. Then I told everyone we had a potential client coming at 10:30 and I hinted that we were going to need to return a favor for Doreen regarding an insurance investigation. I didn't go into detail about that because really, I couldn't handle thinking about dead parrots and a broken jump rope all in the same day.

Brittany said she'd typed reports, filed papers and entered three pages of phone numbers and email addresses into a database. Dave said he couldn't tell us anything because it would violate client confidentiality. I could have pointed that it wouldn't, since everyone in the firm had access to the case files, but then he'd just make up another reason to keep from reporting, so I made no objection.

Then it was Rodney's turn. "I have a plan for the office that I know you will be excited about," he began in his cool polished professional unexciting voice. "My girlfriend gave me a desk calendar with a new surefire success business idea for each day of the year." He held up a square pad of paper labeled "Surefire Success," illustrated with a smiling raccoon on the cover.

I wondered if each day had its own coloring page, too.

"I've seen a couple of weeks' worth now," he continued, "and they've included some really outstanding ideas. So I'm going to incorporate the best of them into our business plan. Let me read you some of these pearls of wisdom." He began to thumb through the pages.

"I don't believe it," Dave muttered.

"I didn't think we had a business plan, either," I whispered back.

"No, I mean I don't believe this guy has a girlfriend. He still lives with his mother."

Brittany leaned over toward both of us. "He dresses well," she whispered as Rodney continued to flip through his calendar. "And he drives a really hot car."

"Yeah?" Dave countered. "I'll bet half the time his mother is in the back seat."

She shrugged. "Tinted windows. No one can tell."

"Listen to this." Rodney looked up at us and cleared his throat. "'If you fail to plan, you may as well plan to fail.' So true!" He flipped to another page. "And this one: 'It takes as much energy to wish as it does to plan.' Eleanor Roosevelt said that."

So far this didn't look too bad. If Rodney's new business plan just consisted of him reading a 10-word quote each week, it wouldn't be too painful at all.

"And how about this." Rodney waved his calendar with a flourish. "Shakespeare said, 'Our doubts are traitors, and make us lose the good we oft might win, by fearing to attempt.' Wisdom from the best-selling writer of all time."

I wondered whether Shakespeare's sales figures had been eclipsed by the Harry Potter books or the Twilight series, but decided that really wasn't the point of the exercise. We'd listen to Rodney read once a week—

"So," he said with the light of zeal in his eyes, "I will be sharing these ideas with you each day"

—Or day. It still wouldn't be a huge waste of time and energy, and it would cost nothing. Even the calendar was already paid for with outside funds.

I think Rodney would have continued to share several more days' readings with us, but Dave stood and pointed to his watch. "Got a client comin' any minute." He stuffed the last handful of Pop-Tart in his mouth and wiped a spray of crumbs from his shirt front onto the floor.

"Next time let me vacuum you off first," I admonished.

He made a face and started for his office. Then he turned back and pointed to the chair he'd been sitting in. "Get that for me, will you?"

"He means you," I said to Rodney, and I wheeled my own chair back into the old coat closet before he could argue.

I had a meeting to prepare for, after all. A meeting about a broken jump rope was still a meeting.

The buzzer to the security door downstairs sounded promptly at 10:28, allowing our client one minute to walk up the stairs, 30 seconds to catch her breath, smooth her hair and freshen her lipstick, and another 30 seconds to saunter into the office precisely on time. For some reason, I was sure this woman would be precise and well groomed.

I hit the button to unlock the downstairs door.

"That foul sounding 'buzz' is really not a friendly welcome for clients, you know," Rodney admonished as he pushed Dave's chair past me. "We shouldn't lock potential customers out."

"It is the potential weirdos we need to lock out," I reminded him. Sometimes they were one and the same. Even though I expected Gina Callaghan to look, act and pay like a normal person, I still had my doubts about a woman willing to hire a professional investigator to find out who broke her daughter's playground toy.

I picked up an extra chair to move into Dave's office since we'd have to meet in there. He might not ask me to stay; in fact most of the time he met with new clients alone. But I insisted on being part of this meeting because I had a feeling he'd assign this case to me, and I'd have to take it. I still needed to prove I could satisfy a client without getting fired.

A pungent fishy odor assailed my nostrils as I entered Dave's inner sanctum. "Ugh. How can you eat those things for breakfast?" I nodded toward the open can of sardines on his desk.

He shrugged. "They were leftover from lunch yesterday." Then he popped the last two into his mouth.

As he started to toss the can into the trashcan I reached over to grab it. "Disposal of this stuff requires a hazmat team, or at least double ziplock bags. Open your window to get the smell out before Gina Callaghan arrives."

"They still haven't picked up the trash," he reported as he shoved on the window to hoist it open.

"Good," I called over my shoulder as I hurried out of the room with the offensive fishy tin, "then maybe you can rummage through it and find something better smelling for today's lunch."

A frantic search in the kitchen came up empty for ziplock bags, and our client would be walking in any second. "Here." I shoved the can into Brittany's hands. "Find something airtight to wrap this in."

She's been around Dave long enough that, to her credit, she didn't even bat an eyelash. "Ok."

Then I ran to the bathroom to wash my hands like

Lady Macbeth.

From the bathroom I could hear Rodney's greeting in his most obsequious voice. "Good morning, Mrs. Callaghan. Welcome to DS Investigations. Would you care for some coffee or cappuccino?" He put an extra little zing in that last word.

"No, thank you."

I could visualize a just barely perceptible slump of his shoulders in disappointment. "All right, then. You will be meeting with the head of our firm, Dave Sarkesian, and his assistant, Karen Maxwell."

I shut the water off with a fierce tug on the faucet handle and nearly ripped the paper towel rack off the wall. His *assistant?* Rodney introduced me to clients as my little brother's assistant?

"I'll show you back to Mr. Sarkesian's office," Rodney was saying as I stormed out of the bathroom.

"I am not Dave's assistant," I hissed in Rodney's ear as I pushed my way past him and into Dave's office where Dave was already shaking hands with our potential new client.

"Sure, I'll be happy to bring you a cappuccino, Mrs. Maxwell." Rodney gave me the world's most patronizing smile before turning to our guest. "Are you certain you don't care for anything, Mrs. Callaghan?"

"Yes." She smiled politely. "Nothing for me, thank you."

I offered her my hand. "I'm Karen Maxwell; I spoke to you on the phone when you called yesterday." *And I should have given you my name then*, I finished to myself *so that I can start building up a potential client base*. I had a lot to learn.

She did not seem comfortable with a hand shake, at least not from me, so I let her hand drop quickly and we all seated ourselves.

I deliberately had not told Dave much about the client ahead of time so that he'd have to include me in the meeting. "Mrs. Callaghan contacted us yesterday about a matter concerning her daughter."

She leaned forward slightly. "As I told your assistant, it is very important to proceed with discretion in this case."

Dave nodded, to all appearances looking the very soul of discretion and attentiveness.

"In fact," she continued, "I really hesitate to say any more about the matter until that man comes back with your coffee, Mrs. Maxwell."

"Please, call me Karen," I cut in so quickly as to almost be rude. Even though I hadn't asked for it, I was embarrassed about the cappuccino since it was delaying our client's confidence.

"Very well, Karen, and please call me Gina." She pronounced her name in a drawn out fashion, almost with three syllables.

I somehow felt this was going to be the most formal use of first names I'd ever experienced.

"I see that you have a teenager in the office," she continued gravely. "I know how they talk. I'd hate for the door to open at a moment when embarrassing information might leak out."

Now I experienced the very novel sensation of wanting to defend our inept intern. "Brittany is not a teenager, ma'am, she is a senior in college," I pointed out, "and a professional member of the staff. We trust her as we would any other employee." I hoped God wouldn't strike me dead on account of my lying tongue.

Gina offered a simpering smile. "Young people can't help themselves sometimes, I know. And with the texting… well, it's just better to be safe than sorry."

We waited in silence for a few moments until we heard Rodney's deferential scrape on the door.

"Come in, Rodney," Dave boomed. He turned to me with a grin. "You know, Karen, you really shouldn't make our office administrator wait on you like this."

I wanted to hit him but I guessed that would be unprofessional, even in a business like ours which people associate with danger and violence.

After I took a sip of the drink Rodney handed me, I wanted to hit him, too. He'd put so much sugar in the coffee it was almost the consistency of frosting. Now I was trying not to gag in front of a client, and I was going to look ungrateful and wasteful for not drinking the beverage I'd "asked" for. Grrr.

"So," I said as I swallowed a lump of undissolved sugar in the back of my throat, "please explain the matter you would like us to investigate."

"I need someone to find out exactly what happened at the regional competition last Saturday. And we need proof in two weeks before the trials for the Worlds team begin."

"The 'Worlds team'?" Dave asked. He probably wondered if it was some strange sci-fi competition.

She nodded. "My daughter is a senior. This is her last chance to make the U.S. team that will compete at the world championship. And she deserves to have that chance."

Dave's forehead creased in puzzlement. "But what kind of a team are we talking about? Soccer? Basketball?" He grinned as he suggested something he seemed to think was far-fetched. "Chess?"

She turned a brief, disapproving gaze on me before facing Dave again. "I thought your assistant would have related the information better."

"I prefer to hear our clients describe their situations to me in their own words," Dave said quickly, although this was not actually true. He was trying to keep me from looking incompetent, and I appreciated the gesture. "So." He leaned toward her. "What is this world team your daughter is trying to make? Are we talking about the Olympics?"

She sighed and laced her hands together on the desk in front of her. "I wish, but our sport has not been granted that privilege just yet. My daughter wants to try out for the Team USA to compete in the FISAC World Championship in South Africa this summer."

Dave frowned in annoyance. "Yes, but in what sport? And what's a fee-sack?"

"It's an acronym," she explained as if it were obvious. "It stands for Federation Internationale ... er..." her face flushed as it became obvious to all of us that she had no idea what it stood for. "It's French," she concluded dismissively. "The English translation is 'International Rope Skipping Federation.'"

"Rope skipping?" Dave cleared his throat. "Did I hear you correctly?"

"Yes."

I didn't know what hackles were, but I would have sworn that Gina Callaghan's rose sharply as she heard the skepticism in Dave's voice.

He cleared his throat again. "As in skipping over a rope?"

"Yes." She nodded impatiently. "Jump rope. My daughter has been a regional champion in the past and we expected her to win the category again this year so she could qualify to try out for the US team. Instead, due to some unknown treachery, she didn't even make the top four."

"Treachery," Dave repeated slowly. "So you think someone did something deliberately to hurt your daughter's chances of qualifying?"

"Of course." All the Botox in the world would not be able to erase the frown lines on Gina's forehead now. "That's why I'm hiring you. I really thought Mrs. Maxwell would have explained it all to you already."

"Karen," Dave and I said at once.

"Yes, yes, first names, I understand." She rolled her eyes as she sat back somewhat. "You want to appeal to the young crowd, I get that, and for my purposes it may be just the thing. I need you to conduct your investigation without anyone knowing of it."

Dave leaned back in his chair. "Why? Why not let everyone know there's a suspicion of foul play and see who gets nervous? You'd be surprised how effective that can be."

Gina pursed her lips and looked down for a moment. "Because I promised Hayley no one would know."

"Hayley is your daughter?" Dave asked.

She nodded. "She's a senior in high school, as I said. You know how it is. Her reputation might suffer if the others on her team knew we suspected them."

"So," Dave clarified, "you want us to investigate in secret."

Again she nodded.

"You realize this will increase both the length and the cost of the investigation." Ignoring her continued nods, Dave sat forward and stared straight into her eyes with a look that even I found a little intimidating. "How much is this worth to her? Or should I say, to you? How much are you willing to spend? We can't guarantee that we'll find any evidence of wrongdoing. And there may be nothing to find. So do you really want to do this?"

I was surprised at his intensity. Usually, Dave listens to the money and says the customer is always right until the money runs out. I'd never heard him challenge a potential client before—at least not one who appeared to have good credit.

Gina did not hesitate. "Yes. Of course. Whatever is necessary."

"Okay." Dave sat back again, his voice suddenly much lighter and almost distant, as if he was getting ready to leave. "Karen will take the lead on this investigation since she's got kids and can fit into the 'hanging out at practice waiting' thing much more convincingly than I can." He rummaged around in a desk drawer and pulled out a small digital recorder. "I've got a meeting with another client in a few minutes, but I want you to tell Karen everything you can think of that might be relevant, and we'll record it for future reference, if that's okay with you."

She looked like it was not okay but couldn't think of a good reason to object. "Is that really necessary?"

"Necessary?" He shook his head. "No. A good idea so that I can listen in later and help out with the case? Yes. So it's up to you." He stood and held out the recorder.

With a grimace, she took it gingerly from his palm. "Do you have a private conference room where we can speak without being overheard?"

He stepped around to where we sat and patted the back of her chair. "Just stay right here. My meeting is off-site. Gotta run. It was a pleasure to meet you, Gina." He shook her hand and flashed a look of instant sincerity that fooled everyone in the world except me.

I tried to catch his eye as he slipped out the door, but he evaded me.

He was willing to take this woman's money, but not to do any work for her. Why?

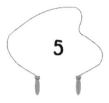

5

I had a case again. I should have been happy. Instead, I resented Dave for just assuming I'd take it without asking me first.

Trying to hide my resentment under a businesslike smile, I closed the door firmly behind my brother and turned to Gina.

She looked tense and unhappy, too. For some odd reason, the situation reminded me of a meeting with my son's assistant principal last year, after Evan had kicked another kid's soccer ball onto the roof of the school. The way Evan told it, the boys were having a contest to see who could kick the ball the farthest, and he won. But his prize was two weeks' detention.

The school administrator's demeanor had appeared to ooze empathy, and she was very soft spoken and polite. But she didn't listen to a word I said, or at least didn't give any credence to it. Was I going to be the same way with this woman? After all, I thought her concern over the jump rope was as meaningless as my son's sense of injustice for being punished for a contest with a soccer ball.

I needed a fresh approach, some way to better understand what she was going through. I let my gaze roam as I returned to my seat, desperately seeking inspiration. The screen on Dave's computer had the answer. It was blank.

His screensaver usually had pictures of sports cars morphing from one design into another. But now, for some reason, the screen was blank, and I missed the colorful pictures.

I needed visual.

"Do you have any pictures of your daughter jumping?" I asked. "Or is there a video we could look up?" That would give me an idea of what we were talking about. In my mind, I still couldn't reconcile the image of singsong playground rhymes with a sport that had international competitions.

She blinked. "Of course. I didn't bring my iPad with me, and the image will be too small to see on my phone. May we use one of your computers?"

"Oh, yes." But not Dave's. I was sure the keyboard would be covered with mustard or anchovy paste or something. On the other hand, Dave's was the only computer with any privacy.

I stepped around to the back of the desk and perched on the edge of the great creaking chair that used to belong to the founder of the firm. I was pretty sure it would tilt backward and flip me over if I shifted my weight wrong, so I tried to stay as close to the front edge of the chair as possible. Then I pulled a tissue from my pocket and laid it over the keyboard before hitting the return key a few times to bring the monitor to life.

Within a few seconds, a Maserati materialized in front of my eyes and then dissolved into a search engine page. "Okay." I turned to Gina. "Where to?"

Her brow furrowed in thought. "Have you ever seen a jump rope team before?"

"I've never *heard* of a jump rope team before."

"Go to the Jumptastics website then."

The homepage showed a row of smiling kids in yellow and blue uniforms doing chorus line kicks. After a second I realized they each had a yellow and blue rope arching over their heads. I turned to Gina. "So they do, like, dance routines with jump ropes?"

She nodded. "More or less. At least, that's part of what they do. And of course it photographs well." She waved to the screen. "Most of the pictures are from shows we've done."

I turned back to the website and clicked on the "About our Team" page. It showed big kids turning long ropes while joyful little kids jumped in the middle, kids turning cartwheels toward jump ropes that looked like they were about to decapitate them, rows of kids smiling for a class picture, kids smiling as they held up ribbons and medals, more kids smiling as they posed with ropes wrapped around their legs and arms. Too many smiles. I felt like I was watching a PBS show for toddlers.

"It's a happy sport, isn't it?" I couldn't help myself.

She gave a harsh laugh. "We wouldn't get many new members if the website showed the competition team doing push-ups or the bloody welt on a jumper's leg when he's had a bad miss with a wire rope."

"No, I guess not." I turned back to her. "I take it that everything is not as happy as it seems in the pictures? And what was your daughter doing exactly when you think someone interfered with her rope?"

"It was the power competition. That's not on the website."

"Oh? I saw kids with ribbons. That was from competition, wasn't it?"

She gave a dismissive shake of the head. "Parents take pictures of the fun things, the shows, the award ceremonies, the freestyle tricks. No one videos the speed and power competitions—they all look the same."

"What do you mean? Explain the difference."

She ticked off three different options on her fingers one at a time. "Freestyle is where jumpers make up their own routine using as many fancy tricks as they can. Speed is where a jumper sees how many jumps she can do in a minute, and power is where they count the number of triple-unders she can do without a miss. So speed and power looks virtually the same for everyone. Whereas with freestyle…"

"Each routine is different." I nodded. "I get it. And your daughter was doing triple-unders? Are those what they sound like?"

"Yes. The rope goes under her feet three times with each jump."

I wished I knew how to whistle. "That's impressive. But what makes you think someone interfered with her rope?"

"It broke."

"Like, in half?"

"No, the wire came loose from the handle. That's not unusual, it does happen, and the jumper automatically gets a re-jump." Her forehead creased with consternation and her voice began to rise, giving me a glimpse of the real mom beneath the veneer of poise. "But it's so tiring – she can only do so many triples before she's shot for the day. Whoever broke her rope knew that she'd be tired on the re-jump. And she was – she missed on her 15th jump. Fifteen!" Her voice had grown so sharp I almost winced. "Usually she finishes at least 90 before she has a miss."

"That's a lot of whatever they are—triple-unders."

"Fifteen is nothing. In fact, you can't qualify for Nationals with less than 30 even if you come in first place in your region."

I was still trying to grasp the fact that there were more than four girls in the state of Maryland who could get a rope under their feet three times on one jump, let alone do it more than 15 times in a row. What if her daughter wasn't a superhuman and had simply gotten tired? I tried to get her to look at this reasonably. "You said it wasn't unusual for a rope to break. Why do you think someone did something to make it break on purpose?"

An ugly sneer grew on her face. "The other girls are jealous of Hayley because she was the only one on the team to win a medal at Nationals last year – in this same event. We all expected her to take first place this year at Regionals and Nationals. I just know she would have if someone hadn't messed with her rope. She always checks her rope before a jump to make sure nothing's loose. Always. This could not have been just a loose screw or some other accident."

I was pretty sure it had been an accident and mom just didn't want to accept it. But if she wanted us to pay to investigate the accident, it was not my job to turn her down. It might give her a sense of closure, at least. "What does your daughter—what does Hayley think?"

"I—I don't know." She looked away for a moment. "As I said, she doesn't want the matter investigated at all. But that's because she feels enough resentment from the others as it is. If it were known we suspect one of them of sabotaging her rope, well, that would be social suicide, wouldn't it? As if that matters. She will never have another chance to go to the world competition. Never. This is it." She sighed. "She just doesn't understand how important it is."

"They never do," I agreed. My daughter would rather have the good opinion of friends over the good opinion of her mother any day.

"So you will need to be very discreet."

I looked at her for a moment. "You realize that may make it next to impossible to find the answers you're looking for."

"I'm sure you can find a way. That's your job, isn't it?"

My job. Doing the impossible. "Sure." I opened up the folder I'd brought in with me. "Here's our client agreement. Please read it through and let me know if you have any questions." Normally I'd explain the terms and emphasize that we could not guarantee results, but the terms were spelled out in plain English and I figured she could read them for herself.

While she read the contract, I poked through Dave's file drawers to see if there was anything in the files I didn't know about that I should. It was a waste of time since most of the file folders seemed contain only what I'd put in the to begin with. I did find three candy wrappers, another sardine can and a pile of fortunes from the Chinese buffet on Route 40. I stuffed them all inside the sardine can and wrapped it in the tissue that I'd used to cover the dirty keyboard. Then I threw it where the trashcan used to be. Since it wasn't there anymore, the can clattered against the old wooden floorboards and all the wrappers and fortunes sprang out like confetti.

Gina looked up. "Is there a problem?"

"Oh, no." I surreptitiously kicked the trash under Dave's desk. "Do you have any questions?"

She tapped her pen against the page. "I want to

know what your plan of action will be. Before I sign this contract."

I had no plan of action. At this moment, I couldn't even find the trashcan, let alone find whoever had tampered with this woman's daughter's rope. I needed time to think. "Fine," I said as I stood up. "I'll send you a written description of the proposed operation and after you've had time to review it, you can mail me the signed agreement with your retainer." I didn't think the delay would sit well with her and I was hoping she'd drop the demand to hear my non-existent plan. If I was wrong and she left without signing, however, Dave would not be pleased. And what was worse, he would think I didn't have what it takes to run a case.

Gina frowned at the contract.

I crossed my fingers behind my back.

Finally she looked up. "I don't want to wait. We have so little time before the tryouts—we have to get this settled."

"Okay." I hoped she couldn't actually hear my sigh of relief. "Sign right here." Then I remembered I had forgotten to turn on the recorder. Oh, well. Dave would never ask about it anyway.

"I will email you a list of questions I need you to answer to the best of your ability," I continued. "The more information you can give me, the faster the investigation will go."

She nodded.

After we exchanged email addresses and other basic information, I let Rodney show Gina out because I knew it would make both of them feel better. He likes to give clients the sense that they're VIPs and I don't have time for that. But the real reason was that I felt like I could hardly trust myself to be civil to the woman, let alone gracious. Why did she bother me so much?

It bothered me that she bothered me, but I was wasting time just thinking about it. Instead I had to create a list of questions, draft a plan of action for this case, finish the week's invoices and figure out what to say to say to Dave about Doreen's dead parrot case so that he might be tempted to handle it himself. Maybe I could hint that the parrot's owner was attractive and rich.

I created an account for Gina Callaghan and started a list of questions covering things like the location of the competition, names of competitors, etc. When I got to the "plan of action" my mind went blank.

I finished the invoices instead. And then to entice Dave to take on the parrot investigation instead of assigning it to me, I decided the parrot's owner would be rich, lonely, and fascinated by the life of a private investigator.

The plan of action for the jump rope case was still blank when it was almost time for me to leave. I couldn't avoid it any longer.

What on earth would I do with these people?

Okay, at a bare minimum I had to attend practices to get information from jumpers and parents and I had to make it look like I wasn't attending practice to get information from jumpers so the obvious plan was to be like one of the other parents. I think I was trying to avoid the obvious plan. Because that meant I had to involve my kids in a case again. It wasn't fair to them and it really wasn't fair to me because Dave didn't pay me nearly enough to listen to their complaints.

But I didn't have any other ideas. Of course I would need to ask Alicia first. You can't just tell a 12-year-old that she's going to do something for you and expect her to go along with it.

If I waited to ask her, though, then I'd couldn't get started until I had an answer, and the clock was ticking. I had to solve or at least fully investigate the case before the trials for the world competition team, or Dave might not ever trust me with another case. And that was in a little more than two weeks.

I picked up the phone and called the Jumptastics to see how my daughter could join the team, willing or not.

Of course I got an answering machine. It was Friday afternoon. I would still have to wait until next week to get started.

With a sigh, I went for my last swallow of Diet Coke, only to find it was already empty.

Dave walked in as I was shutting down my computer. I focused my mental energy on the parrot case and hoped I could hide my bad mood long enough to become persuasive. "Hey, Dave," I said casually. "Doreen called in a favor we owe her."

"We?" He shook his head. "I don't even know a Doreen."

"Smith Insurance. She looks stuff up for us all the time."

"Okay." He didn't sound convinced.

Appeal to his ego as an investigator. "She's got this investigation that has her team all puzzled," I began. *Appeal to his sense of greed.* "A ceiling collapsed on a sun porch addition one of the houses on Church Street, you know, those big Victorians." And *now the double whammy—appeal to his professional pride and tempt him with the prospect of an attractive client.* "The owner has been trying to sweet talk her way past the insurance adjusters and Doreen wants to bring in someone who won't be persuaded by a pretty face." Of course that attractive client would be more of an adversary and might not be attractive at all, but I hoped he wouldn't think of that.

"Oh, well," he considered for a moment. "I don't think *you* would be persuaded by a pretty face."

My hopes plummeted. "Me?"

"Yes, you. And you park up Church Street half the time, don't you?"

"Um, sometimes, but I don't like to."

"Yes, but you do. So you could stop by on your way in one morning."

"But I thought—"

"You thought you could tempt me with your logic." He grinned as he shook his head. "Way too obvious, Karen. A 'Hardy Boys' mystery would be enough to stump insurance investigators."

"I don't know. Some of those mysteries are really puzzling." I used to read them aloud to Evan. They were pretty awful, but he liked them, at least until he reached the age of reason.

Dave laughed as he sat down on the corner of my desk. "It was a good try. So why don't you want to help your friend Doreen with her Victorian house mystery?"

I sighed and shook my empty Diet Coke can, wishing it had somehow miraculously refilled itself. "It's about a dead parrot."

"Ooh," his eyes grew wide. "Maybe we *should* call in the Hardy Boys on this one."

"I'm serious. The owners claim it was worth more than a Corvette."

"Hardtop or convertible?"

"I don't know. Hardtop."

"Not really worth buying in the hardtop."

"More worth buying it than a parrot."

"Well, duh. And since the parrot won't bring in any money, we don't need to use our senior investigator on it. From a financial perspective, you have to see that."

"I do."

He paused and gave me a sly glance. "We could send Brittany."

"Do we carry malpractice insurance?"

"She's not that bad."

I just looked at him.

He shrugged. "Do we really need this Doreen person?"

"No, not at all. Instead we could subscribe to the Integrated Underwriting database so we can look up our own claim information."

"Okay, I get it, we need to keep this Doreen happy. And you're right, Brittany shouldn't take the lead. But let her help you out. She can be useful."

I was disappointed, and it looked like I was going to stay that way. And now I had to fight back a ridiculous urge to cry. I turned away from him. "Okay. I gotta go."

"Sure, but answer that call first."

"What?" But the phone rang before the word was out of my mouth. He'd been looking over my shoulder and had seen the light blink on the phone base.

I reached over the desk at an awkward angle to pick up the receiver."Good afternoon," I said through clenched teeth.

"Hi, this is Maggie with the Jumptastics," a friendly voice piped up. "I'm returning a call from Karen Maxwell."

My teeth unclenched. Finally, something was going right. "Thanks for calling me back." I moved around the desk so that I was no longer in danger of being strangled by an overstretched phone cord. "My daughter would like to join your team, so I'd like to know how to sign her up."

"Does she jump?"

"Oh, yeah." Everybody knew how to jump rope.

"Well," Maggie said, "we just started a new session last week. I think we could catch her up. We'll have a coach evaluate her. Can you bring her in on Monday? We meet at the Throckmorton Athletic Center."

"What time?"

"Four o'clock?"

"Sure, that'd be great." And it was, at least from my perspective. But what was Alicia going to say about it? Could I come up with enough threats or bribes to get her to go along?

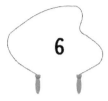

Friday night dinner was not planned, as usual. It was our junk food night.

"Let's have waffles," Alicia suggested with an evil gleam in her eyes. She looked pointedly at the toaster oven just in case we didn't get her reference.

"No," Evan and I said at once.

"But some of those firefighters are pretty hot," she insisted.

"How would you know? You weren't even here when they came," Evan pointed out.

I didn't say anything. The thought that my not-yet-even-a teenage daughter was paying attention to "hot" guys was bad enough. And these would be guys way too old for her.

"Anyway, they wouldn't pay any attention to you," Evan continued. "You're too flat-chested."

"Mom!" Alicia whined.

I actually found his observation comforting.

"What?" Evan stopped rummaging through the refrigerator and spoke over his shoulder. "I didn't say any bad words. And Mom calls herself flat-chested all the time."

"Really!" Alicia turned to me. "I can't believe you're letting him say that."

"He has a point."

He stuck out his tongue at his sister.

"Can we go back to disagreeing about dinner?" I asked.

"Let's just get hamburgers." Alicia said dismissively. "I might be going to a movie later."

I gave her a skeptical look. "Oh, really?" She hadn't asked permission. I decided to wait to see if she would.

Evan scowled. "We had hamburgers last Friday."

"But we were at Dad's last Friday," Alicia countered, hands on hips.

"So?"

"So it doesn't count."

"Yes." Evan nodded with vehemence, making his hair stick up in front even more than usual."It counts."

"No, because we never get to decide what we have at Dad's. Ellie always decides."

Ellie was the daughter of my former best friend, Linda, now living with my former husband, Jeff.

Linda, incidentally, was not flat-chested.

"Waffles are starting to sound pretty good," I said. "But I think we're out of syrup. So I guess it will be tacos."

"Tacos?" Alicia recoiled as if I'd just slapped her. "I thought you were gonna say pizza."

I shrugged. "Brian's coming over later. He's probably tired of pizza since they have that at every youth group meeting."

She sniffed in derision. "He can bring his own tacos then. I want pizza."

"I thought you wanted burgers."

"I do, but I was sure it was gonna be pizza anyway."

"So get a slice of pizza at the movies," Evan suggested.

"She hasn't asked if she can go yet," I pointed out.

Alicia sighed. "Can I go to the movies?"

"Maybe."

She looked hopeful. "Can you drive?"

I started to groan at the thought of having to go back out on a cold wet night, but then a thought occurred to me. "Maybe. I'll drive you to the movies if you'll do me a favor next week."

"What is it?"

"What movie do you want to see?" I asked.

"I don't know yet. We have to decide. What's the favor?"

I crossed my arms in front of my chest. "I'm not sure I have to tell you until you tell me the movie."

"I would know the movie if you let me have a cellphone."

"Your friends don't know how to use a regular phone?"

She rolled her eyes. "You can't text on a landline. Do you want me to go back to be one of those reenactors at the 1776 House?"

"No." I was surprised how close she'd come to guessing it, though.

Evan poked his head out of the fridge. "I'm not wearing those dorky clothes again."

"I don't need you for this one," I assured him. "And close that door."

"Ah-ha!" Alicia leaned in close with a grin of triumph. "So it is an investigation that you want me to help with,"

"Maybe," I admitted.

"You have to pay me."

"What?" This time I was the one who acted like I'd just been slapped.

"If I'm working, I should get paid. Same as anyone

else."

"But…" I hadn't expected that at all. "I don't know. You're too young."

"Do you need my help?"

"Yes."

"Then I'm just the right age."

Evan held out his hand. "I'll wear the dorky clothes if you pay me enough."

"No," I shook my head. "This is a girl thing. I need Alicia to join a jump rope team so I have an excuse to be at some practices."

"Jump rope team?" Alicia pursed her lips. "Sounds tiring. That will cost you extra."

"I'm not even sure I'm paying you anything."

She leaned against the counter. "Tell me what role I'll be playing this time."

"You play my daughter. A girl who wants to be on the jump rope team."

"Yes." She rolled her eyes. "But what is my motivation? Why do I want to jump? Am I restless?"

"You have lice and they're making you itch," Evan suggested.

Alicia ignored him. "Do I have a fear of stability? Or maybe I'm anorexic."

"Or on meth, like the guy who tried to eat people on that TV show." Evan reached over on the counter for the remote, leaned toward the opening toward the living room, and pointed it at the TV.

"He didn't jump," Alicia pointed out.

"He twitched a lot though." Holding the remote out like a beacon in front of him, Evan left the kitchen and headed toward the living room "I'm gonna find him."

"Hmmn," Alicia mused as she drifted across the

floor toward the refrigerator. "Maybe I could play an addict of some sort."

I followed her. "No you will not. I'm directing this production and you're an ordinary girl who does not have parasites or an addiction."

"Little do you know," she scoffed as she stuck her head in the fridge.

"What?"

She turned to me with a gaze of disdain. "There is no such thing as an 'ordinary girl'"

"Okay, you're average then."

"Really? That's so lame."

"I need you to be lame." *Wait*. "Not literally. I just need you to be normal, and to not attract attention so people don't realize I'm investigating."

She pulled out a Diet Coke and shut the door. "*We're* investigating, you mean." She made a face at the can in her hand. "Why do you always buy diet soda?"

"I buy diet soda for me. If you don't like it, you can buy your own." I slipped the can out of her fingers, opened it and took a drink. "And I mean it when I say that *I'm* investigating this case. Even if I agree to pay you, and I'm not saying I will, I don't want you getting involved. That's not part of the deal."

"But you do want me involved. That's the whole point."

I sighed. "You're involved, you're just not *involved*. It's too obvious if you start asking questions, too."

"But everyone asks questions. How will I know where the bathroom is if I don't ask questions?"

"You know what I mean."

"I won't be obvious. But don't you think you'll find out what's going on sooner with two of us paying attention?"

"Yes, I suppose."

"And," she reached over and took a sip of my drink, "what is supposed to be going on?"

I looked over toward the living room to see if Evan was paying any attention to us. He was engrossed in something on the screen involving a polar bear and a skateboard. When I spoke again, my voice was much lower, just in case. "We are trying to find out if someone sabotaged a competition. Our client's daughter was favored to win but she didn't even place. Her mother thinks someone deliberately tampered with her equipment so she would lose."

"Really? Very interesting." Alicia paced a few steps away and then spun around. "But wait. This is jump rope, right? Her mom thinks someone tampered with a jump rope? Or was it other equipment like the time clock?"

I was impressed – I'm not sure I would have thought of that. "Her mom thinks someone did something to make her rope break. But she also admits that ropes break all the time. So it may be nothing. If there is something, though, I need to prove it soon so her daughter will have a chance to make it to the next level of competition."

"How old is the daughter?"

"She's a senior in high school."

"On the threshold of life's great adventure."

"What?"

"Teen Life." She pointed to a magazine in a rack behind the butter dish on the counter. "That's what they call college."

"They should call it Life's Great Overpayment."

She shrugged. "Does she think she knows who messed with her rope?"

"I haven't talked to her yet."

"I can."

I shook my head. "No, you can't. You'll be jumping so I have an excuse to be there talking."

Alicia grabbed her magazine and flipped through a few pages. "Should I do my hair like this?" She pointed to a picture of a model leaning over the edge of the Eiffel Tower. "Or like this?"

"You really just need to have it out of your face."

She gave me this look that I knew very well, accompanied by a slurping noise that indicated I was sucking all the fun out of things.

"Okay. " I looked at the magazine. "The one on the right then. But where are you going to find a starfish in January?"

She studied the picture for a moment. "I think I can use a hair clip and some of those ties from the trash bags."

"Okay, great. Now call your friends to find out about the movie."

She reached for the phone. "It's about a boy," she said as she punched in the number.

"Which movie is that?"

"No, the jump rope girl and the broken rope. I'm sure it's all about a boy."

"You think so?"

She nodded, then addressed her next words into the receiver. "Hi, it's Ali, is Darrell there?"

Ali? Darrell? When did she start calling herself Ali? And who the heck was Darrell? Was it a boy? And was that why she thought this case was about a boy? I suddenly felt like I had a lot to learn about my little girl. Maybe hiring her wasn't such a bad idea after all.

Later, when I was in the kitchen trying to decide what to do with the remains of dinner, I heard the front door open.

"Hey Evan." A familiar deep voice called in greeting. "Watcha watching?"

I had told Brian he didn't have to knock when he came over, but I guess I didn't actually expect him to listen to me. It was a little weird just having him come in like that and head right into the living room to talk to Evan.

I shouldn't have been annoyed. Ignoring Evan would have been rude. But Brian spent so much of his time with kids that I sometimes wondered if he preferred them to adults. Like me.

Using more force than was probably necessary, I wadded up the bag of wrappers, unused sauces and sporks and stuffed it into the trash can.

"I should have guessed I'd find you in here."

I looked up to see Brian peering around the doorway. "Messes don't clean up themselves. At least not around here." I held up a box of fried chicken with a cartoon face on the front that was either a disturbingly happy chicken or a customer in danger of turning into a chicken. "Would you like any of the pieces we didn't want?"

"Wow, when you put it that way, how can I refuse?"

"Well, it's true." I opened the box. "Evan eats the wings, and Alicia and I tear up all the thighs thinking that they're chicken breasts. But they never are. So we eat the drumsticks and we have a pile of torn up scraps left over. If you don't want them, I'm sure Molly will."

"I hate to deprive the dog, but it does smell good."

"Help yourself. There's coleslaw, too."

He reached for the bag on the counter. "I know Molly won't want that."

"I wouldn't be too sure. She likes anything that doesn't have the word 'dog' on the package."

He laughed as he pulled out a mangled piece of chicken and turned to lean back against the counter. "So what's going on tonight?"

"I think I should be the one asking you that."

"You already know I had basketball. But it was just a practice. What are your kids doing tonight?"

"Evan is watching—" I suddenly remembered Alicia's phone call. "Alicia might be going to the movies. With a boy."

I watched for his reaction to this news.

He chewed and swallowed and took another bite.

"She's twelve." I reminded him.

More chewing and swallowing.

"If she was your daughter, you wouldn't be so calm."

"I might. Who's the boy?" He turned to open the cabinet and took out a glass that said "Toby's Dinner Theatre" on it.

"I don't know. She was talking to someone named 'Darrell'."

"Could be Darryl Hannah." He picked up the plastic pitcher from the counter and poured the contents into his glass without asking what it was.

"Yes, and it could also be a mermaid, too, but I don't either one is likely."

He started to reach for another piece of chicken, but I slapped down the lid of the box. "Are you paying any attention? My extremely too young daughter might have a date for tonight."

"Have you asked her?"

"Asked her?" I grimaced. "No. That's way too direct. She would never talk. I need to use more subtle means."

He shrugged and looked at the box of chicken.

I let go and reached for the phone. "I think the call history can tell me who she called." I pushed a button and the phone beeped so loudly at me I dropped the receiver. "I guess that wasn't it."

He nodded "That was probably the locator."

I picked up the receiver, looked at a round dial with four arrows on it, and pushed one of the arrows, bracing myself for a loud noise. Instead, it gave a soft chirp and dialed 911. "That's not it, either." I pushed "End Call" about 67 times. "I hope they won't bill me for that."

"Why don't you ask Alicia to help you with the phone?" he asked with a mischievous grin.

"You think this is funny, but it really isn't." I sighed and leaned back against the counter. "I don't know if I can trust her, but I don't want her to know that."

"Why not?" He shrugged and reached for the chicken again. "I start out telling all the kids in my group that I don't trust them. They have to earn my trust."

"It's different if they're your own."

"Okay."

Alicia stormed down the stairs, her heavy boots making her sound like she'd been split into at least four different people, or one person with eight legs. "We're ready to go now. You can still drive, right?"

"Uh, yeah. How many people are we picking up?" If I was driving, I'd get to see who was going and if I didn't approve, I could say so then.

"Three. What do you think?" She pointed at her

head. "I copied the style from the picture." Her hair was pulled back on one side with a combination of clips that looked like a lopsided sea urchin. Not quite a starfish but close.

"It's really, um......have you got money?"

She held up her wrist to reveal a tiny purse dangling like a lopsided bracelet. "Yep. Let's go."

"Just a minute." Brian stepped over to her, wiping his greasy hands on a dishtowel. "What movie are you going to see and who's going with you?" he demanded.

Her eyes widened in surprise but she answered without hesitation. "*Herbie the Love Bug*, with Abby, Sarah and—"

"Are you kidding?" I nearly gagged on my soda. "*Herbie the Love Bug?*"

She shrugged. "It's dollar classic night."

"That," I pointed out, "is not a classic."

"No," Brian agreed, "but at least they got the price right. So who's going—"

I put a hand on his arm. "Don't worry," I whispered. "I've got this figured out." I didn't need him to interfere with his high handed I'm-the-youth-group-leader-approach.

"Okay," he whispered back. "But when we're old and gray, don't go all subtle with me. I want you to be direct. It's a lot easier."

"Yeah, alright." I grabbed my purse and shooed Alicia out the door.

Old and gray. He pictured us growing old and gray together? We'd only been dating since, well, not that long and I didn't think we'd hit "serious" yet. And you don't get much more serious than old and gray.

There was no Darrell in the group I picked up and no guys waiting outside the theater when I dropped off

Alicia and her friends. And I didn't really think any would be inside, either. *Herbie the Love Bug?*

Even people who were old and gray didn't watch that kind of cinematic waste.

Old and gray. I took my time driving home, not sure what I was going to say after that comment. But Brian and Evan were watching something about the Titanic when I got back, so I joined them. We ate popcorn and talked about how we shouldn't have eaten so much popcorn so the "old and gray" thing didn't come up again, and I didn't have to deal with it. It scared me, and I didn't want to think about why.

7

On Monday, Evan's after-school bus was late the one day I needed it to be early.

"How's my hair?" Alicia asked as she came into the kitchen.

"Fine," I answered, still watching out the window for the bus.

"You didn't even look."

I looked. "It's still fine."

"I want to make a good impression on my first day."

"I want to make an on-time impression," I countered, trying to keep myself from venting my frustration on my daughter during one of the rare times she wasn't responsible for it. "But if Evan does get home soon, we will be late."

"Why do we have to wait for him to get home?"

"Because." I had already hidden the waffles and unplugged the toaster oven, but I wanted to give him instructions and make sure he'd be safe while we were at the jump rope practice. "He doesn't have a key."

"You could give him one."

"He's only nine."

"That's old enough."

I didn't answer. I had told myself last week he was old enough to be on his own, and I was planning to leave him again to show I trusted him, but really I didn't.

I texted my neighbor Amy for about the sixth time. "Don't forget to keep an eye on the house. We'll be leaving soon."

"I'm going out to the car," Alicia announced. Her footsteps were unusually quiet without the heavy boots.

After a few more minutes of staring out the window, I decided to wait outside, too.

Amy came out of her house. "Just go on ahead," she called with a wave. I'll meet him at the bus."

"Okay, thanks!" I hated to impose on her like that, but I also hated to be late. Next time I'd pick Evan up at school or something.

The building where the Jumptastics held their practices seemed big enough inside to be an airplane hangar – it was a giant vault of space divided with big green curtains that stretched up into infinity. The walls were mustard yellow. To our right as we walked in, I saw an army of teenage girls with padded knees popping volleyballs off their forearms like popcorn. To the left, preschool kids hit plastic golf balls with oversized plastic golf clubs.

"Are we in the right place?" Alicia asked, looking down at her unpadded knees.

"I don't know." A door on my right was labeled "Park Administration." I knocked and got no answer. "Maybe behind the curtain?" We threaded our way past the preschoolers and as we got close to the curtain, I could hear a strange whirring and tapping noise.

"Time!" a voice called as we stepped around the curtain.

"I think we're in the right place," I murmured as I looked around at the red-faced kids gasping for breath as they paced around clutching the plastic handles strung with pieces of thin wire. One of the older girls was probably Hayley.

"You will definitely have to pay me extra for this," Alicia murmured as she looked at the exhausted faces around the room. There were about twenty kids, some nearly as young as Evan but most in middle or high school. I was surprised to see that at least a third of them were boys. Obviously this wasn't a "girl thing" after all.

Over in the corner parents sat huddled in awkward heaps on a set of portable bleachers. I wondered if the Maggie I'd talked to was one of them.

"One minute for water," a male coach called out from the side. "And I'm timing it." Some of the jumpers scurried over to a pile of backpacks scattered on the floor and pulled out water bottles. Obviously something was going to happen at the end of sixty seconds, so I had only that much time to ask that coach where to find Maggie. I grabbed Alicia's arm.

"Mom," she protested as I dragged her over to the coach who'd called out a few moments earlier.

"Fifteen," a toneless voice announced over a speaker.

The coach, a muscular young man who was probably in his late 20s, was talking to a girl with big dark eyes and a lush ponytail of thick brown hair that bobbed up and down as she spoke. She reminded me a little of Gina Callaghan, but didn't look old enough to be a senior in high school, so I assumed it couldn't be her daughter Hayley.

As I drew closer, I could see she was blinking back tears, so I didn't come any closer. But I strained to catch what she was saying. She didn't say much. Just "okay," each time the coach said something, and his voice was so low I couldn't hear without being really obvious.

"Thirty" the recorded voice announced from the speaker.

The coach patted the girl on the shoulder and nodded for her to rejoin the others on the floor. As she turned away and headed out, I stepped closer to the coach.

"She looked upset," I observed.

"I was just trying to give her tips on how to improve her speed. Lindsey tries hard. But…" he turned, hands on hips, to give me his full attention. "What can I do for you?"

"I'm looking for Maggie. She said she would have a coach evaluate my daughter for placement on the team."

The coach nodded. "I'll have my mom take a look at her."

"Forty-five" the voice insisted firmly over the speaker.

"Let's go guys." The coach hollered. "Three minute speed."

A few jumpers groaned.

"Let me get them started," he said to me. Then he hollered again. "If you don't want to do this again today, do it right this time. No slacking. Count yourselves." He went over to the speaker and fiddled with an iPod sitting on top of it.

"Three minute speed," the toneless voice announced. "Judges ready, jumpers ready…set…go!"

The whirling noise sounded all around the room as jumpers started turning their ropes at a frantic pace. They alternated their footsteps in quick succession, like football players doing that funny drill where they run on their toes. Ropes moved so fast I couldn't even see them. Some of the jumpers turned their bodies slowly in a circle as they jogged, their mouths open, skin turning red.

"Fifteen." That same voice announced.

"Okay," the coach motioned for us to follow him around the side of the room to the bleachers. "Coach Nan will take care of you." He nodded toward a blonde in a purple track suit as he led us over to her.

"Thirty."

I was feeling out of breath just from watching all those kids work. As I looked back at Alicia she appeared to be in shock. Then I turned my attention to the female coach ahead of us. Though her athletic build was as trim as any of the girls jumping on the floor, when we got close I could see a thinness to her face and wrinkles around the corners of her brown eyes that put her age at about 50.

"I realize she was out of line," she was saying to a dark-complected woman who stood frowning with her hands crossed in front of her chest. "But she's off the committee, and it will be up to the board to decide what to do next. It's out of my hands."

"It's not fair to the others," the frowning woman insisted. "They should all have the same chance."

"I'm sorry." Coach Nan laid a hand on her arm. "You're right, it's not fair. But I doubt there's anything we can do about it now." She offered the woman an apologetic smile before turning to us.

"Excuse me, Mom," the young male coach began, "we have a jumper who needs to be evaluated."

She smiled first at Alicia, then at me. "Hi. I'm Nan Daniels."

Her son waved and turned back to the jumpers.

"One minute," the loud toneless voice echoed across the gym.

"Keep up the pace, don't slow down," the young man ordered as he jogged into the center of the practice space.

"And who was that?" I asked Nan.

"He didn't introduce himself?" She shook her head. "No manners. That was my son, Eric. The kids call him Coach Dan."

"Do you both coach the team?"

She nodded. "I'm the head coach. Eric was one of the little jumpers when I started the team." She laughed. "Thinks he's ready to take over now, though."

"Is he?"

"No." She laughed again. "But I'm might let him anyway. I've been doing this too long."

"Yeah, I can see where it might get pretty tiring." I glanced meaningfully at the woman with the dark skin and even darker expression who'd she'd been talking to moments before. "All those disgruntled parents to deal with." I tried to think of some way to find out who they'd been talking about without appearing too nosy.

Never mind—I was paid to be nosy.

"What was that all about, anyway?" I added quickly. "Was somebody caught cheating or something?" I wasn't sure how you could cheat in jump rope, but there were ways to cheat at anything in this world. Sabotaging someone else's rope for starters.

Her lips drew together in a thin line. "I really can't talk about it. Let's just say that every parent wants their child to succeed, and we share that goal. Now how can I help you?"

As much as I wanted to keep asking questions, I decided I'd better remember that I was supposed to be an interested parent. "My daughter wants to join the team." I pulled a reluctant Alicia forward. "Remember, you are an actress," I whispered.

"I love to jump," she said with an almost-convincing smile.

"Great." Coach Nan smiled. "Were you on another team before or did you do Jump Rope for Heart or..." The coach let her words trail off with another smile of encouragement.

"Um, no."

"Okay, well if you don't mind, I'd like to see what you can do and we'll see what class you should be in."

We all waited for a moment.

"One minute, forty-five seconds."

The toneless mechanical voice that called out the time intervals sounded in stark contrast to the intensity of the action surrounding us. I could almost feel the jumpers grasping for every last ounce of energy and oxygen in the room as they spun their ropes and sprinted in place, grimacing with determination. Just watching their impassioned exertions left me breathless. I never would have guessed anyone could inspire teenagers to work so hard at anything.

"Did you bring your rope?" the coach asked.

Alicia shook her head.

"I'll get one for you. Do you wanted beaded? Licorice? Wire?"

"Um..."

"Okay, just a minute." The coach walked off and disappeared behind a door in the back wall.

I tried not to look at the faces of the jumpers, even though I needed to know which one was Hayley and which ones were her potential rivals. I would look after they finished their marathon of cardiovascular torture.

"One minute left." Coach Dan hollered. "Keep it up. No slacking."

"I'm not sure about this, Mom," Alicia whispered.

"I'll pay you," I promised.

Worry lines gouged her forehead. "I don't think I can do it."

"Be brave."

She gave me a wavery smile.

"Act brave, then," I suggested. "Use your acting skills."

"Two minutes, fifteen seconds."

Coach Nan reappeared with a big duffle bag slung over her shoulder.

It looked heavy. By the time she reached us, the awful cold voice on the speaker had called out two minutes, thirty seconds. Lindsey, the girl I'd seen talking to Dan earlier, got her foot tangled in her rope and hopped around trying to get untangled.

Two boys jumping near us seemed to increase their speed, and one of them actually smiled. Well, it was more of a deeper grimace, but he seemed to be trying to smile.

Nan unzipped the bag and pulled out a bunch of smaller bags that sounded as if they were full of macaroni. From one of these bags, she extracted a jump rope with green and white beads. "Try this."

"Two minutes, forty-five."

Alicia reluctantly stepped forward and took the rope from her hands. "You want me to do three minutes?" The dread in her voice showed that she had now learned just how long three minutes could be.

Nan shook her head. "No, just show me some of your favorite steps."

Alicia put the rope behind her feet and took the

handles in each hand, but she didn't start to jump until after the emotionless voice called "Time" from the speakers, and the other jumpers stopped jumping. Some paced in circles, a few went for their water bottles, and others hunched forward, breathing heavily, hands on their knees. A cluster of high school aged girls were soon leaning against the wall with water in one hand, cell phones in the other.

"Okay, go ahead," Nan encouraged.

I turned back to see Alicia lift the rope over her head. As she brought it down in front of her, I held my breath. She would be mortified if she missed.

She jumped. The rope went under her feet. Then she did it again, and again. I let out my breath. She could jump, thank heavens. She wasn't anywhere near as fast as those other kids, but at least she knew how to jump rope.

"Can you go faster?" The coach asked. "Take out the double bounce?"

She stopped. "Double bounce?"

"You're taking two jumps for every turn of the rope," Nan explained. "Try to go faster—only one bounce."

After a few attempts, she got into the faster rhythm and grinned in triumph. "Is that it?"

"Yes, great. Can you do a cross? Or a double-under?"

Alicia shook her head, her forehead creased in confusion. "I don't know what that is."

"Try this." The coach jumped her feet out and together again like a jumping jack. "A straddle jump."

Alicia copied the move, and the rope made it under her feet, but very slowly.

"Okay, great. Great job." Coach Nan turned to me.

"She should sign up for our Juniors class. It's on Tuesdays and Wednesdays."

I had looked at the team schedule online and seen that the competition team jumpers practiced on Mondays, Fridays and Sundays, so bringing Alicia on another day wouldn't help me much at all. "She doesn't qualify for the practice team?" I asked. They met along with the competition jumpers on Mondays and Sundays.

The coach smiled. "Not just yet. But she can work up to it."

This was not going well. "I work late on Tuesdays and Wednesdays," I lied. "Do you have any classes on Mondays or Fridays? Those are my best days. And weekends."

I crossed my fingers.

"We do have a class on Fridays…"

My heart leapt—

"But it's only for boys."

"That leaves me out," Alicia muttered with obvious relief.

"Oh." I turned to Alicia. "Maybe I can sign your brother up for classes and he can teach you what he learns."

Alicia smiled. "Great idea!" Again there was that wicked gleam in her eyes.

Nan directed a smile at me too. "You have a son that wants to jump?"

"Yeah. Yeah, I sure do." I forced myself to match their smiles, wondering how many video games this was going to cost. We probably didn't have room for them all.

I decided there was no point in mentioning the

class to Evan until just before he had to go on Friday,
since I'd only have to listen to him complain about it all
week. The note I put on the calendar was discernible
only to me: JRWRB (jump rope with reluctant boy). But
there was another note on the calendar that was equally
mysterious and it was for Tuesday. Tomorrow. It said
"MOM. 7:30." It wasn't my mom's birthday. Had I
promised to call her? Did I expect her to call me?

The phone rang. It was almost 7:30. If my mom
was on the line I would freak, since she almost never
called and I had never had a premonition about her
calling. But it would be just like her to call a day early
and complain that I had it wrong.

I steeled myself for the sound of her voice just in
case. "Hello?"

"Hi, Karen." Fortunately, the voice was way too
low for Mom.

"Hey, Brian. I thought you were my—never mind."

"What? You'd better not say ex-husband."

"No. I saw this weird note on my calendar and
thought my mom might be calling."

"Were you expecting your mom to call?"

"No. But the calendar says MOM in capital letters
followed by 7:30"

"Hmm." He paused for a moment. "Didn't you tell
me you were joining Mothers on a Mission? They're
always listed at church as 'MOM'."

"Oh, that's right." I'd forgotten. Brian said I'd enjoy
going to his church once I got to know some of the
people, and the best way to do that was to join a group
with similar interests. The "Mothers" group seemed an
obvious choice. I liked being a mom. I was good at it—
I'd raised two wonderful kids without much help from
their low-life father. So I would find other moms like

me and make friends. In theory, at least. Making friends had been easy when I was a kid, but starting over after the divorce everything felt all wrong. It was forced. So far about the most I'd been able to manage was a few short talks with my neighbor. I hoped things would be easier at church, but I was still a little nervous.

"Do you have any youth group meetings or anything at church tomorrow night?" I asked. It might be sort of like a date. We'd be in the same building, at least.

"No, I don't think I do."

"Oh."

"But there's a light that's not working right in the Sunday School hallway, so maybe I'll take a look at it."

"And then you'll need to go out for coffee after that, right?"

"You know it." I could hear the smile in Brian's voice. "We really do think alike."

I was suddenly reminded of his "old and gray" comment from the other night and decided to steer the conversation in another direction. I also didn't want to think about my job, so I asked about his. The conversation ended fairly painlessly with a funny story involving crazy glue and someone's telephone.

The best way to not worry about work was just to go to bed, I decided. But I dreamed of giant parrots jumping rope.

8

Before I went into the office the next morning I had an appointment to visit the parrot house with the collapsed sunroom roof. I'd told Dave it was a big Victorian house to make him think the owner was rich, but I actually had no idea what the house looked like even though I sometimes parked near it. Church Street wound up the hillside above Main Street and was lined with large, old houses. I didn't know much about architecture, so I wasn't sure they were Victorian, but some of them had elaborate gingerbread trim and they all looked like rich people could have lived in them. None of the houses on the street looked like they had much back yard, since they were set on a hillside that sloped sharply up on one side of the street and dropped to nothing on the other side. I parked in the street as close as I could to the Flaglers' house. Theirs sat on the side of the street where the backyards sloped down and seemed to disappear in the air above Main Street. It was three minutes to nine – so I wasn't that early. I knocked on the leaded glass of the door.

A dog barked in a high yippy tone, and then another low baying bark joined in. Maybe the dogs kept Doreen's investigators from getting close enough to learn anything. After a minute, a face appeared behind the leaded glass, eyes distorted and framed by dark hair and a long nose. It disappeared. There was a muffled sound of voices and some more barking. Then all at once the door swung open, and I was standing face to face with a red-headed woman who looked really familiar. She wore a blue sweater that was probably made of something expensive and a greater than average amount of makeup. Maybe even false eyelashes.

"Mrs. Flagler?" I asked.

"Yes."

"I'm with DS Investigations." I waved a clipboard as if it were a symbol of authority although the only thing on it was the packing list from Evan's Cub Scout camping trip. "Your insurance agent made the appointment for me to come by and take some information regarding the incident with your sunroom."

"Oh, yeah." She stepped back to allow me in. "I've been expecting you, but you weren't what I was expecting, if you know what I mean."

"Er, no."

"Like I thought the investigator would be a young man, like on TV."

"Sorry."

"So do you want some coffee?"

I did, but of course I had to pretend I didn't. "No, thanks." I flipped over the pages on the clipboard to reveal a blank sheet of paper and wrote down *Mrs. F wears too much eye makeup*. She looked so familiar. Had she been a former neighbor of mine? Or a mother of one of the kids at school? I gave up trying to place her and just asked, "Can you show me to the sunroom?"

"It's right back here." She led the way through a narrow marble hallway next to a big staircase with dark, rich looking wooden balustrades. We passed through a kitchen with brightly painted tiles in intricate patterns on the floor and a dining room with textured carpet that pushed back when you stepped on it. Finally we came to a room at the back that was blindingly bright even on a cloudy day. Light came in from every angle, since the entire room was paneled with glass, except for the floor which was covered in a flat carpet that looked like dirty red felt.

"This is the sunroom."

Nothing appears broken, I wrote in my book. Then I looked up at her. "I assume this is where the ceiling—"

"We had to have it fixed, of course," she cut in. "We couldn't wait for you guys. It's January, for heaven's sake."

If the room had been damaged, it was hard to imagine now. The glass ceiling and walls were all intact, the carpet, though ugly, was unmarred and the futon sofa, bean bag chairs and little tables in the corners all looked brand new.

New carpet, new furniture, I wrote.

"Of course we had to replace everything, too."

"Did you take pictures of the damage?"

"I thought you were supposed to do that."

If I had been a dog I probably would have growled at her. "No one answered the door when the first investigator arrived. He could only take pictures from the outside."

She rolled her eyes. "Well, you could see from outside just as well as inside that the roof had collapsed."

"Yes. But we need proof of the items that were damaged. The easiest way to prove that would be to show us a picture of the damaged furniture, etc."

"Oh. Well we have pictures of the room from before the roof collapsed. But when it happened, we were too upset to think of taking pictures."

"That makes it difficult."

She planted her hands on her hips. "It doesn't take a rocket scientist to know that if a roof full of snow collapses on your Stanton Shaggy Plush it's going to be ruined."

"Shaggy plush what?" Nothing in the room looked plush to me. Or shaggy.

"Oh." She sighed with impatience. "It's just a... a general carpet expression. The carpet that was in there was the exact same as what we've got in there now, of course. Indoor/Outdoor Supreme."

What was with those carpet descriptions? She sounded like—then it hit me. She sounded like a carpet commercial. Because she *was* a carpet commercial. Flagler Flooring. She did local commercials where she and her husband rushed in to save people from bad carpet deals. I think they both wore capes.

That's why she seemed familiar.

"We're in the carpet business," she explained, as if she understood the dawning look of recognition in my eyes. She seemed proud, but a little embarrassed too. Maybe those cheesy commercials weren't her idea.

I decided not to ask about the capes. "So, um, I need to take down a list of what was damaged or destroyed when the roof collapsed."

"Well there was the Stanton—I mean Indoor/Outdoor Supreme carpet," she corrected herself quickly.

May be lying about carpet I wrote.

"And the futon and chairs, and there were three tables," she continued.

"Did they look like the ones you have now? I only see two tables."

"Are there only—maybe two then. I'll get the

picture." While she walked into the kitchen, I went over to examine the futon and chairs. Definitely from the lower end of the retail market. They could not be claiming much for those. It was all about the parrot, apparently, which Mrs. Flagler had yet to mention. And some value for the carpet. I didn't know how much carpet was worth, but if they could afford to advertise it on TV so often, it couldn't be that cheap.

Futon with frame, two bean bags, two cheap parsons tables, I wrote. *Hasn't mentioned parrot yet.*

When Mrs. Flagler came back clutching a picture frame, she was either blinking back tears or having trouble with her contact lenses. "This was the worst part," she said with a loud sniff. "The kids were so attached to Pencils."

"You lost some pencils, too?"

"Pencils was our parrot. He was a blue mutated yellow napped Amazon. The rarest breed in captivity."

"A yellow mutated what?"

She held up the frame so I could see. "He was the blue mutation of a yellow napped Amazon."

The picture she held out showed the room just as it looked now with the addition of a Christmas tree in the corner and a big blue bird in a sizeable cage on a stand. "I see."

"Amazons are usually green. But he was blue. So he was worth a lot more."

"How much more?"

She pursed her lips. "Average price for the mutation seems to be $18-20,000. I think we paid $15,000 for him, but of course prices always go up."

"Do you have the receipt?"

"Oh, no, we never keep receipts. Too much clutter."

"Well, without a receipt, it's hard to prove that you lost such an expensive bird." I pointed to the picture. "I know nothing about birds—all I can tell is that it's blue. It could be a blue jay or a plain old bluebird for all I know."

"Hmpf. The vet can confirm that we lost a blue mutation Amazon parrot."

If that was true, I could find out the value on my own, at least roughly. But there had to be something she could show me. "Can I see the parrot's cage?" I asked.

"Oh, no." She shook her head with vehemence and it was disturbing to see just how little this caused her hair to move. "It was totally destroyed, of course, and the kids were horrified. We had to dispose of it right away." She blinked rapidly again as if trying to hold back tears.

Not much evidence of bird I wrote on my page. *And scary hair. Eyelashes look like spiders.*

To force myself to ignore her appearance and focus on finishing Doreen's business, I started making a list. "Okay, as you know, the company has already settled with you the value of the structural repairs and the only thing at issue is the contents of the room at the time of the incident. You're claiming the loss of your bird at $18,000—"

"Maybe $20,000."

"Or $20,000, the furniture at...you don't have receipts for that either, I suppose?"

She shook her head.

"I'll look it up in the Ikea catalog," I muttered, pausing to see if she would object. She didn't. "And the carpet. What's the value on that?"

"The room is 12 x 15 and that carpet runs $3.89 per

foot plus padding and installation so $1,060.20."

I was sure they didn't pay that much since they owned the company, but I wasn't going to argue carpet. Doreen wanted me to investigate the bird, and that's what I was doing. If the vet confirmed it really was the mutated blue thing, then the claim might be valid. The Flaglers said the roof collapsed January 4, so if the parrot was in there before Christmas, he was probably there when the roof collapsed. It would be difficult to prove he wasn't, and I had no reason not to believe her. Now if the vet reported that the bird had been spray painted blue or something, that would be different. I got the name of her vet, made a few notes about the room and had her email me a high res copy of the picture she'd shown me.

Then I was done and could go to the office and work on something important, like hiding sardine cans.

After I'd finished with the initial flurry of activity at the office and had settled in at my desk with a cup of coffee, I considered four names: *Gwen, Juno, Danielle, Morgan*. Those were my most obvious suspects in the jump rope case. Gina Callaghan emailed me the results of the qualifying competition where her daughter placed fifth in the "power" category. The four girls who placed ahead of her were my obvious suspects. Right now they were just names on a computer screen, since the only jumper I'd heard called by name yesterday was "Lindsey." Though we had stayed at practice "just watching" for over half an hour after our conversation with Coach Nan, no other names had come up. So I had watched the high school girls, but didn't know who they were. I hoped Gina could tell me a little about them.

I dialed her number and the phone was ringing when Rodney announced that we had a "pre-visioning" meeting in fifteen minutes. I had no idea what that was, but I knew I would want to be on my lunch break by then. Or I could distract him by getting him to make lattes for everyone and while he was happily engaged with his steamed milk, the rest of us could sneak out.

"Hello?"

I suddenly remembered I was on the phone. Who was I calling? "Hi, this is Karen Maxwell with DS Investigations." I paused, hoping whoever I'd called would say something to remind me who they were. The "hello" was a fairly generic woman's voice.

There was an awkward pause.

"Did you get the results I emailed you?" the voice asked, sound more refined and less generic now.

Ah, that's right, it was Gina Callaghan.

I relaxed back in my chair, feeling kinda like my brother. "I did, thank you. I was hoping you could tell me a little about the girls who placed higher than Hayley on that list. And do you have any pictures of them?"

"I can send you a team picture. What else did you want?"

"Well, you think someone deliberately damaged Hayley's rope. Are any of those four girls likely to have done that, in your opinion? Or Hayley's opinion?"

Skepticism sounded in her voice. "None of us likes to think our child would be capable of such a thing."

"Of course."

"It could have been one of the girls' mothers."

"I'm not saying that it couldn't. But let's start with the girls." I sat forward and grabbed a promotional pad of paper advertising wart cream. "How about Gwen?"

"Hmmmn." She considered for a moment. "Gwen's a good jumper, but this is her first year in this age group, so she's new to this event. None of us expected her to do well enough to qualify."

"So it's possible that she might have wanted to do something to increase her chances?"

"It's possible. But not likely. She's part of the group routine so she was almost guaranteed to qualify for that."

"Maybe she wanted to qualify in two events."

"Maybe." I could almost hear her shake her head. "But she doesn't seem like the type."

"Okay, then how about Juno?"

"Oh, she's been the best speed jumper on the team for years and her power numbers are usually almost as good as Hayley's. Everybody knew she'd qualify. I don't think she'd take a chance on getting disqualified for bad sportsmanship." She paused for a moment. "I think it would be somebody desperate, someone who thought her daughter would not otherwise qualify."

"So you really think it's more likely to be the *mother* of one of the competitors rather than one of the competitors themselves?"

"I didn't say that."

"Okay." I tried not to make any judgmental noise as I scribbled some notes. "Next on the list is Danielle."

"Who?"

"Danielle Beckett."

"She's on the Frederick Flyers. I don't know much about her except that she's usually very competitive in freestyle."

I wrote down the name of the other jump rope team. "And then the last is Morgan."

Gina went silent.

"Are you still there?" I asked after waiting what seemed like a ridiculously long time.

"They say if you can't say something nice, don't say anything at all."

"Would you consider Morgan a possible suspect?"

"The most obvious. If Hayley scored in her usual range, Morgan would be the one who didn't qualify."

"And is that typical for Morgan? Would she be likely not to qualify?"

"I'd say so. It seems like she'd rather talk than practice most days." Even without the obvious disgust in her voice, it was pretty easy to tell that Gina didn't have a high opinion of this Morgan girl.

Of course, I couldn't imagine anyone talking much during practice based on the exhausting workout I'd seen the day before, but maybe some practices were different than others.

"So let me get this straight," I clarified. "You think Morgan wants to go to Nationals or to try out for the Worlds team so badly that she would cheat to make it happen."

"I wouldn't put it past her. Bonnie is really out of control."

"Bonnie?"

"Morgan's mom. She's just—well, you have to meet her."

"Okay." I wrote *Morgan** Bonnie*. Then I read off the next four names on the list who placed after Hayley. After all, one of those girls could have damaged Hayley's rope and yet still failed to qualify.

"I don't know any of them," Gina admitted. "There were three other teams at the regional qualifier besides us and Frederick."

"Were there any other members of the Jumptastics

who didn't qualify in that age group?" It looked like there were at least 15 girls competing in the event against Hayley.

"Hmmn." Gina paused again. "Well, Lindsey moved up to that age group and she didn't qualify. But we didn't expect her to. She's just not that good."

Lindsey was the girl I'd seen at practice. I immediately felt sorry for her.

"Do you think she might have sabotaged Hayley's rope out of desperation?" I asked. "Or maybe she tried to damage a lot of ropes, and Hayley's is the only one we know about."

Gina surprised me by laughing in a lush, rich musical tone. "No, I really don't. She fights with her sister a lot, but I don't think she'd break her rope."

"Lindsey is Hayley's sister?" I'm sure the shock was evident in my voice. "Your daughter?"

"Yes." Gina didn't seem to think it was odd that she hadn't mentioned this to me before now.

So what else wasn't she telling me? I tapped my pen against the picture of a bottle of Wart-Away. "Do you have any other offspring that jump competitively?"

"No, just the two girls."

"So you don't think Lindsey might have had anything to do with this?" I tried to keep the cynicism out of my voice, but really, most crimes are committed by people who know the victims. And having grown up with an obnoxious younger brother, I was well aware of the lengths siblings could go to sabotage each other's chance at happiness.

"I really don't."

I tried to get her to look at this objectively. "You said Lindsey's 'not that good.'" And her coach had said it too, in so many words, but I decided not to repeat that. I cleared my throat. "Don't you think there's a chance she could be jealous of her sister's success?"

"That's a horrible thing to suggest."

It would be an even more horrible thing to learn after paying hundreds of dollars for an investigation, but I didn't point that out. "I have to consider all of the suspects," I explained, "or I'm not doing my job."

"Well, leave Lindsey out of it. I know my own daughter."

"Okay." I scribbled, *Talk to Hayley about her sister* on my notepad. Mothers think they know their daughters but my mom didn't know half of what went on in my life during high school, and I was starting to realize the situation might be just the same for me and my own daughter, whether I liked it or not. A teenager's life seemed like a puzzle, where parents see a few pieces, friends see different pieces and sisters might see something completely different.

I suddenly wished Evan was a girl so Alicia might have someone to confide in who would come tell everything to me.

Then I remembered something Alicia had said earlier. She said this would be about a boy.

"One last question for now, Mrs. Callaghan. Does Hayley have any friends who pick her up from practices or competitions? Any boyfriends, for example?"

"Oh no," she laughed again as if this idea was completely ludicrous. "She doesn't have time for that."

Find out about boys I wrote on my notes. That might be a piece of the puzzle her mother had never seen.

9

Despite multiple orders for cappuccino, not a single one of us was able to sneak out of the office, so we spent a large part of the rest of the day coming up with our "visions" of how business should be conducted at DS Investigations. I think Dave spent most of his "visioning" time watching a movie on his iPad. When we reconvened, all the visions were translated onto post-it notes stuck all over the office. And then it was time to leave, and even though I'd stayed until five to finish the exercise, we still weren't done.

"Good work, comrades, we can pick up where we left off tomorrow," Rodney chirped happily.

I reached over to peel a purple Post-it note off his back. "Are we just going to leave all these notes out?"

"Yes, tomorrow we can document the locations and then synthesize them into a coherent symbol of office success."

"Half of them will fall off overnight."

"Then we can approximate the locations from where they've fallen on the floor."

"Except that the janitor service comes tonight and so their location will now be at the bottom of a trash can." Which is admittedly where they belonged, so I don't know why I was complaining. I looked at the note I'd pulled off of Rodney's back. It said "visualize talking less and saying more" and I think it was in Dave's handwriting.

"Was that on my back?" Rodney asked.

"What?" I shook my head as I crumpled the note into a ball. "No."

He reached out. "What did it say?"

"Nothing." I tossed it into the trash.

"Ah," he shook his head, "by throwing that away, you're saying that your comrades' opinions are not worthy of consideration." He stepped over to the trash can and reached in.

"Sometimes they're not." I really hoped he wouldn't open it.

He uncrumpled the note and read it silently, his forehead creased with a frown. "Okay," he said slowly. Then he folded the note into quarters and tucked in his shirt pocket.

I cleared my throat. "Like I said, sometimes other people's opinions aren't important."

"That's not true." He was shaking his head slowly as he spoke. "If we want to perform like a winning team, we must hear the voice of every player."

That sounded like a quote from a football coach or something so I was sure it had come off his motivational calendar. "Maybe you don't need to hear what they have to say at every practice." I pointed out.

"It's my job to listen."

I found that an odd thing for him to say, since we grumbled about his plans and changes all the time and he never seemed to hear.

He moved away and went over to shut down his computer and I couldn't really think of anything else to say, though I felt I should. He reminded me of a balloon interrupted while someone was blowing it up. Half the air emptied out in a sudden rush, leaving behind a mere shadow of what once was.

I hope he doesn't take it too hard. Please help him to feel better.

I stopped moving. Who exactly was I asking to help Rodney feel better? There was no one else left in the office. Was I talking to God? I didn't want to be a religious weirdo. Maybe it was okay if I talked to God occasionally, but if I started to hear God talk back, then I would know I was in trouble.

It was probably just because I knew I would be going to church tonight. I had God on the brain or something. But it didn't make me a religious nut. Not yet, anyway.

I arrived home to a strangely vacant house. The kids were with their dad, so my dinner consisted of a bag of microwave popcorn and a Diet Coke, along with the slightly brown apple I'd cut up for breakfast that no one had eaten. I arrived at Brian's church about fifteen minutes early and sat in my minivan with the radio on. Cold air seeped through the windows, since I'd turned off the engine, and I had goosebumps, but I didn't want to go in too early to sit in a room full of people I didn't know. Even though the purpose of going was to get to know them. Pretty lame. I just didn't want to force myself on people. *"Hi, I'm Karen, and I don't know anyone here. Be my friend."* No, not happening.

So when I walked in a few minutes before the meeting started at 7, I felt a little guilty, like I was sabotaging Brian's plan. He said I'd like the place better once I got to know people, and I wasn't really doing my best. On the other hand, I was here and that had to count for something.

I'd hoped to come in and take a seat in the back,

but I couldn't because there was no seat in the back. Everyone was sitting around two long rectangular tables. I paused in the doorway.

"C'mon in," a woman at the far side of the table said warmly. "Are you looking for MOMs?"

I forced myself to smile and my feet to move forward. "Yes."

"Always glad to see a new face. Have a seat. I'm Siobhan." She looked as Irish as her name, with pale skin and red curly hair and a wide infectious smile. Maybe this wouldn't be so bad.

I sat down in an empty chair that was almost directly across from her. The women to my right smiled, but seemed to be engaged in a conversation about math books, and I didn't want to interrupt. On my left, a thin woman with bobbed chestnut hair turned to face me as I draped my jacket over the back of my chair.

She held out her hand to shake mine. "Hi, I'm Elise. Are you new to the area?"

Suddenly everyone seemed to start talking at once.

"You look really familiar," another woman across the table blurted out.

"I've seen you in church," someone down at the end of the table said.

"You're a …friend of Brian's, I think," the woman next to Siobhan said. "Right?" she asked me.

My face heated so fast I could have sworn my head was being pumped full of boiling oil. "Um…"

Siobhan held up her hand. "Okay, ladies, let's not interrogate the poor woman. Why don't you tell us a little about yourself and your kids, and then we'll introduce ourselves, too."

"Yeah, okay." I took a deep breath. "I'm Karen

Maxwell and I have a daughter Alicia who's 12 and my son Evan is almost 10. And I work in Old Ellicott City and live in Langley's Choice. The townhouse part of the development, not the part with the really big houses."

Everyone nodded politely. Then the women on either side of me both started to introduce themselves at the same time and then they both laughed, and again I thought this might not be such a bad group. I began to relax a little.

Elise ended up going first. "My oldest is 12 like yours," she started off. Then she listed about six more names and ages in rapid fire.

The woman next to her did the same. At the end of the table was a young woman with her hair in a disheveled bun. She had a three week old baby. Everyone at in the room seemed to have either tons of kids or very young kids. I felt a little inadequate, since I could barely manage my two, and they were at an age where they didn't need a whole lot of managing.

When the introductions were finished, Siobhan lead us in a prayer and then everyone pushed away from the table and headed to the refreshments table up against the wall. Popcorn, potato chips, Diet Coke and brownies. So what if I didn't have the superhuman parenting skills that these women did? We shared a common taste in snacks, at least.

When we settled back at the table, Siobhan wiped chocolate crumbs off her fingers and opened the Bible in front of her. "We've been reading Paul's Letter to the Colossians and this week we're discussing a pretty unpopular section—"

"The 'wives submit to your husbands' section," Elise interrupted with a shudder. "I hate this one."

A woman on the other side of the table wearing a

family tree necklace full of different colored birthstones leaned forward. "But it says 'husbands, love your wives,' too," she put in quickly. "The obligations go both ways."

Just like before, the voices suddenly rang out from all around the table.

"Love is not the same as submit."

"If you're acting out of love, the decisions will essentially be the same."

"I don't think I should have to submit to my husband if he doesn't have to submit to me."

"It's really hard to function as a family unit without one person in charge."

"We function just fine, thank you very much."

Siobhan waved her napkin in the air as a signal for a truce. "Ladies, please, enough. Let's read it first, shall we? We'll start at the beginning of Chapter Three. Who needs a Bible?"

I was the only one to raise my hand. Most of the other moms had Bibles with special covers like leather zipper cases or something covered in pastel quilted stuff with white eyelet edging.

Maybe a shared preference for Diet Coke was not enough. I was pretty sure we had a Bible at home somewhere, but it didn't have a fancy cover, and I didn't know how to find things in the way these women all seemed to.

And they were all so... married. Most of the discussion centered on their relationships with their husband. I didn't say anything. Once Elise asked me for my opinion about sharing household chores with my husband and I said we couldn't share because we were in two different houses. I said that was a good thing because we couldn't fight about it, either, and everyone laughed, but still I could tell they felt sorry for me. Some of them might have been offended, too, because maybe they thought divorce was a sin. I know some of the discussion was about how there was too much divorce in society and people saw marriage as disposable. I didn't, and I never had, but when something is broken, you can only glue it together so many times before you finally throw it away. And if one of the pieces decides it wants to live with a dish from the other side of the cabinet, there's not much you can do to hold it together.

Everyone was friendly throughout the meeting and they all talked like they assumed I'd be back for the next session in two weeks. But on my way out I looked at the bulletin board to see what other group I might try instead. I was not a "Mother on a Mission." Or at least not the same mission.

What other group could I join instead? Gardening club? Sounded like work. Quilting? No, quilting was very big with my mom's friends in Arizona. I was not ready to follow in her footsteps. Foreign missions? My mind instantly pictured an exotic rainforest with monkeys swinging from trees and a waterfall cascading over rocks to the piranha-filled waters below. Sounded kind of cool, actually. But tough to fit in on a school night. What else was there?

"How'd it go?" Brian asked from behind me.

"Oh, great."

"Siobhan scares the living daylights out of some people. She tends to take charge of things."

"No, she was great, I really liked her." And it was true, I did. I liked all of them. But together they were just too much. Some of them even homeschooled their kids. I wasn't in that league. On the Christian Life scale they were grad students and I felt like I was in my first few sessions of preschool. I couldn't keep up and didn't want to try.

"Well I can arrange to do some work around during their next meeting, too."

"Oh, um, I don't think I can go to the next meeting."

Disappointment creased his face. I couldn't let him down like that. I had to try harder. "Yeah," I continued, "I liked the MOMs group, but it meets at the same time as another group I want to join."

"Oh," curiosity sounded in his voice. "What's that?"

Yeah, what was that? Like I couldn't see that question coming. My eyes scanned the bulletin board nearest to me frantically. There was a calendar – what met on Tuesday nights besides the MOMs? "Knitting for Neighbors in Need," I said triumphantly, so grateful there was something else on the schedule. "I really want to join the knitting group and make…whatever it is they make for people."

"Oh," he said again, this time sounded almost shocked. "I didn't know you were into knitting."

"And you know everything about me?" I turned away from the bulletin board and we started to stroll toward the door.

"Uh, no, obviously not. You just, uh, didn't seem the type."

"There's a knitting type?"

"Okay, okay, I give up." He held the door open and nodded toward one side of the parking lot. "Do you want to go to Bean Hollow or the place next to the Trolley Stop?"

"The Old Mill Bakery? That place isn't open this

late, so let's see if Bean Hollow is. If it's not…" I didn't know what to suggest. Neither of us liked the chain coffee places on Route 40.

We stopped walking. Our breath made heavy clouds that glowed in the lights shining down on the parking lot.

"We could go to the Trolley Stop," Brian suggested.

"That's a bar. Won't they revoke your youth leader card or something if you're seen going in there?"

He laughed. "I'm not taking the kids there on a field trip. I am allowed to have an outside life."

Are you? I sometimes wondered. He seemed tied to the church by an invisible band. Well this would be a test. Would he park in front of the bar or hide his car in the big lot behind the stone wall?

His pickup truck was actually too big to fit in one of the spaces in front, so he had to park in the lot on the side. But I parked my minivan in front and waited for him there, almost daring people to pay attention. I wanted to shout out "I'm meeting the youth leader at a bar on a Tuesday night." How daring. Never mind that I ordered Diet Coke and he had iced tea and French fries. It was something different, something I hadn't predicted either of us doing. That was a good sign.

The next morning, the kids were crabby, like they usually are after time with their dad. I'm never sure if that's because it bothers them to spend time with him or whether it bothers them to return home to me. Of course I assume it's the former. I mean, if the man irritated me, he probably irritates everybody.

I was tired, as if I'd been drinking shooters in that bar the night before instead of soda. So I nearly ran over Brittany when I was backing my van into a space along the curb on a street that was farther away from the office than I liked.

"Sorry," I called out the window.

She must not have held it against me because she waited on the sidewalk while I shut off the van and gathered my lunchbox and book bag.

"I think I'm early today," she said with obvious pride as I joined her on the sidewalk.

I started to point out that I was actually late, but then I decided that if I agreed with her, we would both look better. So I just nodded and zipped my coat up higher to try to block the winter wind and frigid rain spitting in our faces. As we walked down toward Main Street, I yawned and tried to calculate how many seconds it would be until I was in the warm, dry office with a cup of hot coffee in my hands.

"Isn't that the parrot house?" Brittany asked.

"Huh?" Parrots had nothing to do with coffee.

"3775 Church Street. I remember seeing the report on the computer screen."

I looked up at the house as if I expected to see the Carpet Queen standing in the front window. "Yeah, that is the house."

She walked a few paces into the front yard and tried to peer around the side of the house. "Oh, you can't see the sunroom from here."

"It's not that exciting. They've fixed all the damage." All the same, I looked around the side, too, hoping the house might give up its secrets if I just stared at it long enough.

"Oh." Brittany went back to the sidewalk.

"Can you see anything from down below on Main Street?"

I shook my head. "It's blocked by the stone

building with the shop that sells clothes knit out of rope."

She considered for a moment. "The one with the crystals and wine made from tree bark?"

I nodded.

"Hmmn." She looked up at the house again. "Did you see the parrot?"

"It's dead." I started to walk down the hill toward Main Street.

"I didn't know if they might have had it stuffed or something. Since it's worth so much money. Hey!" Her voiced spiked with sudden interest. "What's all this junk?"

I turned back to see Brittany pointing her boot toward a pile of boxes along the curb. "Guess recycling doesn't get picked up much here, either."

Right then I realized I'd walked past a big box with a picture of a really fake looking Christmas tree on it, as well as boxes of lights, garland, ornaments and a big star. These were all things from the picture the owner had shown me. I hadn't even noticed them. But Brittany had. I immediately headed over to the pile.

"You'd think they would have thrown these boxes out weeks ago, if they put the stuff up in December," I murmured as I bent down to examine the tree box. "I wonder if they could have faked that picture."

"Do you want me to search through the boxes?" Brittany sounded unusually eager.

I thought about it for a moment before shaking my head. "No, I guess it doesn't matter. Even if they took the picture after Christmas, it doesn't matter as long as the parrot was alive at the time the sunroom was in use. But the insurance agency thinks the room wasn't finished at the time of the collapse." I stood back up.

"What do you think?"

I shrugged. "Too early to say for sure, but the picture makes it look like the room was finished and in use while the parrot was still alive, so it's hard to prove he wasn't in there when the roof collapsed. I'm waiting for a report from the vet."

"Like an autopsy?"

"Yeah."

She shivered. "It's cold out here."

"It's winter. Let's go." I was annoyed that I hadn't noticed the pile of boxes, which could have turned out to be important. I couldn't even remember if they'd been there yesterday when I talked to Mrs. Flagler.

We hurried the rest of the way down the sidewalk. As we turned onto Main Street a man passed us with a tray of steaming paper coffee cups. Only a block up this street and one block down Merryman Street and then we'd be within striking distance of our own cappuccino machine.

A trash truck rumbled past, spitting diesel fumes in its wake. Not trash, today was recycling. Did I remember to put out the recycling bin? Wait, they didn't pick up recycling at home in our housing development on Wednesdays, just in Old Ellicott City. The piles of boxes hadn't necessarily been sitting out long at all. Were those Christmas decorations new? Did it matter? What if it did?

I stopped. "I'm going back to the parrot house," I called to Brittany, who was now a few steps ahead.

"I'll come too." She turned around, raced past me and by the time we turned onto Church Street, she was several paces ahead of me. But the trash truck was ahead of both of us, with sanitation workers hanging off both sides ready to grab whatever was sitting at the curb.

"What are we looking for?" Brittany asked over her shoulder as she ran.

"Anything." My shoulder bag slammed into my hip with every step, slowing me down considerably. By the time I reached the house, all the boxes would be gone.

"Do you want me to save all the boxes?" Brittany called out.

I thought frantically. Daily walking workouts hadn't prepared me to run flat out with a book bag bumping against my legs. My breathing was frantic—everything was a little frantic at this point. "No," I called to her breathlessly, "unless it's dated or gives some other hint of the purchase date."

With an admirable burst of speed, Brittany dashed ahead and reached the pile of boxes in front of the parrot house before the sanitation workers. She started pawing through them, reading the sides, shaking them and peering inside. The sanitation guys caught up about the same time as me. I grabbed one box microseconds before it would have been swept into the crushing mechanism in the back of the truck.

"We're keeping this stuff," I told the surprised sanitation worker.

He shrugged and moved on to the next house.

"Hey, I found a Santa's elf Chia pet," Brittany chirped. "Or at least the box for it. What did you get?"

I looked down. "Packing peanuts."

Brittany made a face. "Those aren't even recyclable in this county. Hey!" She held up the picture of a round faced elf with a green beard. "This box has a clearance sticker. That means they bought it after Christmas, right?"

I shook my head. "Not necessarily. Lots of stores

put Christmas stuff on sale ahead of time. Did you find any receipts?"

"One, but it was just from the grocery store. I don't think it has any of this stuff on it." She handed me a crumpled piece of paper.

I scanned the list eagerly hoping she was wrong, because the date on the top was January 8. But it seemed to be mostly the usual bread, milk, toilet paper and a few craft supplies. I smoothed it out, folded it carefully and tucked into my book bag to examine later in detail. Then I pulled out my phone and took a picture of the boxes in the wild hope that they might turn out to be useful.

"So we didn't find anything important?" Both her posture and facial expression sank like a fork in cotton candy.

"I don't think we did," I admitted. "But at least we're pretty sure we didn't miss a chance to find something important. We looked – because you noticed the boxes."

I hoped she felt better. I didn't, but then again, it was Wednesday. I never could quite see the point of Wednesdays.

Friday afternoon is usually the best part of the week. Even though weekends for parents can be busier than weekdays, I still have this sense that weekend=freedom. But this weekend, I had the sense of a giant ticking clock with an alarm that was going to ring loud enough to cause physical pain. This work week had gone by too fast, though it wasn't quite over yet.

My son apparently saw nothing but the freedom sign on the road ahead.

"Except for soccer practice I'm going to watch TV all weekend," Evan announced after he threw down his book bag and kicked off his sneakers. "There's a cinnamon sea creatures marathon."

I tried to make sense of that. "Cinnamon sea creatures? Is that a new breakfast cereal?" I watched the boxes that Evan pulled out of the cabinet to see if one of them featured spiced sea horses or something.

"No." He rolled his eyes. "It means movies with fish. Like Spongebob."

"Oh, Cinematic sea creatures, maybe?" I suggested.

"Whatever." He yanked open the silverware drawer and grabbed a spoon.

"Please close the drawer." That "please" would not have been there if I hadn't felt guilty for the little surprise I was about to spring on him. "Your soccer practice is tomorrow, not today, right?"

"Uh-huh." He pulled a bowl out of the cabinet, sat down at the table, and dumped a heaping mound of sugar-covered crunchy things into the bowl.

I started to tell him to close up the bag of cereal so it wouldn't go stale, but then I remembered I had to be extra nice so I reached over to do it for him. Then I poured him a glass of milk and asked if he wanted chocolate syrup in it.

His eyes narrowed. "Does it have extra vitamins or seaweed or something in it that's good for me?"

I looked at the label. "No, just lots of sugar. Do you want some?"

"Why?"

"Why? Because I know you like chocolate milk. And it's Friday. You can celebrate the end of the week."

"You never offer chocolate milk."

"That's not true." I sighed and reminded myself that I wasn't supposed to argue. Instead I just held up the bottle. "I'm offering now."

"Okay."

When I handed him the glass, he sniffed it suspiciously. Then he took it tiny sip. "Tastes fine. I thought it might be sour."

"Would I give you sour milk?"

He nodded emphatically. "Yes."

"This isn't sour." But he was plainly suspicious, so I decided to go ahead and spill the bad news. I pulled out a chair and sat down next to him. "I need you to come with me someplace this afternoon. Then we can go get whatever you want for dinner."

"Dad is picking us up for dinner," he said through a mouthful of dry cereal.

"Then I'll buy you ice cream on the way home."

He chewed and swallowed nervously. "Am I going to the dentist?"

"No." I debated for the millionth time how much to tell him. I really shouldn't be involving my kids in investigations but it just seemed to happen. Alicia really wanted to be involved. Maybe Evan would, too. And then it wouldn't be that wrong, would it? I was taking him to a legitimate youth activity, not a backstreet fight club.

I cleared my throat. "As part of an investigation I have to sit with parents during a class, and I need you to take the class so I have a reason to be there."

"No." He dug his spoon back into the bowl with ferocity.

"What do you mean 'no?' You haven't even heard what it is yet."

He shook his head. "It's not good or you wouldn't have offered chocolate milk."

"I offered chocolate milk, not a trip to Disney World. It isn't that big of a deal."

"Okay." He dropped the spoon and looked up at me. "What is it?"

"It's a boys conditioning class, to make you stronger. By jumping rope."

He sighed and gave me the classic *Parents Don't Know Anything* look. "I don't need a class for jump rope. I already know how."

"You do?"

"We do it in gym class every year." He picked up the spoon again and started flipping pieces of cereal into the air like tiny circus performers.

"So this won't be a big deal, then."

"I don't need a class."

I bent down and looked him in the eye. "I need you

to take it anyway. Please? Just for a while."

"How long is a while?"

"Just a couple of weeks. Probably." Actually, it had to be. If I didn't find the answer by then it would be too late and I would have failed. "Yes." I nodded. "A couple of weeks at the most."

He pushed a piece of cereal around the rim of his bowl faster and faster until it scooted over the edge and shot onto the floor.

I bent down to pick it up without complaint.

Then he looked up at me. "If I don't go to the class then you can't go and you can't get paid, right?

Yikes. I hadn't expected that. "Well, it's not that desperate. I could find another way. But this is the best idea I have right now."

He pushed another piece up to the rim of the bowl. "If I can think of a better idea, can I stop going to the class?"

"Well, yeah. That seems fair. But you'll at least go to this first one, right?"

"I get as much ice cream as I want?"

"Okay." There was no guarantee that his dad planned to feed him anything more nutritious for dinner anyway.

I tried to keep him away from Alicia before we left so she couldn't either taunt him or warn him about how much work it would be.

When we arrived at the gym, I guided Evan over to the section in back where the team had been practicing on Monday. It was filled with tiny children tossing basketballs toward nets not much taller than they were.

"I thought you said it was jump rope."

"It is." I listened closely to see if I could hear that

whirring sound I'd heard last time.

"Freestyle event," said the flat mechanical voice I'd heard calling time increments at the last practice.

"Let's go." I nodded toward the curtain. "They must be in another section of the gym today."

"Judges ready," the mechanical voice continued, "jumpers ready, you may begin."

This time instead of a roomful of whirring ropes, we walked toward a pulsing drum beat and the techno sounds of some musician with enough talent to have hit it big in the 1980s if he had the right hair.

"Alicia hates this song," Evan murmured.

"Sorry." This was not a good sign. We hadn't even actually reached the class yet, and already there was a problem.

"No, that's okay. I think I like it."

"Just because she doesn't?"

He grinned. "Maybe."

When we got to the other side of the curtain, instead of a floor full of jumpers, we saw only one, a boy of high school age who was swinging a jump rope in all directions, letting go of the handle, flipping it around and catching it under his leg, behind his back, or while twisting in the air. He did a round-off, back handspring and back tuck, all while still turning the rope. There was something involving push ups and handstands, too. He ended by throwing his rope high in the air, spinning around, catching it and somehow tangling his feet in it to make a pattern as the music stopped.

Evan had his mouth hanging open, looking as dumbfounded as I felt.

"Time," the mechanical voice called.

"Okay," Coach Nan called from where she sat at a

table by the sound system. "You know your routine, now I think you need to practice it more without the music."

The boy grinned sheepishly as he struggled to catch his breath. "I like doing it with the music."

"I know, but you won't have it at Nationals. Can you put another quad in that last power sequence? And you don't even have a single quint in there, do you?"

"I have one."

"Hmm. I think you can get more points out of it. Try to add one more quad at least."

"Okay." The boy walked over to a pile of matching blue backpacks on the floor, reached over and pulled a water bottle out of one of them and took a long drink.

"Hey, Jacob," a woman called from a chair over near the bleachers, "looking good, baby. You've developed some man muscles. Who-hoo!" She laughed.

He flushed and pretended not to hear.

I made note of the woman, tiger-striped hair, a low cut tank top and big heavy gold earrings. Definitely someone to watch. But first I had to get Evan settled in his class.

Once we'd finished watching Jacob's amazing performance, we noticed a small group of boys in one corner with Coach Dan. Jacob jogged over to join them. "That must be your class," I pointed out. "C'mon."

"Am I gonna learn to do stuff like that guy did?" Evan asked as we walked.

"Do you want to?"

"I don't know. It looks really hard."

"Most things in life that are worth having are hard to get. That doesn't mean you stop trying to get them."

He shrugged.

"Excuse me, Coach Dan?" I called to get his attention as we got close. "This is my son, Evan. He's joining your boys' class."

The coach grinned. "Great, Evan, good to see you. We'll be having lots of fun today. We're working on toads and cougars."

Evan's eyes widened, and his mouth crinkled with uncertainty as he looked at me.

I shrugged. "Ice cream," I whispered. "Think of the ice cream."

"Jacob?" Coach Dan turned to the boy we'd just watched, who had come over to join the boys' class. "Evan is new. Can you help get him started?"

Then, as hard as it was, I had to turn away and leave my boy. I had only an hour to work now and my effort and Evan's would be wasted if I didn't make the most of it.

"I need everybody to show their routines today," Coach Nan was calling out as I walked back over toward the parents on the bleachers. "And that means everybody."

A few jumpers stood by her, as if waiting their turn. Most of them were scattered on the outskirts of the floor practicing skills or talking with each other. One girl was rummaging through her backpack. Or at least I thought it was her backpack. After a few seconds she moved to the next backpack and looked through that one. So I kept watching. Like all the other girls at the practice, she wore a t shirt and short shorts, but hers said "Just Jump" on the back in big black letters. I couldn't imagine wearing a message on my butt, but then I wasn't exactly in the same excellent physical condition as these girls. Hair the color of wet sand bobbed in a ponytail as her head moved up and down while she searched for something in the bag. She went through two more bags in similar fashion before she noticed me staring at her.

"Are you looking for something?" I asked.

She shrugged. "Someone's cellphone was ringing." Then she stood up and went over to a group of girls in the corner opposite from where Evan's small class was meeting.

I couldn't resist—I had to look over and see how he was doing. There were six boys altogether, most of them not much bigger than he was and one of them quite small. They were trying to do something that involved lifting one leg and sticking the rope handle under it. Two of the boys had mastered the skill and were doing it on both legs. Evan was not even close to getting it. I forced myself to look at the older girls instead. That was my job, the reason we were here. I recognized Hayley from the pictures her mom had sent. She was jumping by herself, not doing fancy tricks like most of the others but just jumping with both feet at a really fast pace. Morgan, the girl who probably had to be my prime suspect just because of where she placed in the competition, was talking to the girl with the "Just Jump" shorts who had been rummaging through the backpacks and another girl whose dark hair was held back with a wide orange headband. The "Just Jump" girl whispered something to Morgan and then looked over at me coldly.

I sent a few ice cubes back her way before turning my attention to the parents on the bleachers.

"Hi," I said to Gina as I approached. I had emailed her asking her to introduce me to other moms as a friend of hers from another setting, like church or PTA. She hadn't responded, so I didn't know what she'd come up with or whether she'd play along at all.

"Hi, Karen." She flashed a professionally-whitened smile. "How's your son liking the class?"

"Hard to tell from over here, but he was real excited about it before we started."

"Great." She turned to the others on the bleachers. I'd hoped the woman I'd heard complaining to Coach Nan during our first visit would be here, because disgruntled people are usually happy to share their complaints. But I did not see her. Instead, there were three other women, one grading a stack of school papers, one playing "go fish" with a small girl, and one gazing intently at a tablet in her lap.

"Ladies," Gina announced to the group, "this is my friend Karen from Rolling Road. Her son Devin just joined the boys' class."

I barely noticed that she'd gotten Evan's name wrong. What was Rolling Road? Her street? School? Garden club? I hoped no one would ask me about it.

"Hi." I tried to smile. "Quite an impressive group you've got here." I turned to the woman sitting to the right of Gina, the one grading papers written in big uneven letters. "Which jumper is yours?"

"That's my son Jacob over there." She pointed to the boy we'd seen earlier.

I had to stop myself from asking her a bunch of questions about how her son got to be so good. Right now it was the girls I needed to concentrate on. "He's amazing," I said quickly before turning to the woman on her right who was holding a tablet and looked like she'd rather be reading whatever was on it than talking to me. "How about you?"

"I'm Debbie. My son Sean is waiting over by coach Nan." She nodded toward a thin blond boy a few years older than Evan.

I stifled a sigh. Apparently only the boys' moms came to practice today.

"And I brought Stephen, Gwen and Rachel in the carpool," Debbie added, "so you won't see their parents here today."

At least she gave me an opening to ask about the jumpers' names."Which ones are they?" I ignored Stephen as she pointed him out, but saw that Gwen was the girl with the orange headband and Rachel was the one who'd been sifting through the backpacks. And she was obviously friends with Morgan, my suspect. That made Rachel a suspect, too. And Gwen—she was on that list, and on friendly terms with Morgan and Rachel. Maybe they were in on it together.

Loud cheering and clapping rang from the other side of the gym. "Great job, guys!"

I glanced over at Evan's class. Maybe I'd forgotten that this was little more than a playground sport and nobody was "in on it" because "it" was most likely an accident. I was losing my perspective.

But I had been hired to lose that perspective, at least temporarily. Gina wanted me to find a culprit, and so if there was one, I had to find it. Her. Him. Whoever.

There were no other parents on this set of bleachers, but the woman with the tiger-striped hair who'd practically given a wolf whistle to a boy who was young enough to be her son was sitting in a reclining folder chair nearby reading a magazine with more pictures than words. I definitely wanted an introduction. I caught Gina's eye and nodded in the direction of the tiger lady. She smiled and stood, immediately understanding.

"Bonnie," she said, changing her smile from smug to what I assume had to be fake sincerity, "I'd like you to meet Karen. She's a friend of mine from Rolling Road and her son just joined Dan's Friday class."

"Oh, a golf buddy of yours, huh?"

Golf? I tried not to shudder. I couldn't imagine a sport I knew less about.

Bonnie's face settled into a smile that was half sneer. "I don't recognize you guys without your little white skirts."

"That's tennis." A hairline crack appeared in Gina's smile.

Bonnie waved dismissively. "Whatever."

Gina flashed a dismissive smile in response and then excused herself.

That left me alone with Bonnie, who Gina considered our prime suspect. *Please don't ask me a question about golf. Please don't ask me a question about golf.* I needed to go on the offensive to steer her off the subject of Rolling Road, which I now guessed was a country club somewhere. "So this jump rope is quite a sport. Do you have a son here or a daughter?"

"Morgan." She nodded toward the corner where the three girls were still talking. "She's the blonde with the All-Stars shirt."

"Oh, yes, I see." Her shirt didn't look different than anyone else's, but I already knew that she had blond hair and big teeth and wore more than the usual amount of eye makeup for an athlete.

"How long has Morgan been doing this?"

"Years. Seems like forever. Course she's also a cheerleader, too, that's why she's so good at tumbling. Qualified to go to Nationals in two events this year."

"Is that unusual?"

"Oh, yeah. Most of the jumpers like Morgan who are good at freestyle don't have the speed and power scores to qualify in those events. But she qualified in power, too."

I was a little surprised. If she knew she would probably qualify in the freestyle event, was she likely to sabotage a rope to qualify in a second event? "So she's real excited?" I prompted.

Bonnie's face split into a proud parent grin. "She's got a good shot to make the U.S. National team to go the Worlds competition in South Africa."

"Wow."

"I think the whole family's gonna go. Might even take her boyfriend, Jack. He's real cute." She winked.

I tried not to gag at the woman's cougar aspirations. "That's got to be an expensive trip."

"Oh yeah, but it's the world championship. My baby's gonna be the best in the world."

"Girls!" Coach Nan yelled from her place in the front of the room. "This isn't chat time." I cringed inwardly for a second, thinking she was talking to us, but her attention was directed toward Gwen, Rachel and Morgan who were still standing in the corner. "Put down your phones and get back to work."

"But we weren't using our phones," Gwen objected.

"You weren't jumping, either. Get back to work. David, I need to see your freestyle. Juno, I want you and Hayley to lead a speed drill at 5:30. And Hayley, the hair looks much better, but I've told you that rope is too short. Either lengthen it or get a new one. Okay, Lindsey, you're next."

Gina looked up and watched as her younger daughter danced her way across the floor with the jump rope. She had a cute smile on her face, but she missed several times and one time the rope got caught in the tread on the bottom of her shoe. Gina stopped watching and started to read something on her phone.

I continued to watch her routine. There was a nice but boring cartwheel and some more jumps, mostly without misses. Then she struck a pose with her rope wrapped around her arm and smiled.

"I like your ending," the coach told her, "but the misses are killing you. You may have to take out some of those tricks."

"Ha. She's hardly got any tricks worth scoring to begin with," Bonnie said under her breath. She glanced toward Gina, but she was still reading her phone.

I decided I'd had enough of the moms for a while and wandered closer to where the jumpers were practicing.

I couldn't hear much of what they were saying to each other, and what I did hear sounded like it related to whatever they were working on. As we got close to the ending time of Evan's class, two high school-aged boys walked into our side of the gym. They were dressed in jeans and hoodies, not looking like they were ready to work out.

"They've got another hour," Coach Nan told them right away. "So you boys take a seat right there on the bleachers."

They ignored her instruction and started toward the girls in the corner, but then they noticed Coach Nan following them and they sat down against the wall.

"If you disrupt practice, I'll have to ask you to leave," she warned.

Hayley put down her rope and started to jog around the gym.

Soon after that, Lindsey came over to get a drink, and I decided to try to talk to her before I had to leave.

"Hi, I'm Karen Maxwell," I said in a low voice. "Did your mom tell you about me?"

She nodded warily.

"Don't worry, I won't embarrass you and there's no one close enough to hear us talking. Why is your sister running?"

"She does that a lot. Part of her training. For endurance."

"Oh, okay. I saw you jump for your coach a little earlier. You were really good."

Her face lit up. "Thanks."

I wanted to ask her about Rachel but wasn't sure how. "Does your coach have a rule against using cellphones?"

She nodded.

"All your bags look alike. Do you ever grab something out of the wrong one by mistake?"

She shook her head. "They all have our names on them. And I can tell mine by the kangaroo on the outside." She pointed toward a tiny stuffed kangaroo hanging on a carabineer as if it had been strung up for some crime.

"Did you see anyone looking through your sister's bag on the day of the competition?"

"Leave her alone," a girl's voice ordered sharply from behind me.

"What?" I turned to see that it was Hayley who'd spoken, but she ran past so quickly that she was gone before the word was even out of my mouth.

Lindsey immediately went back on the floor and started jumping furiously.

Across the room, I could see Evan's group had

stopped moving, and Coach Dan was handing them each a piece of paper. His class was over.

I was almost out of time, and I hadn't really learned much at all. Juno was pretty near me so I decided to ask her a few questions. But as I walked toward her, Hayley nearly ran me down from behind.

"Oh, I'm so sorry," she said in a loud voice, stopping and pretending to be embarrassed. But in her eyes, I saw a look of cold fury. "I know why you're here," she growled in a low voice. "And you're embarrassing me. Just leave things alone."

"I can't. Your mom hired me to find out the truth."

A look of pain flashed across her face. "I can figure this out on my own. "

"Your mom thinks someone messed with your rope. Someone did something to make it break. Is that what you think?"

"I told you, I can handle this. I don't need your help."

My gaze wandered to Morgan, who was giggling and showing off for the boys sitting against the wall. "Your mom thinks you do."'

"Well she's wrong." She sighed and rolled her eyes. "Look, go ahead, and do your little investigation, but don't ask any questions and don't be so obvious."

"I won't have to ask so many questions if you can ask them for me. Or answer them."

"Okay." She pushed a loose strand of hair out of her eyes, revealing deep frown lines on her forehead. "Like what?"

"Like who do you think might tamper with your rope, even for a joke."

"I don't know. I'm thinking about it."

"Did you see anyone hanging out around the rope

bags on the day of the competition?" I thought of Rachel earlier, rummaging through several bags.

She shook her head. "No, I wasn't paying attention."

"Can you ask Lindsey if she did?"

"I'm sure she was busy too. And the other jumpers were, too, so I'm not going to ask them and you shouldn't either."

"Can I ask those boys?"

The frown lines seemed to spread across her whole face like a sudden rash."I wouldn't bother. They weren't hanging around here then." Without another word, she took off running again.

Evan walked up to me red-faced but smiling. "Can we get ice cream now?"

"Um, yeah." I still felt like I hadn't learned much, but a bargain was a bargain. My eyes scanned the gym one last time as I followed Evan slowly toward the exit.

Hayley had been joined by another girl in her jog around the perimeter of gym. The second girl was a little shorter, with darker hair and skin. I thought it was Juno but it was hard to tell from this far away. Rachel and Morgan were doing handstands and walking a few steps on their hands. Gwen was jumping high in the air with some kind of kick and a twist.

Did they do this every day? It was a lot of time to spend practicing a sport no one had heard of except them.

"So, do you want to learn more of this?" I asked Evan as I held the door open for him.

"No! I want ice cream." He paused and looked back. "Well, maybe. If I can get ice cream every week."

The ice cream would last as long as the investigation. But given the negative response of the person this investigation was supposed to benefit, it might not last long at all.

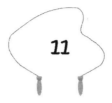

11

Monday morning started with coffee and a still, silent office where the only sounds came from recorded voices on the phone that I could switch off with the press of a button. I was a little surprised Rodney wasn't there yet, but the others wouldn't be in until later, if at all.

There were two messages on voicemail about lowering the interest rates on our credit cards and one asking if we wanted to take a survey about the color of school buses. I was tempted to call that one back. Would they give us a chance to suggest other colors? I was a little tired of that yellow. The next call was a deep voice I recognized very well.

"Hi, Karen, just wanted you to know I missed you over the weekend. It was hard not to call or text, but it was my rule not to allow electronic devices during the retreat, so I had to live by it. I'm sure you're busy now, but I'll call you at home tonight. Keep the faith!"

I'd missed Brian, too. But I couldn't imagine calling to tell him that. Couldn't we go three whole days without talking to each other? I was touched and a little horrified at the same time.

The last voice on the answering system reminded me that I had work to do. "Karen, it's Doreen. Have you got a report yet on the Flagler investigation? They've had a lawyer contact us about it."

They hired a lawyer to handle the case of the dead parrot? That had to be as embarrassing for him or her as it was for me. I immediately hated lawyers just a little bit less.

Rodney came in just after I grabbed my second cup of coffee and was heading over to check the fax machine. I grabbed a handful of papers and pretended to read them so he couldn't launch a discussion about the quote of the day or have a meeting to plan our next meeting.

He walked by me without saying anything, and I breathed a sigh of relief.

Underneath the standard affidavits and drug test results in the tray of the fax machine, I found something of interest. There was a report from Patapsco Veterinary Hospital about the Flagler's parrot. The report stated that the bird had ceased all respiratory and circulatory functions.

In other words, it was dead.

Well that was a tremendous help.

The report contained a detailed description of the bird and stated that it was a blue mutated yellow napped Amazon, which corresponded with what Mrs. Flagler told me. I would have Brittany do some research on the bird's value. I might be able to finish this one up today. But something still bothered me – Doreen wanted to know if the sunroom was finished at the time of the collapse, and I didn't have an answer on that yet. Maybe the neighbors could tell me something.

On the other hand, this case wasn't bringing in any money for the firm. Wouldn't it be better to just go with the most likely scenario? Mrs. Flagler showed me a picture of the parrot in the room with a Christmas tree, which was proof the room was in use before the roof collapsed in January.

As if she knew what I was thinking, Doreen called again. "Have you got anything on the Flagler file yet?"

"Yes…and no."

"Well that's clear as mud."

I sighed, wondering just how to explain my reservations. "The vet confirmed the bird's rare species and Mrs. Flagler offered a photo as proof that the bird was in room at the time of the collapse, but something doesn't seem right."

"Okay, well let me know when you've got it sorted."

"Will do."

I started the report for Doreen and typed up what we'd done so far.

Brittany arrived just before lunch time.

"I've got a job for you." I leaned up against the edge of her desk, feeling a strange urge to sit on it like my brother always did. "Can you research the value of a blue mutated yellow napped Amazon?"

"Sure." She sat down in her chair, whirled in a circle, faced the computer screen and typed something. "Wait. A blue what? And did you say mutilated?"

"It's a bird, a parrot. Come here for a sec." I headed over to my computer and waved for her to follow. I opened the picture Mrs. Flagler had sent. Then I zoomed in on the bird in the cage. "It should look like this. I need to know how much this bird is worth. Or how much it would be worth if it was still alive."

She leaned in toward the screen? "It's dead?"

"Now it is. This was taken when it was still alive."

"Oh, yeah," she laughed. "I guess no one takes pictures of their dead pets."

"I wouldn't say no one, but probably not most

people."

"Oh, you're right, there was a guy in my intro biology class who—"

I held up my hand. "I really don't need to know about it."

"Right."

The office door opened, and the smell of fried fish and onions instantly filled the room. It did not mix well with the coffee taste in my mouth.

"Hi, Dave." I wished he'd eaten lunch in his car or something.

"Hey." He set a brown paper bag down on my desk. "Want some fries?"

"I thought they were onion rings. They smell like onion rings."

"I don't think they are." He peered inside the bag. "If they are, they're going undercover as fried potatoes." He took an enormous bite from a sandwich wrapped in greasy waxed paper. "'atcha 'orking on?"

"Flagler case. Should be wrapped soon."

His forehead wrinkled in confusion as he swallowed. "I don't remember that one. Is that the one where the employer thinks one of the employees is stealing craft supplies to resell to seniors?"

"No. It's for Smith Insurance."

"Okay." He finished the sandwich with one huge bite. "Have I missed a meeting?"

"Nope. Didn't have any today."

He glanced at Rodney, typing silently at his desk. "Quote of the day? Vision of the future?"

I shook my head. "No. It's been... quiet." I had enjoyed the chance to get some work done in peace. But now that he mentioned it, it was an uneasy peace. I should have been interrupted by some buoyant, happy work-promoting message from Rodney. The lack of an annoying interruption would annoy me the rest of the day. I'd either be waiting for it or wondering why it hadn't happened.

"What's Brittany doing?" Without waiting for an answer, Dave headed over to her desk and looked over her shoulder. "Another bird? What is this, nature class?"

"It's for the Flagler case, too."

He tried to snap his fingers but instead sprayed ketchup across the front of his shirt. "That's the parrot case. You can't both be working on it. Finish it, and move on to the paying clients."

"Since when have you paid attention to paying clients? You never get me your tear-offs until I harass you and then I can't bill—"

He stalked back over to me to interrupt. "I'm not talking accounting, I'm talking about work. I work for the clients who pay us, which is what you should be doing."

"You do favors for people who help you. Well, that's what I'm doing."

"Favors are quick. This—" he waved at the screen "—this is the Stay-Puft Marshmallow Man Giant Out-of-Control Favor. It needs to go away."

"If you don't like the way I'm handling this, you should have done the job yourself." As soon as I said the words, I regretted them. I'd just told my boss he shouldn't have given me an assignment.

"Nobody should be doing this job." After glaring at me, he scowled at Brittany again. "Turn that off. Do something else."

She looked at me quizzically.

"Type in the information from Dave's latest field

reports," I suggested. "That shouldn't take long."

The confusion on her face intensified. "But the box of reports is empty."

"Oh, wow, yeah, so it is." I glanced toward the box that never held anything more substantial than a layer of dust. "Guess you can play computer games then."

"Hold on." Dave rummaged through a shoulder bag that he'd dropped on the floor when he came in. "I got a couple in here." After a few moments he pulled out a wad of crumpled papers. "Receipts, too. All billable to clients." He dropped the mess on my desk.

"I think some of those have dry-rotted in the bottom of your bag. Are any of these cases still open?"

He ignored me.

I held up a small rectangle of thin paper. "Who are we billing for your double cheese fire-eating burrito?"

"Match the date with my log. You'll figure it out."

"The last log I have is from September."

"Then it should match the receipt."

He was right.

I wadded it back up into a ball and dropped in the trashcan under my desk. "I can't bill clients for stuff this old."

He shrugged. "They like getting the bills late. It gives them more time to pay."

I was going to refute that but then I gave up. He'd have another smart-aleck response. Instead, I held up the paper bag spotted with grease stains. "Take your onion-scented French fries and go."

He stepped closer, but made no move to take the bag and just loomed over me with a menacing glare. "I mean it, Karen. I want you to work on something else."

"I will. I'm about to call Gina Callaghan."

"There is still a picture of a bird on your

computer."

"I'm making it my screen saver."

Score one for the big sister. He grabbed the bag out of my hand and turned away without saying anything else, which is pretty rare.

After a few moments, I noticed that though he'd walked away, Dave still hadn't gone into his own office. He was hovering in the big common area the rest of us shared, waiting to see if I really would work on something else.

I had a whole long list of questions to ask Gina that I'd thought of while I was vacuuming over the weekend. I'd stopped so many times to write down notes that I'd nearly worn out the on/off switch. Later I'd organized the list into a logical order. But then I left it home on the shelf by the door. Maybe if I called home, the dog could read it to me over the phone.

Sigh.

I scribbled down what I could remember from the list and dialed Gina's number.

"Hello?"

"Gina? This is Karen Maxwell."

"Yes. Do you have information for me?"

"Not yet. I have some questions."

"Oh, okay." I was sure from the disappointment in her voice that she expected her mystery to be solved in the span of an hour like a TV episode.

"I noticed that one of the older jumpers was helping with my son's class on Friday. Do they do that with the Tuesday and Wednesday classes?"

"Yes, some of them."

"Some of the kids or some of the classes?"

"Both." She paused. "Morgan does, so you'll see Bonnie there. And Gwen coaches. Jackie is her mother, you should investigate her as well."

"Good." I didn't mean that, since I didn't like her telling me who I needed to investigate. "Okay, thanks. So how do the tournaments run? Are they pretty similar to each other or are there different types?"

"They are quite similar, though the events are a little different for each one. They start with short speed events, then longer speed events. At some tournaments they do power events right after individual speed. But at this type of qualifier they wait until the end to do the triple unders because they're so tiring. They take a break to reset the floor before and after the freestyle events."

"Reset the floor?"

"They pick up the tape that sections the floor off into small squares for the speed events and just leave larger squares. The jumpers use a lot more space for freestyle."

"So you have more kids competing at the same time during speed?"

"Many more. Power too, though at this tournament just the older age groups jumped power."

I tried to visualize it. It probably would have looked a lot like the speed practice, with ropes whirring all around the room at the same time. "And lots of kids jumping at the same time during power?"

"Yes. And there are three judges counting each jumper."

"So the floor would be really crowded. It would have been hard for you to see what happened during Hayley's turn. When she didn't score as high as she should have."

"I couldn't see because I was clicking for another jumper at the time."

"Clicking?"

She sighed as if my ignorance was almost more than she could bear. "Counting. I was a speed judge counting another jumper in a different station."

I nearly dropped the phone. "So you didn't even see it. How did you know what happened? Was there a video?"

She laughed. "Heavens, no. That would be too boring for words. Lots of parents videotape the freestyle events, but no one would record the speed or power. It's all the same."

"No one records it? Ever?"

"Well I don't know of anyone who does."

"Can you ask?"

"I suppose."

I made a note to find out whether any parents on other times might have taken video of the power competition. If the floor was as crowded as it sounded, Hayley might show up in the background of someone else's shot. Or maybe the video would show the rope bags.

"So how did you find out what happened?"

"The coach told me."

Was there a way to ask the coach about the incident without letting her know why I was doing it? Did it matter? I was a little embarrassed that until now I hadn't even considered talking to the coach.

"Okay, thanks." I was getting ready to say goodbye and hang up, but she stopped me.

"Mrs. Maxwell, we need the information soon. Tryout for the Worlds team is coming up in little more than a week. And it's in Idaho this time, not the easiest place to get to in February. Every day we wait to buy plane tickets, the price goes up."

I found myself gritting my teeth. "I am doing as

much as I can while maintaining the discretion you required. If I can come right out and start asking questions in the open, this will go much faster.

"Oh, no." I could hear her shake her head. Tones of hushed horror seeped through the phone. "No, you must be discrete."

I wanted to growl but instead had to be nice as I said goodbye. I didn't need the extra pressure of worrying about the price of her plane tickets. But I couldn't help about thinking about the last time I bought tickets online. Every time I checked, the price seemed to jump in huge increments.

I had planned to go to visit the team in Frederick tomorrow while the kids were with their dad. But I decided I could head out there today instead.

Before I left, I called Amy to see if she would mind keeping Evan at her house until I got home. Then I got in my minivan and headed west.

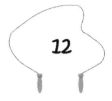

12

The Frederick Flyers headquarters were in an
industrial park between a baseball practice facility and a
shop that repaired tubas and French horns. The space
was a lot cozier than the giant gym the Jumptastics
used. The Frederick Flyers had team banners and
pictures on the wall, trophies on shelves, motivational
sayings pasted everywhere, plus a waiting room for
parents with couches instead of bleachers.

They even had a drink cooler full of Gatorade and
Diet Coke. I wished someone from this team had hired
me instead.

After I wandered in circles around the waiting area
about three times, a woman with short brown hair and
glasses came out of her office and asked if she could
help me.

"I'm looking for a jump rope team for my son," I
said, after giving a fake name. "He's really into this, so I
want to make sure you've got some good high school
coaches to mentor him."

"Oh, we do." She waved toward the windows
overlooking the practice floor. "Our top tier jumpers
coach the other jumpers on designated days. Today is
their own practice, where they focus on developing
their own skills."

"So who's here right now?"

"That's Megan there, and Danielle next to her

and..." After that I stopped listening. I was in luck—my target, Danielle was here. But there was only one parent in the waiting room, and she was sitting on the sofa engaged in a novel, so I didn't know how I was going to ask around to get information about Danielle or anyone else on the team.

"Great," I mumbled when I realized the coach had stopped talking.

"So what does your son like to compete in?" she asked with great enthusiasm.

"Soccer," I answered automatically as I watched Danielle to see how she seemed to interact with the other kids.

"I meant in jump rope."

"Oh, yeah." I forgot I was supposed to be looking for a team for him. "He likes, uh, jumping, uh, high and…"

"Power?"

"Oh, of course. Yeah, power, definitely." I should have said that. That was the event that caused all this brouhaha.

"Does he do doubles or triples?"

"Uh, triples."

"Okay so then he's in high school. How long has he been jumping?"

"What?" *My son in high school? I'd missed something here.* "He's only nine."

She gave me the sort of indulgent smile usually reserved for toddlers and puppies who've just made a mess. "Then your son is probably doing doubles. They don't start triples until they're fifteen."

"Oh, right." I was sounding like an idiot. "Hey, is that Diet Coke for sale?" I walked toward the drink cooler.

The coach laughed. "To you, yes. We don't let the jumpers have soda, but our standards aren't so strict for the parents."

I gave her money, told her to keep the change for the team, and then asked if I could just watch for a while.

"Sure, go ahead. Let me know if you have any questions."

I wandered back over the windows and stared out at the open floor. It was, as Gina had said, pretty boring, like watching runners train for a marathon by jogging in place. I yawned.

The woman sitting on the sofa laughed. "That's my reaction, too. Watching them work so hard makes me tired."

Tired and bored weren't necessarily the same thing, but I decided not to go there. "I assume one of them is yours?" I asked, fingers crossed.

"Kellen, the girl in the red shorts."

I pretended to look. "Oh, yeah. Did she compete in the Regionals a couple of weeks ago?"

She nodded. "They all did. Kellen qualified in Double Dutch and three minute speed."

"Congratulations."

"Thanks."

"You must have been very proud. Did you take lots of pictures? Video?" I was getting a little too hopeful.

"No, I was judging, so I was counting someone else."

Seemed to be a common theme. I was going to have hard time finding a parent who might have seen what was going on off the competition floor at the time, since they all seemed to be judging.

I tried another tack. "Did anyone video the event so

you could watch it afterwards? Since you missed it?"

She laughed a little. "We do have a team videographer. He sets up a camera to cover the whole floor during the competition so you can see your jumper, but you need a magnifying glass to tell who's who!"

This was great news! I could find a magnifying glass. If the camera covered the whole floor, it would show jumpers from other teams, including Hayley and her competitors.

Right after I inwardly did a jump for joy about the video, my streak of luck ended. Danielle crossed the practice floor and entered the waiting room at great speed, dressed in a warm up suit and obviously leaving in a hurry. I would have no time to ask her or her parents anything.

"Is practice over?" I asked the mom I'd been talking to.

"No, she probably just has to leave early. Lots of them have jobs or other sports."

"Oh."

Then I got a break.

"Danielle," the coach stuck her head out of her office. "Can you stay later next Monday?"

She stopped with obvious reluctance. "I dunno."

"Your Double Dutch pairs needs more practice."

"Yeah, but my volleyball coach won't let us miss."

"What if *I* didn't let you miss?"

She shrugged but gave a sheepish smile.

"Go on," the coach urged. "I'll see you Wednesday." She turned to me with a sigh as the door closed behind Danielle. "Volleyball's always gonna come first with that girl, even though she's a terrific jumper. But they don't give scholarships for jump rope."

"Oh yeah, I guess not. Does she miss a lot of practice for volleyball?"

"Not just practice. She missed all the speed events at the USA Regional Qualifier. *All of them* including three minute. Just barely made it in time for power. They were looking for her in the heat lineup when she walked in. And it was a volleyball practice that made her so late. Not even a game."

"So she just barely arrived in time for the power event."

The coach nodded. "Her mother was still looking for a parking place when the event ended. She missed seeing her daughter do the best jump of her life. And neither one of them seemed to care. They just take all that talent for granted." She shook her head in disbelief.

I didn't know what to say. It definitely took Danielle out of the running as a suspect. She didn't have motive, means or opportunity. "That seems, um…"

The coach gazed out the windows leading to the practice floor. "I have kids who come six days a weeks and can't beat the scores of that girl, and she's only here on Mondays and Wednesdays. But that's the way it is." She turned back to me. "So, your son's interested in power jumping?"

I had what I needed and it was time to leave before I wasted any more time—either hers or mine. So I started backing toward the door. "Oh, well, yeah, but just like Danielle, he likes other sports, too. Thanks for the information. You have a great facility here and a great team."

She handed me a business card. "Come back and bring your son. We'd love to have him join us."

"Thanks. I gotta run." I gave her a little wave as I headed toward the door.

"Okay, stay safe out there. I hear traffic's a real mess this afternoon."

That was the last thing I needed. By now Alicia would be home from her practice. Home by herself. I hoped she wasn't making toaster waffles. Or visiting an online chatroom that featured "hot" firefighters. What if she invited this unknown Darrell over in my absence? My mind raced with disagreeable possibilities as I drove the long unsympathetic stretch of interstate between Frederick and Ellicott City. Yes, I could pull over and call her to make sure everything was alright. But a lot can be hidden from a phone. So I decided not to take the time and instead to focus on getting home as quickly as possible.

But when I parked and stepped out of the van, I was torn about what to do first. Should I go to Amy's and get Evan? I knew he wouldn't want to be there a single second longer than he had to. Or go see what Alicia was up to first?

What I should do was stop being paranoid. My kids were fine. Deep down, I knew I could trust my kids to act their age and it was time I started showing it.

I took a deep breath.

"Karen, are you okay?" Amy called out from her front door.

I grinned sheepishly and started toward her. "Yes. Just having a mad mother moment." The biting wind inspired me to run, rather than walk across the street. "Thanks for watching Evan for me," I added when I neared the house.

"It's no problem. Nicole loves having him here." Amy held the storm door open extra wide so that Evan could get out around her.

He stalked past me without making eye contact and stomped over to our house, kicking the pile of unwanted newspapers that I never seemed to get around to picking up.

"Evan, you should thank...never mind," I muttered as I continued up to Amy's porch. "My kids have zero manners."

"No, he's very polite. When you're not around." She smiled and held the door open for me to come in.

I wavered, but only for a moment. Yes, I needed to get home. But I also needed friends now that Jeff and Linda had taken all my old ones away. And developing friends would take time—time made up of strange, unplanned moments like these. Alicia would be okay. I had to trust her.

I stepped inside and sighed. "I feel like I never would have gotten away with that. We were expected to show respect to adults all the time."

Amy leaned back against the wall. "Yeah, well no one does that anymore."

"Some kids do. There are these kids at church that..." I sighed again and rolled my eyes. I didn't think my kids were ever going to behave like those perfect kids at church.

She grinned. "I'll bet they only act like that in church. At home they're probably little monsters."

"Maybe."

"Definitely. Weren't you a little monster when you were a kid? I mean when you weren't pretending to be respectful to grownups?" She took a step toward the kitchen. "I know I was. Do you want some tea? It's cold out." As she started into the kitchen, she nearly plowed into her daughter.

The little girl staggered into the foyer, her eyes red from crying and her tiny face glazed with a shiny layer of tears and snot. "Why'd Evan have to go? I told him to stay."

Amy looked down at her daughter with a surprisingly cool expression, clearly not giving her the empathy that she was giving me. "I'm sure he had homework to do."

"I could have him come back," I suggested, thinking this would be a great way to get even with him for his rude exit.

Amy shook her head and flashed me a warning look as she miraculously pulled a tissue from thin air and bent down in front of her daughter. "No, it was time for Evan to go home. And now it's time for you to blow your nose."

"No." Nicole crossed her arms in front of her chest and snorted, sending out a spray of mucus that made me take a step back.

"I guess I should get home now," I said, retreating further.

Amy mouthed the word "monster" to me as she held open the storm door.

I tried not to giggle.

"See you later,"

"Yeah," I agreed. And for once, I realized I was happy about it.

After I checked around the house for signs of fires or firefighters and found nothing incriminating, I went right to the computer to email Gina Callaghan. I wanted her to get a link to the Frederick Flyers jump rope video and the request would look much more natural coming from the parent of a competitor than from a stranger like me.

The laptop took a long time to warm up. I lured the dog off the sofa with a treat and then carried the computer over and sat down in her place, enjoying the heat she'd left behind but wishing it had not been accompanied by such a strong aroma of dog hair.

Evan stalked over and planted himself right in front of where I sat. "Mom, that was no fair at all."

"Of course not. Life isn't fair." *Opening the operating system, running through security program...*

"You let Alicia stay here by herself and made me go stay with the babies."

The screen reported a "Security Risk" from Quilters Anonymous. That was a site where I'd shopped for a birthday present for my mom. *What kind of security risk did those quilters pose? Was it all the sharp needles?*

"Mom! You're not even listening."

Did I buy a present for my mom or just think about buying one? "I'm listening."

"So why did I have to go to Miss Amy's house? Her daughter put Play-Doh up her nose."

I patted him on the head. "At least she didn't put it up *your* nose." *When was Mom's birthday, anyway? I always got the day mixed up with Uncle Larry's.*

"Then she threw it at me."

"I think that means she likes you." *One birthday was on the 19th and one was on the 29th.*

"Eeew don't even say it. If you make me go there again I won't go to that jump rope class."

I hope I didn't send a super deluxe quilter's kit to Uncle Larry. He wasn't supposed to have sharp objects anymore. Hold on, what had Evan said about jump rope?

Without warning, Alicia suddenly appeared in front of me to pluck the computer off my lap. "Can I use that? I need it for world cultures class."

I tried unsuccessfully to grab it back, wondering how my daughter could have descended the stairs without my noticing. Usually she came down like a herd of clumsy elephants. "Wait, I need to send—what did you say, Evan?"

He crossed his arms in front of his chest "I won't go to that jump rope class if you make me stay at Miss Amy's anymore."

I snapped my fingers. "That reminds me, Alicia, I need to sign you up for a class tomorrow."

"What?" She looked up from the laptop, which she was holding with one hand while typing with the other as she walked back toward the stairs. "I thought Evan was taking the class."

"No!" Evan nearly shouted, "I'm not if I have to stay with the Play-Doh girl again."

Molly barked, but I'm not sure whether she was speaking out in support of Evan or arguing against him.

In any case, I'd had enough. I raised my voice to override all their whines of protest. "I need you both to take the class, but not for long. Evan, you can stay home by yourself if you promise not to cook anything."

"Really?"

I nodded. "You see? I do trust you."

Alicia's gaze flickered between me and the computer screen. "What do I get to do if I take the class?"

"You get to stay home by yourself, too."

"But I already get to do that."

"I can take the privilege away for a while if it will make you feel better."

"No." She scowled.

Evan laughed and plopped down on a pile of

pillows on the floor.

"Good, that simplifies things." I held out my hand. "Now give me back the computer."

"I need it for homework."

"And you can have it for homework. I just need to send a message first."

Slowly—in a way that only a grudging child can be—she trudged over and deposited the computer in my lap. I opened it, sent a message to Gina, and handed it back to her. "That wasn't so bad, was it?"

"Yes it was." She scowled. "I was trying to be one of the first 20 people to 'like' the new Sweet Frog and then I'd get a free cone."

"A cone of frog?"

"It's a frozen yogurt shop."

I considered taking the laptop back. "I thought you wanted the computer to do homework, not to enter contests on Facebook. You're not even old enough to have an account."

She rolled her eyes. "Everybody does. And I'll be old enough in 83 days."

"Until then, I don't want you on Facebook."

"What?" Her eyes widened as if I'd just ordered her not to breathe for the next 83 days.

"You lied to them to get an account," I pointed out. "You told them you were at least thirteen."

"But everyone does it." Her voice rose to Whine Level Five, the classic *it's not fair* pitch. "They know that. It doesn't matter."

"It matters to me."

She snorted in derision. "It doesn't matter to anyone else."

I took back the computer. "I'm not going to argue with you. What's your password?"

"I don't have to tell you. Passwords are supposed to be—"

Evan sat up. "It's vampirecarrots, pushed together as one word."

"You little twerp." Alicia glared at him. "You spied on me."

"You hogged the computer and said I had to wait to use it."

I turned to Evan. "You don't have a Facebook account too, do you?"

"No."

"Ha." Alicia smirked. "He's using the computer to play Zombie Poker."

Zombie Poker? What, did they gamble for, body parts? "Okay," I admitted. "I don't think I like that use of my computer, either."

This time both kids glared at each other.

Things were about to turn ugly, so I proposed a compromise. "Okay," I announced.said, "Since the computer upstairs doesn't work anymore and we only have this one, we will use it just for work—homework for you, work-work for me—for the next week. Then I'll think about letting you use it for other stuff."

"But it's not fair," they both said pretty much in unison.

"You're right, it isn't." I nodded in agreement. "It's my computer and very often I don't get to use it when I want to because one of you is using it. But I'm willing to share if you play by my rules. Got it?"

There was no sign of assent, but I didn't push it. I knew they heard me.

In the glum silence that followed, I congratulated myself on taking a firm stance as a mother with principles. I thought the MOMs group at Brian's church would approve. But then, they probably had such good control at home that their kids would never dream of opening an underaged Facebook account or using the computer for paranormal gambling. I was still way out of league with those women.

13

I didn't get the computer back until after dinner when Alicia was in the shower and Evan was parked in front of the TV flipping back and forth between a dinosaur movie and the Monday night football pre-game show. "You know you have to go to bed before the actual game starts, right?" I reminded him.

"Yeah."

Gina Callaghan had sent the username and password for the Members Only section of the Frederick Flyers website, where they had links to video posted. I found the videos of the Regional competition and watched the power event. It basically looked like a roomful of people jumping high. I couldn't see any ropes at all. I had to watch it three times before I spotted Hayley. I saw her stop about ¾ of the way through the event and hold up one of the handles of her rope. But I didn't see her re-jump the event. And I couldn't see any of the jumpers' bags.

My mood plummeted.

I did a Google search on the competition to see if I could find any other videos from the day, but didn't find anything. Then I looked for Zombie Poker. It was gory with players betting brains and body parts, but I couldn't help but laugh when the players went "all in" quite literally.

Then I got on Facebook, typed in Alicia's email

address and the password Evan had given me.

Almost half of her 75 friends were boys. That I knew of. Anybody could pretend to be anything on Facebook. Alicia's posts seemed to be pretty innocent—mostly about boy bands, dessert, and cute cat videos—but there were a lot of them, and it would take time to go through all of her posts. She used a picture of Daphne from Scooby Do as her profile picture, so at least she wasn't posting pictures of herself. Not yet, anyway.

I was just about to close out her page when one of her posts caught my eye. "Mom thinks she gets it but she has no idea."

What did that mean? What was "it?" Was "it" life in general? Or something Alicia was up to?

Loud music screamed from the television and someone started telling us why football was better than breathing.

"Okay, Evan," I called over to him. "Time for bed."

"Whatcha doing?" he asked as he came over.

I closed the computer. "Dishes." I stood up and made myself leave the computer on the sofa. It was time to move on. The Facebook remark wasn't important. I would monitor to make sure she wasn't posting anything, but that would be it. I would not obsess over this.

The phone rang while I was up to my elbows in a sink full of warm, soapy water. The soothing water (with new "Nasturtium Nirvana" scented dishwashing liquid) felt so good after my long day that I debated just standing there for a while and letting the phone ring over to the answering machine. But by the third ring curiosity won out and since I couldn't see the caller ID from the sink, I dried off my hands and stepped over to pick up the receiver.

"Hi, Hon." It was Brian's voice. I couldn't remember him calling me "Hon" before, but we were close enough to Baltimore that the word "Hon" could be tacked on to anyone's conversation without attracting much attention so maybe I'd just never noticed.

"Hey."

"How was your day? For that matter, how was your weekend?"

I headed back over to the sink. "Good." I washed a bread knife, rinsed it and laid it in the dish drainer.

"Did Evan win his game?"

I felt around in the soap suds for other dishes but all that was left was the pan from inside the bread machine that had crusty stuff stuck on the bottom that couldn't be scrubbed with anything scrub-worthy since it supposedly had a non-stick coating. "The game was rained out."

"How can an indoor soccer game be rained out?"

"The gym flooded." I scratched at the bottom of the pan ineffectively with my fingernail.

"Maybe it should have been changed to a swim meet."

I grinned. "Then we'd have to pay a pool membership fee for the use of the flooded area."

"True. Did you guys do anything fun?"

"No." I pulled out the little piece from the bottom of the bread machine that mixes the dough around. It had gooey, watery bread dough stuck in the middle like glue. I dropped it back into the sink with a sense of hopelessness. The layer of soap bubbles parted enough for me to see just how dirty gray the water had become.

I grimaced when I realized I'd been soaking my hands in greasy water full of decomposing food.

"Is something wrong?"

"No." I felt like I had spent most of the weekend cleaning, just like I was doing now. I didn't want to be reminded of it. Time to change the subject. "How was your retreat?"

"Oh, it pretty good. The speaker was boring, but the kids liked him because of his tattoos. Guess that's better than nothing."

I nodded sympathetically, then realized he couldn't see me. "Yep. Better than nothing." I pulled the bread pan out of the sink, not at all surprised that it had not miraculously soaked itself clean, but disappointed nonetheless. Utensils clattered in the drawer as I pawed through it looking for something I could use to scrape off the burnt bread dough.

"So are we still on for tomorrow night?"

I stopped. "What are we doing on a school night?"

"You have your knitting group right? Then we'll go out afterward."

Knitting group? The phone slipped off my shoulder, bounced off the counter and landed in a clump of dog hair right next to Molly's water bowl. "Sorry" I yelled down toward the receiver. Then I grabbed a paper towel to pick up the phone, which was now coated with wet dog hair. After I'd wiped most of it off, I put it back up to my head. "Sorry," I repeated. "Dropped the phone."

"Good. For a moment I thought you'd been overrun by zombies or something."

"Only on my laptop."

"Do I want to know?..."

"No," I assured him as I went back to drawer to

find something to clean out the bread machine.

So, anyway," he continued, "I thought tomorrow night we could go out for ice cream."

I laughed. "I can tell you've been spending time with teenagers."

"Why?"

"Adults don't just go out for ice cream. Unless they're trying to reward kids."

"But I like ice cream."

"I do, too."

"So it's a date."

"Yeah, I guess." I'd forgotten about the knitting group I supposedly "wanted" to join. I didn't know if I could find any knitting needles, and I was pretty sure Evan had used all the yarn to make an (unsuccessful) rabbit trap last summer.

"What's wrong?" Brian asked.

"Nothing. Why do you keep asking me that? Does something always have to be wrong?"

"You sound unhappy."

"Can't I be unhappy without something being wrong?" I slammed the drawer closed.

"Um, no."

"Oh."

"So what is it?" he demanded.

"I don't know." I gave up on the bread machine and opened a cabinet to search for chocolate instead. "I don't even remember what we were talking about when you decided I was unhappy."

"You just admitted you were unhappy."

"I did not. When?"

"When you said you could be unhappy even if nothing was wrong."

"I was speaking theoretically." I pulled out a red

cardboard box that was empty except for a lopsided chocolate Christmas ornament covered in green foil. When I peeled back the foil, it smelled like fake chocolate.

"So you're not unhappy?" he asked with a note of challenge in his voice.

"No."

"You sound unhappy."

"Is that the same as sounding annoyed?"

He was silent for a moment. "So I'm annoying you?"

"No, not really. Well, kinda." I sighed and threw the questionable ornament into the trash can. "I think you're trying to be funny. But I'm not always in the mood to laugh. Sorry."

"Okay. I'll stop annoying you tonight as long as I can see you tomorrow."

"Yeah, I'll meet you in the hall like last week."

He paused. "I have a better idea."

"Oh, where do you want meet, then?"

"You'll see." A note of mystery sounded in his voice.

"I will?"

"Yeah. G'nite."

I just held the phone for a few moments after I'd said goodbye and hit the "end" button. Was he planning some sort of surprise? His surprises could be hit or miss. Showing up unexpected to take me out to lunch had been good. But taking me for a "romantic dinner" at his church youth group spaghetti supper hadn't been my idea of a great first date. And I couldn't meet him anywhere if I didn't know where I was going. But I'd let him figure that out.

I left home before Evan the next morning so I could stop by and see if any of the Flaglers' neighbors knew whether the family had been using the sunroom before the ceiling collapsed. By going early, I hoped to catch them before they left for work. I parked several houses away near the old firehouse. As I walked up the hill, I kept watching the doors and windows of the Flagler House, expecting to see Mrs. Flagler's red hair through the glass. What would it matter if she saw me in front of her neighbors' houses? She already knew I was investigating. But she didn't know I didn't trust her.

I stayed as far out of the sightline of the Flagler house as I could and even avoided the front door of the next-door neighbor's house and knocked on the side door instead. I think it led to a laundry room. Not surprisingly, no one answered.

There were no cars parked in front so it didn't come as a shock when no one answered the front door, either. Was I surprised? No. Disappointed? Yes.

But the neighbor on the other side looked much more promising, with two cars in the driveway and smoke curling out of the chimney. I just had to get there without being spotted by Mrs. F.

I could drive up and park at the other end of the street. But that seemed ridiculous.

If I just walked along the street at a normal pace, she probably wouldn't notice me even if she happened to be looking out the window.

I took a deep breath and started walking.

After taking about five steps, I spotted a face in the window of the Flagler house. I held my hand in front of my face. That looked stupid. So I put my hand at an angle, pretending I was keeping the sun out of my eyes. It was cloudy, however, so I still felt stupid. I fished around in the pockets of my jacket to see if I had anything that might help. One pocket was full of plastic grocery bags for walking the dog. I pulled out a bag, shook it open and pulled it over my head, but I knew it was no good. She may have already seen me.

So I ran (in kind of a zigzag fashion, since it's not easy to run holding a bag over your head) along the street and up the walkway to the porch of the other neighbor.

That didn't look suspicious at all, did it? I was very glad Dave or Brittany hadn't seen me because I never would have heard the end of it. It had to be one of the worst ideas I've ever had. But no one would ever know.

The doorbell at this neighbor's house didn't seem to work. I pushed it three times and didn't hear anything and couldn't see anyone inside responding. I was a little hesitant about knocking on the door because the outer storm door was all glass and the door behind it was antique looking with beveled panes of wavy glass and a crystal door knob. I knocked tentatively on the varnished wood along the edge. Then, since nothing shattered, I knocked a little louder. A man in a plaid shirt shuffled into view. He had white hair and was a little hunched over, but he didn't seem old enough to be walking quite so slowly.

I waited patiently.

I waited less patiently.

I started to hear elevator music in my head.

Eventually, he reached the door, pulled it open, and pushed open the storm door. "If you're selling Girl Scout cookies, my wife already bought some."

I looked down to see if anything I was wearing vaguely resembled a Girl Scout uniform. "Um, no I'm a little too old to be—"

He chuckled, revealing a mouthful of ultra-white, perfect teeth that looked like they could have been taken out, wound up and chattered themselves across the floor. "I know, it was a joke. A little one." He stepped back and held the door open for me. "Come in."

"Thank you." I stepped inside the foyer and inhaled the scent of vegetable soup and Vicks VapoRub.

He pointed to the bag slung over my shoulder. "Are you here to peddle religion or politics? You see we have a sign out to protect against your kind, but I'm letting you in anyway. He pointed to a sticker on the storm door that said *We Support the Neighborhood Watch. No solicitors or peddlers allowed.*

I smiled. "I'm not here to peddle, I'm here to beg. But not for money. And this is my purse—no pamphlets, I promise." I held it open for him to see.

He grinned and again I couldn't help imagining those teeth popping right out of his head and chattering right across the dark-stained floorboards.

"Whatcha beggin' for?"

"Information. Have you ever considered putting a sunroom on the back of your house like your neighbors have?"

"Ah." He nodded. "So you sell aluminum siding and the like."

I decided to let him think that until I found out his attitude toward his neighbors. "Well, you have to admit, your neighbors have a nice addition. Lets in a lot more light." I waved toward the living room to my right where heavy green drapes made the room feel like a funeral parlor.

"And snow!" He snorted with laughter. "Doug told me all about how this sunroom was gonna increase the value of their house. Then the roof collapses with the first snowfall." He shook his head. "Not the kind of value I want to add, thank you very much."

"It collapsed?" I pretended to be shocked. "Was anyone hurt?"

"Nah. Rose said they were all fine." The way he wrinkled his nose made him seem a bit disappointed at the lack of injury.

"Rose?"

"My wife."

"Maybe the room wasn't finished yet when the roof collapsed," I suggested, watching for his reaction. "So that would explain why no one was hurt."

"Could be." He sniffed. "Gonna be impossible to heat that room. Too much glass."

"Did you see them using the room? Before the collapse?"

"No. But I don't see them using anything, including all that fancy patio furniture and the trampoline. Don't s'pose I pay much attention, though. They hire someone to keep the lawn mowed so that's good. But sometimes the lawn company blocks our driveway and they don't pick up the clippings and then all that grass blows into our yard."

"That must be difficult." I tried to figure out a way to talk to his wife. It sounded like she paid more attention to the neighbors than her husband did.

"And it's hard to see around that big trailer of theirs." A frown of consternation expanded the longer he spoke. "Shouldn't be allowed to have a big rig like that on our narrow street."

"Oh, well, then," I put on a plastic smile, "it's good that I got the chance to talk to you. I'm with the neighborhood association, and I'm taking a survey of how businesses are serving the community. I can file a complaint about the landscapers your neighbor is using."

His nose wrinkled. "We have a neighborhood association?"

"I'm sure your wife handles all that. So maybe I should talk to her?"

"Yeah, sure. I'll go call her." He took three steps toward the back of the house and then stopped and bellowed in a deafening voice. "Rose! Neighbor complaint people to see you."

I tried not to wince. A moment later, a woman with obviously dyed dark hair curled, teased and sprayed into a grandmotherly helmet bustled out with a concerned frown on her face. "Someone has complained about us?"

"No, no, it's nothing like that," I assured her. "I'm here on behalf of the neighborhood association to see if you have any complaints against businesses operating in—"

She shook her head to interrupt. "We don't have a neighborhood association. You must be on the wrong street."

I thought every homeowner was stuck belonging to a neighborhood association. Oh well, I could make one up. "Yes, ma'am, it's the Old Ellicott City Association and I'm here to—"

She interrupted again. "We don't pay any dues to an association."

"We're new and we haven't collected any dues yet." I tried to hurry to get to the point. "I understand you have some complaints about businesses used by your neighbors."

The wrinkles on her forehead deepened to epic

proportions. "I don't know about this," she said slowly. "It could be a scam."

"I'm not asking for any money," I promised. "I just want to know about—"

Her eyes narrowed. "You could be here to steal our identity."

"No, I'm just trying to find out whether the contractors hired by your neighbors are doing their jobs properly." I talked as fast as I could, hoping I could get it all out before she cut me off. "I understand the roof on their new addition collapsed, so maybe there was a building code violation. So I'd like to know if you noticed anything unusual about the contractor, and when they finished the work and so on."

"Oh." The woman relaxed and looked thoughtful for a moment. I breathed a sigh of relief.

Her husband spoke up. "She asked me if the room was empty when the roof collapsed."

Rose's frown lines returned in full force. "I know what she's doing. She's trying to find out if the Flaglers were out of town. This woman is checking the neighborhood so someone can come in and rob houses when they're empty." She started to shoo me toward the door.

"No, no really," I struggled unsuccessfully to hold my ground. "I heard you have trouble with the landscaper's truck blocking your driveway. I'd like to report that."

She shook her head, still bulldozing me toward the door. "Oh, no. Then they'll know when we want to use the driveway, and they'll know we're leaving to go somewhere."

I sighed and decided to tell the truth. "Okay, look. I'm really working for the Flaglers' insurance agency.

The last thing we want is for anyone's house to be robbed. We just want to find out whether the sunroom was finished and in use at the time the roof collapsed."

The man wrinkled his nose again. "Shouldda said so in the first place."

His wife looked unconvinced. "What company is it? If you work for the insurance, then you should be able to show us an ID card."

Oh, boy, I should have seen this coming. I took a deep breath. "I don't know the company the Flagler's policy is with—I'm working for the agency and they represent a couple of different insurers."

"What's the agency, then?"

"Uh, the Smith Agency."

She looked dubious, and it was about to get worse.

"And I don't have an ID card," I continued, "because I don't actually work for the agency. They asked me to do them a favor."

"Out!" She marched to the door. "I want you out right now. And if I see you again around here I'm going to call the police." She pushed on the storm door and held it open.

"I actually park on this street a lot for work," I explained somewhat forlornly as I stepped out.

"You can try to explain that to the police. I mean it. And we have a Neighborhood Watch. We'll know if anything suspicious is happening because we watch over our neighbors' houses very closely."

"Well, the parts we can see, that is," her husband corrected as he shuffled toward us. "Can't see most of the Jensens' backyard, and we can only see the back side of the Flaglers' from the spare bedroom. An' we never go in there."

His wife waved at him to be quiet as she pulled the

glass storm door closed behind me. "Shush. Don't tell that woman anything that might be used against us."

"I'm not going to use anything against you," I argued through the glass. "I can get a letter from the agency if that will make you feel better."

She shook her head, black curls remaining fixed in their orbits. "You'll just have your accomplices write a fake letter. No, just go away and don't come back."

"Thanks for uh, your time."

The wooden door slammed shut.

I slunk down the street in disgrace. Did I need to pursue this any further? The neighbors on the other side might know something, but it would have been difficult for them to see the sunroom. And the houses on this side of the street backed up to a steep hill with patches of exposed granite. That sunroom was very private, so it was unlikely anyone had seen whether the room had been used or not.

I had done my duty toward Doreen. It was time to cut my losses and move on.

14

"You're late." Dave pointed a spoonful of ice cream at me as I walked into the office. I'm not sure whether I was more surprised by the fact that Dave was standing right in front of the door or the fact that he was standing at all, given that it was earlier than 10 a.m.

I suppressed a sigh as I set down my bag and hung my coat on the nearest antler. I knew what was coming, but that didn't mean I had to go along peacefully. "You're eating dessert for breakfast." I nodded toward the bowl sitting on my desk. "So we're even."

He shook his head before he shoved the spoon in his mouth. "'oure 'ong." He swallowed. "I do this a lot. But you're never late."

"I worked several hours on the Callaghan case after I left the office yesterday. So technically, I'm early."

He considered that for a moment, then gave this little shrug of his shoulders that I took for a concession of defeat. Then he sat on my desk. "How's that case going? Did you find the evil saboteur?"

"Not yet. I'm going back again this afternoon."

"How many hours did she pay us for again?"

"I can check, but I know I'm not there yet. She wanted this made a priority, so we got a big retainer."

"Good." His spoon screeched as he scraped the bottom of the ice cream bowl. "And you're done with the parrot people, right? I have something else I'd like you to start on."

That grabbed my interest. He was offering a new case without me having to beg or even hint. But I wasn't finished with the parrot, not quite. "I'm almost done with Doreen's case."

"Almost?"

"I, uh, just have to finish the report."

"Okay, let me know when that's done and I'll give you the Hernandez file."

"You can give it to me now." I held out my hand.

His grin turned a little wicked. "Oh, no. I know you. You're not done with that stupid parrot case that is earning us zero money. So you don't get a new case until I see the finished report."

"What? You never even look at reports." I shouldn't have said that aloud. I could have just handed him a sheaf of blank paper with a cover page. But now he'd check.

"And if you don't finish by, oh, tomorrow, then I'm giving the new case to Brittany."

"Brittany?"

She looked up from her computer and pulled an earbud out of her ear. "Yeah?"

I must have said that really loud for it to penetrate the cacophony on her iPod. "Nothing."

She looked at Dave. "I'm almost ready for the Hernandez file. Just have a few more background checks to finish."

I glared at him. "But you told me *I* get that file. When *I* finish."

"You mean *if* you finish. If not…" He shrugged. "She won't be done today, you know that. It's Tuesday. She leaves for class soon."

"So is this a race to see who finishes their work

first? We get the prize of more work?"

"Yep." He licked his spoon. Then he stood and headed for his office. I made a face at him, but it didn't make me feel any better.

Then the phone rang and I could see from the caller ID that it was Doreen. This was perfect. I could tell her right now that as far as I could tell, the Flaglers had been using the room at the time of the collapse. No one could prove they hadn't been. And they had that Christmas picture. But something bothered me about that picture.

I let her ring over to voice mail.

Just before we left for the jump rope class that afternoon, I ran around the house unplugging any appliance that had even a remote chance of bursting into flame.

"The TV's broken." Evan held up the remote, his thumb jamming the button over and over.

I gave him my best stern mother look. "You promised you'd work on homework if I let you stay home alone."

"Oh, right." He grabbed his book bag and slunk down into a pile of pillows on the floor.

"Alicia!" I called upstairs. "We have to go."

"But I need to braid my hair."

"You do not."

She appeared on the stairs with her arm twisted over the side of her head and her hands entwined in her hair. "All the girls at jump rope braid their hair."

"You went to practice with me last week. They did not all have braided hair."

"But in the video—"

"You were watching the video?"

She shrugged, despite the contorted angle of her arms. "The guys are really amazing."

"You're twelve. They're in high school."

"Maaaaahhhhmmm." She rolled her eyes. "I was just looking at a video."

Did I really want to bring my daughter into this? Yeah, it would look creepy if I just started showing up to watch classes on my own. I did need her. But I would finish this quickly so I wouldn't corrupt her too badly.

"Your hair looks great. Let's go."

While Alicia learned some dance steps with a jump rope, I sat down on the bleachers as close as possible to the class Lindsey was coaching. She had never answered my question about whether she'd seen anyone going through the jumpers' bags. Lindsey was probably the only jumper I could really press for information, since she knew both why I was there and that her mom wanted her to cooperate. Of course, Hayley knew all that, too, but the cooperation wasn't happening.

The field house was so big that they were holding three classes simultaneously and still only using one half of the airplane hangar-sized space. Each class was sectioned off by green curtains. From the sets of bleachers at the end, I could see a little bit of each class. Gwen and Rachel were coaching a class in the section nearest to me, and Lindsey, Juno and Morgan were coaching a class in the middle. Alicia's class was on the other end, so I was going to look like a disinterested parent if anyone realized I was watching the other classes and not hers. I noticed that her class was coached by two of the male jumpers. Maybe I would have to pay attention after all.

But first I scanned the bleachers in front of the section where Gwen and Rachel were turning a long rope for a line of young children to jump through. The dark-featured woman who had been complaining to Coach Nan on the first day sat on the second row scrolling through something on her phone. I hoped I could get her to share her complaints with me. Casually, I walked over and stood near her. Since she'd been at the practice with the more experienced kids, I knew she had to be the parent of one of the jumpers who was coaching, rather than taking the class. And now to get her attention...

"Oh, they're so good," I murmured with enthusiasm and probably a little too much volume.

She looked up. I think when most parents hear the word "good," their ears perk up, hoping that the word refers to their child.

"Those girls coaching," I added. "They're so good with the little kids." And truly, they did appear to be working well with them, smiling and encouraging them to try again when they missed, which was frequently. Two other older girls were turning a long rope for a second line of young class participants further away from us. I wondered if the complaining woman was the parent of one of those two or of Rachel or Gwen.

"Yes," she agreed. "They love to teach the little ones."

"Is one of the coaches your daughter?"

"Yes." She nodded. "The one with the purple headband."

Gwen. So the woman I was speaking with was Jackie. Gina had said I should consider her a suspect, too.

"Oh yes," I smiled with what I hoped was

enthusiasm. "I think I saw her when we visited a practice to talk to Coach Nan. She's a really good jumper. She was amazing doing those, um, things where they jump really high."

She nodded again, her wide smile in utter contrast to the scowls I'd seen earlier. "Yes, she's doing well. She works hard. And she loves it."

How could I get this woman to focus on the negative? At the moment she was radiating so much happiness that I expected singing cartoon birds to swoop down and start cleaning the floors for us.

"I'm Karen," I announced, mostly because I couldn't think of anything else to say.

She held out her hand. "Jackie. Which child is yours?" She nodded toward the class in front of us.

"Uh, my daughter's over there, actually." I waved vaguely toward the other classes. "I just find it so interesting to learn about all the classes. I'd like to get involved with the team, maybe volunteer."

"Yes, yes. that would be great. It's a great group of people. A great organization." She continued to nod and smile.

This was getting me nowhere. I needed her negative and scowling again and just couldn't seem to make that happen.

I noticed that that the kids in the middle class were taking a water break, so I excused myself and moved over that section to talk to Lindsey.

"Hey, it's me again, the pesky investigator." I said in a low voice.

She gave a tight nervous smile before taking a drink from her water bottle.

"If someone wanted to do something to a jumper's rope to make it break, what would they do?"

"I don't know," she said quickly.

"Can I see your rope?" I asked.

She offered me the one she was holding, which was quite basic—a piece of rope with blue and yellow plastic beads threaded onto it like a necklace, and simple white plastic handles at each end.

I looked at it dubiously. "This isn't the kind of rope I saw in the video. Those didn't have beads."

"Yeah, in competition we use wire ropes."

"Can I see the rope you use for power?"

She glanced toward a woman in a Jumptastics shirt who was fussing with a CD player.

I nodded toward the woman. "Is she in charge of the class?"

Lindsey nodded.

"Don't worry," I assured her, "she won't mind you talking to a concerned parent. So just let me see your wire rope. That you'd use for triples."

Lindsey bent down, reached into her backpack and pulled out a clear plastic bag with a piece of wire coiled inside. At first I didn't think the handles at the ends of the wire looked much different than the ones on the beaded rope, but when she handed the bag to me, I could feel that they were heavier. And they attached to the rope with a screw mechanism. They were actually much more complicated than the handles on the beaded rope.

"If I loosened the screw," I asked, "would that cause the rope to fall apart while you were jumping?"

"Maybe." She looked uneasy.

"Okay everyone." The adult by the CD player clapped her hands. "Drink break's over. Back to your groups."

"I gotta go." She started to edge away.

"One more question. Did you see anyone going through your sister's rope bag on the morning of the competition?"

She shook her head and looked away. "No."

It was the most unconvincing denial I'd ever witnessed.

I let her go back but realized I needed to reevaluate this girl. I'd viewed her as my ally, the one I could go to for neutral information. But if she had done something to sabotage her sister's rope—loosened the screw, for example—then I was letting her know too much about my investigation. After all, she was competing against her sister in the same category. I realized she was not the ally and never had been. I had to view her as the enemy.

I walked over toward Alicia's class and just gave what was supposed to appear to outsiders as a casual glance.

One of the high school boys had his arms around her.

All thoughts of casual went right out the window. I marched forward, ready to let him have it, but words of protest died on my lips as I saw that all he had done was move Alicia's arms so that they crossed in a different position. In fact, by the time my suspicious mind grasped the situation, the kid had already moved on and was talking and demonstrating to the girl next to Alicia.

Overreacting? Just a bit.

I went back to the bleachers.

Bonnie was talking to a mom on the bleachers I'd never seen before. From her lounge chair, her voice really carried. "Morgan found this essay online that she could use for two different classes," she was telling the other mom. "Is that cool or what? Two for the price of one." She laughed.

Had I heard correctly? Was Bonnie bragging that her daughter had bought a paper from a site on the internet so she could cheat in two different classes?

I couldn't hear the other mom's response.

"Well, yeah," Bonnie nodded. "Of course everyone does it and the teachers know that. It's not any different than copying stuff from websites, which is all they do for research anyway. The paper Morgan bought has some book references, stuff we probably couldn't find around here. So it was really good. Should get her an A in both classes."

I tried really hard not to show my disgust. If this woman thought nothing was wrong with buying her daughter's grades, she probably saw nothing wrong with helping her daughter qualify for the national tournament by taking out the competition.

I know Gina suspected her all along, but now Bonnie was officially on *my* suspect list.

I really didn't want to use my number one suspect as a source of information, but I needed information and most of the parents in the room were here with beginning jumpers like Alicia. Bonnie and the woman on the other set of bleachers might be the only parents of competition team jumpers, so I needed to get the information from them. Trying not to look as reluctant as I felt, I stepped over to Bonnie. "Hi, um, I was wondering if I might ask you ladies a question."

She pointed her finger like it was a gun. "Shoot."

"My kids just started jumping, and they really like it. I was wondering if there're some videos we can watch to see more."

The other woman answered first. "Oh, there was

that movie Disney made a few years ago, what was that called?"

"No," I corrected, "I meant any videos of kids from *this* team. Of the stuff they do in competitions, you know, that kind of thing."

"Anthony put one up on YouTube last week that was pretty good," Bonnie offered.

"Oh yeah," the other woman agreed. "That day in Laurel. Most of the team was there."

"Just go to YouTube," Bonnie explained, "and search for Jumptastics, North Laurel Community Center."

I wrote it down on the mini pad of paper that had gotten mangled in the bottom of my purse. "Thanks. Any others?"

She shook her head. "Nah. We used to have a guy who taped everything his daughter did, but then she graduated last year. We all got used to looking at his videos. Guess one of us needs to take over, but it hasn't happened yet. Morgan'll probably be out by the time that happens. Oh, what?" She frowned as she shook her iPad. "Why is this beeping? I just charged it before I left."

With Bonnie's attention on her iPad, our conversation was at an end. I moved on to watch some of Alicia's class, which Morgan was coaching. Coach Nan was in charge of this one, and it seemed to include jumpers who were a little older than the first group I'd watched. They were paired up taking turns jumping and counting each others' jumps. Alicia jumped slowly, wobbling a little as she switched from one foot to the other and not looking at all like the jumpers we'd watched in that first practice.

I turned around and wandered back toward the

middle class, hoping for a chance to talk to Lindsey again, but she stayed far away from me. As the end of class time approached, I headed over to watch Morgan again for any signs of unethical behavior. Coach Nan chastised her and the other coaches a bit after class for not helping to put away the clickers they'd used to count jumps, but if failure to put something away was unethical in a teenager, then I had an ethical cesspool brewing at my house. I waited for Alicia by the bleachers, hoping to overhear something else of interest from Bonnie.

There was a piercing squeal not from Bonnie, but from Morgan. "No fair!" She shouted. "You snuck up on me." But she didn't look unhappy—in fact, she was beaming from ear to ear. Standing next to her, with his hand on the arm, was one of the boys I'd seen come in to the Friday practice. He leaned in and gave her a big, long kiss.

"Ugh." I heard a low voice over my shoulder. "Don't tell your sister about this. That's the last thing she needs."

I turned to see Juno walking with Lindsey toward a storage room in the back, bags slung over their shoulders.

"He knows he's not supposed to be here," Juno continued, her voice laced with disgust. "And she knows it, too."

"Why not?" I asked, moving closer to them and deciding to try the "nosy mom" approach. "What'd he do?"

Juno scowled, glanced at Lindsey, then answered. "He's a loser. Caused a fight between two jumpers. We don't need that."

I looked pointedly at Lindsey, guessing that the

fight had been between her sister and Morgan.

She cringed but then gave a brief nod.

Hmmn. Interesting. But would this guy switch his allegiance from one girl to the other just because she came in fourth at a jump rope competition? Hardly a motive for Morgan to damage Hayley's rope. More like the other way around, depending on when they broke up.

"When was the fight?" I asked.

"Last week."

After the competition. So the stuff involving the boyfriend was probably irrelevant.

Probably, but not definitely.

I sighed. Something else to consider. I was supposed to be narrowing my list of suspects as the investigation progressed, and instead my list seemed to be growing. I was obviously doing something wrong.

15

Brian was going to surprise me at church tonight. I kept hoping it would happen before the meeting of the knitters' group, so I wouldn't have show up and admit that I didn't remember how to knit. But though I waited in the hallway outside the room until just before the session started, I saw no sign of him. Of course, the surprise was that he wasn't going to meet me there, so it didn't make any sense for me to wait, but I really hated to walk into a room full of knitting enthusiasts and admit that not only was I terrible at their hobby, I had no interest in getting better at it.

They were all very nice. It was a smaller group than the MOMs—mostly women about my mother's age, but two of them looked younger than me. All the tables in the room had been pushed against the walls and we sat in chairs forming a loose circle. Each knitter had come in with at least one tote bag which they quickly emptied into a sea of color on the tables and floor surrounding each chair. They started in to work right away, introducing themselves and asking questions without seeming to need to pay much attention to the needles twisting in their grip. I explained that I hadn't knitted since was a kid—which was true—and that I wanted to get back into it—which was not true. And I also said that I had no supplies, which means that two out of three of my statements were true. I decided that wasn't a bad truth ratio, even for church.

On a table in the corner, the group had a big green trash bag full of yarn of all colors and textures wound up into balls which rolled all over the place when I accidentally tipped the bag over. Great accident, too—I was able to use up nearly 20 minutes picking them all up. And then I spent another 10 minutes considering the various merits of each type of yarn. I was just trying to figure out how long I could spend picking out a pair of knitting needles when I heard a low voice behind me. "Crochet is a lot easier, if you want to try that first."

I turned to see a woman with close cropped grey hair and a wide toothy grin. "I'll bet you remember knitting as being pretty difficult, when you were a child, right?" she continued.

"Um, yeah," I admitted in a half whisper.

"You weren't wrong. It is hard. But we've all been doing it so long we've forgotten that. So why don't you start with crochet for tonight?"

"I don't know how to do that at all."

She gave me a motherly pat on the arm. "I can teach you. You've already picked out your yarn, so let me get a hook for you. Drag a couple of chairs over there, by that floor lamp. The light is terrible in here."

She was right, crochet wasn't too difficult. I learned a chain stitch and one other stitch and by the time the session ended, I had crocheted enough rows to make a potholder. A very small potholder, admittedly, probably just about the right size for an EZ Bake oven. But still, it was something.

"Thank you," I said as we were packing up to leave.

"Ellen," she reminded me from our conversation during the chain stitch. "And you're Brian Kieffer's girl,

Karen."

She must have read the dismay on my face.

"Sorry to give you a label," she added quickly "but this is such a big church and my memory is so bad, I need some connection to remember people's names. So you're either so and so's mom, or sister or ...." She let her words trail off with that same infectious grin.

"I understand. See you next week." The words were out of my mouth before I realized it. I really had no intention of coming back, but now I felt like I had to. It was an implied promise made in church, and probably an extra special sin if I broke it.

When I stepped out into the hallway, Brian was not there.

How would I be able to meet him someplace else if I didn't know where to go?

I stood by the bulletin board again wondering if there was some other Tuesday night group I could join to give me an excuse to not come to the knitting group. If I went to something else churchy then it might cancel out breaking that promise to come back to their group.

Of course, it wasn't really a promise. I hadn't said "I promise to be back." So why did it bother me?

"Do you need a ride?"

I turned to see Siobhan from the MOMs group. My face heated and I felt like I had the word "dropout" tattooed on my forehead.

"No, I drove." I added an extra big reassuring smile. "I'm just waiting for Brian."

"Okay, then. Great to see you." She didn't ask why I hadn't come back to their group and I appreciated it.

As the hallway emptied of people, it grew quiet. My shoes squeaked a little as I paced back and forth in front of the bulletin board.

Maybe I was supposed to meet Brian out in the parking lot? Or maybe he'd sent a message telling me to meet somewhere and I hadn't gotten it? I checked my cellphone, but there were no new voicemails or text messages.

I texted him.

I paced again.

I stopped and checked my messages again. No answer. I checked the settings, to see if I'd turned off the volume. I called him. No answer. I didn't leave a voicemail message because he always checks his texts first.

I paced some more. Then I decided to leave. And as soon as I stepped out the door, my blood pressure shot up. Brian's truck was pulled up next to my van in the otherwise empty parking lot. Was he hurt? No. Because when he saw me he climbed out of the truck and waved, carrying a paper bag and a cup as he walked toward me.

In the cold air, the breath literally steamed out of me as I stalked toward him. "Were you just going to sit out here all night until I got fed up and came out? Why didn't you tell me you were here? Is that coffee?"

His forehead wrinkled into a frown of concentration. "In reverse order: yes, I don't know and probably." He handed me the coffee and the bag. "Here."

I took a sip automatically. The coffee was black with one Splenda, just the way I liked it. That almost made up for—wait, why was I holding an oversized lunch bag?

I shook the bag. "What's in here? Thanks for the coffee." The logo on the cup indicated that it was from the convenience store at the gas station—not exactly gourmet—but it was hot.

"I, uh, nothing much." He raked his hand through his hair. "I wanted to surprise you but I couldn't think of anything."

"So you just thought you'd let me wait for you?"

"I ran to the nearest store for a guilt offering. Berger cookies, Diet Coke, and flowers, but they're pretty crummy flowers."

"Guilt offering?" I didn't like the sound of that at all. What had he done to cause remorse? I started walking toward my van.

"Sorry, I know it's pretty lame." He hurried to catch up to me.

"I, uh—why—" I closed my mouth. I didn't want to know. Jeff never gave me a guilt offering and he had a lot to feel guilty about. So what had Brian done? It must have been pretty bad. But I couldn't bring myself to ask about it. "Why didn't you answer your phone?" I demanded instead. "I felt like an idiot waiting around in there."

He looked sheepish. "Well I wanted to surprise you. But as I said I couldn't really come up with anything good. So I figured I'd settle for mystery instead of surprise. Pretty lame, like I said. I hoped the cookies would help."

I stopped walking. "Wait, is that what the guilt was about? That you hadn't come up with a good surprise?"

"Yeah."

I shook my head. "You're kidding me." Breathing a sigh of relief, I gratefully let go of the truly horrid thoughts that had begun to circulate in the back of my mind. Then I leaned over, stretched up on my tiptoes and gave him a kiss.

He pulled me into a big bear hug. "I knew the

cookies would do it. Chocolate frosting can solve any crisis."

"Watch the coffee!" I smiled and tried to keep my cup upright. "I don't know why you felt like you had to surprise me. It wasn't my birthday or anything."

"I wanted to do something unpredictable."

This time I laughed. "Well, I didn't predict this, so you succeeded."

"Good." He looked at me with much more intensity. "I want to keep our life together… interesting."

"It is." I looked down and pretended to be interested in the contents of the bag that was getting crushed between us. That look in his eyes scared me. I was laughing, and here he was, getting all serious. We hardly knew each other.

"What's wrong?"

"We're crushing the poor flowers. Look, they're turning blue." I pulled out a dyed mum with a limp stem and petals that were curling up.

"I think crushing can only improve them. Let's just say that you can't find the best selection of cut flowers in a place that sells antifreeze and oil filters."

I shifted from side to side, suddenly aware that my toes were growing numb. "This was really sweet of you, but it's freezing out here."

His eyes narrowed. "You're looking for an excuse to leave without sharing any of the cookies."

"You're coming over Friday, right? I promise I'll save some until then."

"And you won't let the kids lick the frosting off any of them?"

"Eew." I nearly gagged on my coffee. "I'm not going to ask what made you think of that."

"Let's just say I've seen it done."

I shook my head. "TMI! I did not need to know that."

"You have kids."

"Yeah, but it's not as gross when it's your own kids."

He shrugged. "I don't buy anything with frosting for youth group anymore. So I'll see you Friday, as soon as practice is over. And can we go out Saturday?"

"Yeah, sure." I took another sip of coffee. "Where?"

"Can I try the surprise thing again?"

"Only if I can wait for you at my house. And if you can't think of something good by 7:00 come over anyway and we'll do something not good."

He raised one eyebrow, just like his mother had done during dinner. "Something 'not good?'"

"Yes, something 'not good' together is definitely better than waiting by myself."

"Okay." He nodded. "So I have a deadline."

"If you choose to see it that way, yes. Now I need to go." I leaned in to kiss him goodnight.

He pulled me close and did his best to make me forget that I was standing in a church parking lot, that my feet were cold, that it was a school night and I had to get home and make lunches for tomorrow, that I was worried about him becoming too serious. These thoughts flashed through my mind and disappeared so fast I wasn't even sure I'd had them. I wasn't sure I'd ever had a past or would need a future. There was just this moment.

Until my cellphone rang.

He released his hold on me with obvious reluctance. I fumbled through my coat pocket, found the phone and saw that the call was from home.

"Mom?" It was Alicia.

"Yeah. Is something wrong?"

"No. Dad dropped us off a while ago. I just wondered when you'd be home."

I bit back the urge to ask again if something was wrong. "I'm with Brian. I'm about to get in the car. Be home soon." I hung up before I could ask anything else. She was okay. Evan was okay. They did not need me with them every minute. They could make good decisions without me.

And I was only about five minutes away anyway.

"Everything all right?" Brian asked.

"Yeah. But I should go." I didn't move.

"I'll see you Friday." He didn't move either.

"This is silly. We can't stay in the parking lot all night."

"I don't want to leave you."

"Me neither."

"Maybe we should do something about that." There was that intense look in his eyes again.

"I gotta go." I turned toward the van. "Kids are waiting for me. G'night." I had to get away from that serious gaze. But now I seemed too aloof. I turned back, gave him a quick kiss on the cheek, and then hurried over to the van.

It was freezing inside.

Thursday morning, I parked near the parrot house hoping the sight of it would jolt something in my brain indicating whether the Flaglers were telling the truth or not. The clapboards were silent however, the home gave away no secrets. And even though I walked into an empty recycling bin, nothing jolted heavily enough in my brain to make the case clear one way or the other.

Rodney hadn't cleaned the milk wand on the cappuccino machine, so my first caffeinated beverage of the morning had crusty bits of sour milk floating in it.

Strike two.

A message from Doreen was waiting for me on the voicemail, not quite demanding an answer, but definitely pleading for one. When I got to email, I remembered Bonnie had said at the jump rope practice that I could find a recent video online. So I flipped off email and did a Google search and actually found the video pretty easily.

It showed rows of smiling kids in uniform jumping to music. When the music ended, different kids walked out and jumped rope while bouncing on hoppity hops and pogo sticks. It was definitely entertaining, but I realized I must be watching a show rather than a competition. The video wouldn't help me at all.

Strike three.

And it wasn't even 9:00 a.m. yet.

I made coffee with the old drip machine and starting revising my list of suspects in the Callaghan case.

There was Bonnie,

Morgan,

Lindsey,

Rachel,

Gwen,

Possibly her mom, Jackie

And there might have been other jumpers who finished lower or who expected to do better. And they all had parents who might be suspects, too.

Okay, who had means, motive, and opportunity?

From what I had seen of the ropes, they were simple, and anyone could have unscrewed the handle so it would pull loose while Hayley was jumping. Whoever did it would then hope that she was too tired to score well on a re-jump. All of the suspects had the means to perpetrate the crime. I wasn't really sure altering a rope was covered in the criminal code, but I guess it would come under the heading of vandalism, and it didn't matter because we weren't looking for a criminal prosecution. They were all there the morning of the competition, so they all had opportunity except for Danielle, and I hadn't even counted her.

That left motive.

Morgan, her mom and Rachel would presumably have acted to secure Morgan a spot at the national competition and a chance to qualify for the World competition. Gwen and her mom would have being trying to achieve the same for herself, although she already had a spot with some other event. This list wasn't telling me anything I didn't already know.

What about Lindsey? Revenge? Older sisters could be cruel. Her mother paid more attention to Hayley, and Hayley had been a champion in the past. Could Lindsey be jealous? She had acted more guilty than anyone I'd yet talked to. And if Hayley somehow knew Lindsey had something to do with it, that might explain her reluctance to have the matter investigated. She was protecting her younger sister.

Sheesh. I banged my pen against the paper. In all this time I'd only really ruled out one suspect. I hadn't learned much of anything.

The phone rang.

It was Gina Callaghan. Of course. "What have you found?" she asked, after we'd exchanged pleasantries.

"It's coming together," I lied. "It would be potentially damaging to say more at this point." *Yeah, damaging to my reputation to admit I'd learned almost nothing.*

"Did you get my daughter's email?"

"Uhmm…" I hated to admit I hadn't finished checking email yet, but I'd actually forgotten, what with the sour milk and all.

"Lindsey told me to tell you she sent you an email. She didn't tell me what it was about." Gina paused as if waiting for me to enlighten her.

"I haven't had a chance to read it yet," I finally admitted.

"It might be important."

"Yes, it might. Maybe I should hang up, so that I can continue reading our email."

"But I wouldn't give it too much weight." She sounded suddenly nervous. "You know teenagers."

"I don't need to read it at all if you don't think I should." Now I was grinning and actually having fun at her expense which was totally wrong but also totally fulfilling after the rotten start I'd had this morning. What did she *not* want me to know?

But she gave me no hints and instead repeated her same old suspicions. "You should investigate Bonnie," she said flatly. "I don't trust that woman."

"I have been." I found that a staple remover was good for fishing the dried milk flakes out of my coffee. "And I'll keep that under advisement. Do you have anything specific on her? Was she seen near any of the jumper's bags, for example?"

"She's always sitting very close to them."

"On the day of the competition, was she sitting near the bags?"

"Her chair was there."

I smothered an exasperated sigh. "Was she in it? Or was she judging, like all the others?"

"Well, during the competition she was judging of course. We all have to judge, or tabulate or serve as runners or some other job. Those of us who've been around for a while make better judges."

"So she's been around for a while?"

"Oh, yeah"

I did let out a sigh this time. "I have to admit, it's hard to find someone who might have seen anything that happened to Hayley's bag, since all the jumpers were competing or getting ready to compete and all the parents were on the judging panels."

"Maybe one of the jumpers noticed something while they were practicing. What did they say when you asked them?"

"Hayley didn't want me to ask them."

"What?" Her voice sharpened to a hard point. "Hayley's not paying you. I am."

"I think this embarrasses her."

"But this is her chance to go to the world competition. In two years when they have trials again, she'll be too old. She won't be able to stay in competitive form in college. This is her *only chance*." Gina's voice had grown so strident that I had to hold the phone away from my ear. "I want you to ask the jumpers, *all of them,* what they saw the day of the competition. That's what I'm paying you for."

I rolled my eyes, grateful that she couldn't see me. "Just so you understand, at the point I start doing that, I destroy any trust I might have built by appearing as a regular mother of a jumper. I become the investigator, and people may not be honest with me. And you can forget about discretion."

"Dishonest people will not be honest with you anyway. But I'm sure someone saw someone tampering with Hayley's rope, or at least taking it out of the bag. We need to know who it was."

"Okay," I agreed. "As long as you understand that your suspicions will be out in the open now, I'll come to practice today."

"I'll be there to help."

"Oh, great. Thanks."

Not. Now I had to re-think my approach entirely.

I hung up and got more coffee before I faced the email.

There was the receipt from the Flagler case that Brittany had scanned and emailed to me because it was easier than delivering a paper copy to my inbox. The receipt she'd found was from Walmart, dated in early January and it looked pretty ordinary. Mostly groceries, some office and craft supplies. No bird food, but birds that expensive probably would turn up their noses up at food from a discount chain store. If they had noses. Did they smell with their beaks? I had to stop myself before I went online to learn about the olfactory organs of birds.

There was the email from Lindsey. She "just remembered" that she saw Rachel going through several people's bags on the morning of the competition. That immediately pointed suspicion at Lindsey herself, rather than Rachel, in my opinion. She was trying to divert me. Did her mom suspect? In that case, she'd be better off dropping the investigation.

For the moment I put jump rope out of my head and went back to the email from Brittany with the receipt from the Flaglers dated from early January. Could this morning have a strike four? I'd hoped the receipt would list Christmas decorations, which would suggest the Flaglers had faked the picture, trying to make it look like the bird was in the room at Christmas when it really wasn't.

But there were no Christmas decorations on the receipt.

I brought up the picture again. There was something odd about it. There had to be. I checked the carpet, remembering how Mrs. Flagler called it Shaggy Plush when it clearly wasn't. But the carpet in the picture was the same it was when I'd seen it. The bird looked just like birds in the pictures on rare bird vendors' websites. So what was wrong with the picture? Why did it bother me?

"Are you okay, Karen? Why are you staring at your computer from such a funny angle? Oh, wait." Dave's voice from behind turned quite grim. "That's a parrot. You still haven't done with that parrot case, have you?"

"Almost."

"Brittany!" He hollered in an unnecessarily loud tone. "You can keep the Fernandez file."

"She's in class," I pointed out.

"I'll leave her a note then."

"Fine." It was probably a bad idea, but I ignored his obvious hints that I was destroying any hope of a career. Instead, I kept staring at the picture, willing it to give up its secrets. There was something there that I was missing.

Dave waved a hand in front of my face. "Why won't you realize it's over? Time to move on."

"I'm missing something."

"That's okay. Still time to move on."

"What?" I shook my head and finally looked at him. "If there's something I'm missing, I need to find it."

"No, you don't." He sat down on the edge of my desk. "This is not an industry of perfection. It is an industry of getting what you pay for. While clients are paying, we do what they ask. When the money runs out, the job is over. If we investigated ever miniscule possibility like they do on TV, our clients would go broke."

"Not if—"

"Or *we'd* go broke," he added quickly. We do the work we get paid for. Then we move on. A client can only pay for so many hours. We work for those hours, then we tell them what we learned. And move on to the next client. And this client hasn't paid us a dime."

"Yes, she has."

"Well, we've used up the dime. Time to move on." He stood, leaving a trail of crumpled papers on the desk behind him.

"But I want to get it right." I picked up the papers he'd been sitting on to see if any of them were important.

"Fine." He pushed the papers away from my face and leaned in so that he had my full attention. "Do it on your own time. Not while I'm paying you." Then he leaned back, pulled a candy bar out of his jacket pocket and tore off the end of the wrapper. "And finish up the Callaghan case so we can wrap that, too. Can't imagine that woman is willing to pay much more for such a trivial thing." He stuffed the chocolate into his mouth and bit off about half of it.

"It's not trivial in her opinion. It's her daughter's swansong."

"Okay then," he said in a thick, food-filled voice, "but 'on't 'et it go on." Mercifully, he swallowed before continuing. "Try to wrap it today."

"I have to finish the quarterly tax filing today, among other things. But I'll be working on the case. I'm going to another jump rope practice to question suspects."

"Good." He nodded with satisfaction and started toward his office. Then he stopped and turned back around. "Oh, and see if you can find Rodney. I sort of fired him yesterday but I want him to know I didn't really mean it."

I blinked at him in surprise. "What?"

He stuffed the rest of the candy bar into his mouth as he walked away, and at the same moment, the phone rang, so I couldn't pursue him.

"Good morning," I answered, only half aware of what I was doing. I couldn't believe Dave had just—well, I could believe it, but how was I supposed to—

"Karen, this is Doreen. I'm calling because I really need—"

I couldn't talk to Doreen. Not now.

"So sorry," I said quickly in some sort of totally made-up fake foreign accent. "You must have wrong number. No Karen here." And I hung up.

Then I began the hunt for our missing Office Maximizer, which kept the phone lines busy most of the rest of the day.

16

I had no luck finding Rodney, but I think I left enough messages in enough places that he would eventually find out he wasn't actually fired and could return to work tomorrow. I hoped. Then I wondered *why* I hoped it. Wasn't this what I wanted? The pesky guy might be gone forever. Our office could go back to the way it used to be, as much as possible, anyway. We couldn't use the split molding on the edge of Brittany's old desk as a letter opener any more since Rodney had replaced it with a new one. And I didn't really want to go back to the old filing system because we had created a much more efficient one now. But still…life would be easier without Rodney, wouldn't it? I'd eventually learn how to clean the cappuccino machine myself.

I had been so busy leaving messages for Rodney that I lost track of time. I would need to hurry to get to the Jumptastics practice and wouldn't have time to go home first to check on the kids. "I need to work late," I texted Amy. "Glance at the house every once in a while, and let me know if it's on fire."

After calling Alicia to tell her I'd be home before dinner, I left the office and drove straight off to the practice.

The jumpers were stretching in rows when I arrived, and I cursed myself for having missed the opportunity to talk to them individually before the practice officially started. Despite what Gina had said, I really hated to let the jumpers know the reason I was there. It seemed to cheapen them all, somehow, to suggest that one of them had deliberately cheated to win a place at the national competition. They didn't deserve that.

After the stretching session, Coach Nan called them all in together for announcements. "I want to go over our show this Saturday. It's at..." she consulted her clipboard. "It's at the Columbia Interfaith Center. Their annual health fair. Who's planning to come?"

About half of the group raised their hands, including Hayley and Lindsey.

"We'll do our standard opening, and a Double Dutch routine. Then I want a speed and power demo. Who wants to demonstrate speed for me?" A few jumpers held up their hands.

"Good." She made notes on her clipboard. "How about power?"

A couple others raised their hands, including Hayley.

They went on to discuss additional things about the show, but I was still thinking about the power demo. If there was one in this show, there might be one in that video I had started to watch but had given up on before finishing. I'm not sure it would help, but it wouldn't hurt to take a look at it.

I made a note in my own book to remember to watch the rest of the video. At least I tried to make a note. My pen wouldn't work. Eventually I just scratched the letters "wv" for "watch video" into the page, ripped the page out of the notebook and stuck it in my pocket.

"Wear your uniforms with the blue sleeves," Coach

Nan continued. "Remember to bring water. And turn off all cellphones like during competitions and practices. Um…" She checked through the paper on her clipboard, running her finger along the page before looking up." That's it for the show. You'll be getting heat sheets for the Aberdeen Invitational, those of you who registered for that tournament, so check to make sure your entry is correct. And registrations for Nationals are due soon."

"Monday," one of the moms called out from the bleachers. "They're due Monday. Some of the hotels are already full."

"Okay, get them in soon. Dan will bring all his rope equipment Friday. Check to see if any of your ropes are wearing or frayed or need longer wires. Make sure you have backups of everything." She glanced at her clipboard one last time. "Alright, that's it. We'll start speed drills at five o'clock."

Jumpers dispersed to all parts of the gym and started working. I'd have to interrupt them to ask questions. They didn't deserve that either. Sometimes I didn't like this job.

Hayley and Juno had started jogging around the gym. At least if I jogged with them, I could talk without interrupting their workout.

The next time they came around, I jumped in front of them and tried to match their pace. "Hi, can I join you?"

Hayley shrugged.

"Sure," Juno said.

"Does she know why I'm here?" I whispered to Hayley.

Hayley shook her head.

I tried to keep my voice low and leaned toward

Hayley. "Your mom wants me to start asking everyone openly if they saw anyone going through your bag the morning of the competition."

"What?" Juno looked at both of us but didn't break her stride. "Why?"

Hayley sighed. "There's a chance someone may have 'sabotaged' my rope at the qualifier so it would break during triples so I'd get a low score."

"That's—that's—really weird." Juno shook her head and laughed in disbelief, again with out slowing her pace. "Who'd do a thing like that?"

By now I was getting a little winded and could only say a few words at a time without pausing for breath. "The obvious suspects would be (gasp for air) the girls who Hayley would normally beat"(another gasp). "Including you."

Juno's eyes's widened in surprise and she turned toward me, sort of jogging sideways. "But I *want* her to go to Nationals. We've been roommates every year. This was supposed to be our last year together."

"Juno's practically guaranteed to qualify in speed," Hayley explained, not sounding out of breath at all as her feet pounded rhythmically against the floor. "She breaks 160 and auto-qualifies almost every time."

"Yeah," Juno considered for a moment. "Though I guess if my rope broke, and I was really tired or didn't have a good back up rope…"

"You all do have back up ropes, though, right?" I asked between breaths. "I heard Coach Nan remind you."

Juno nodded. "Yeah, we all do."

"Including you, right?" I peered at Hayley, who seemed to be looking past me rather than at me. Or maybe my eyesight was growing dim from the blood pounding through my veins at an unnatural rate.

"Of course." Hayley's gaze strayed across the gym to the main door which had opened to admit a group of boys carrying basketballs.

"So," I panted, "the back up is what you use if there's a problem with your regular rope?"

"Yeah." She nodded but was still looking toward the door.

I turned to the other girl. "Okay, Juno did you see anyone going through Hayley's (I almost made it without a breath but not quite) bag?"

"Nope." She shook her head, sending her ponytail swishing in all directions. "I didn't pay any attention, actually. All the bags look alike."

I turned back toward Hayley, and this made me a little dizzy, especially since Hayley had fallen behind us somewhat so I turned my head farther than usual. Which was stupid. I should have just slowed down.

So I did slow as we rounded the corner and headed toward the main entrance. "Your sister told me she saw Rachel going through the bags."

"Maybe,'" Hayley allowed. Suddenly she grimaced and started running much faster.

Juno glanced ahead toward the door. "Just ignore them."

"I can't," Hayley called over her shoulder, "when she throws it in my face like that."

As we neared the doorway and Hayley sped past in a sprint, I slowed and looked over to see her former boyfriend—who was now Morgan's prize—walk in with another boy.

Thank God I had an excuse to stop running.

I wondered if I was really thanking Him or just

using "Thank God" as a random expression in my head. That would probably be bad. But maybe God was just happy to be thanked in any case.

So was I earning good points or sending myself on the slippery slope to—

I shook my head to force me to focus and followed the boyfriend over to the corner where Rachel and Morgan were practicing handsprings. While Morgan shrieked in exaggerated surprise at something the boy did, I motioned to Rachel.

"I need to talk to you," I said in a low voice.

"Oh?" She looked at me as if I were a cockroach that was maybe a little too big to step on.

"Oh, yes. Right now."

Rachel waved toward Morgan, who was now locked in a giggly embrace with her boyfriend. "I'm practicing."

"Would you rather have me ask your coach what you were doing going through other people's bags during practice a few days ago?"

"I told you." She scowled, but came closer. "Someone's cellphone was ringing."

"But your coach said you're supposed to turn off your phones during practices."

She rolled her eyes. "No one does. We're not preschoolers. We don't have to do everything she tells us to."

"Okay, so what were you doing going through jumpers' bags on the morning of the qualifying competition?"

"What?" She froze, eyes wide and suddenly wary.

"Other people saw you going through bags, just like I did. But I'll bet your coach does a phone check, just like she does a rope check, to make sure phones are turned off. So you can't tell me you were answering a phone." This was a complete bluff so I wouldn't actually bet on it at all.

Fortunately, I guessed right. Her chin dropped and her face flushed slightly, her defiance now replaced with embarrassment. She glanced away. "I was looking for something."

"What?"

"It's personal."

I moved closer. "Do you want to be accused of stealing? Or worse?"

"No."

"Then tell me why you were searching through other people's jump rope bags."

She finally looked at me, pursed her lips and lowered her voice. "Just the girls. It was just the girls' bags. I needed girl stuff, you know? It was that time of the month. Morgan didn't have anything, but she said to check the other girls' bags. There wasn't time to ask around."

"Okay." I felt a little deflated. Her excuse was plausible and nearly impossible to prove one way or the other. Not much help. I let her go.

My neck felt stiff, and I really wished the gym had a soda machine because it was definitely time for me to ingest something unhealthy and carbonated. But the only liquid refreshment in sight appeared to come from a pair of smudged stainless steel water fountains set into the side wall.

I turned to the bleachers. To give myself a reason to ask the moms if they'd seen anyone looking through the backpacks and duffel bags on the morning of the competition, I came up with a ruse about someone missing money from their bag but being too embarrassed to ask about it. But there weren't many parents there to hear my fake excuse and, as I expected, they all said they were in a judges' meeting and then went right to their stations for judging. No one saw anything.

Morgan's mom, Bonnie, had set up her lounge chair in between the bleachers. Though she was clearly thrilled that her daughter had succeeded at the Regional tournament, she paid very little attention during the practices I'd seen. Today she was watching a movie on her iPad. Would someone that disinterested really sabotage a rope? Would she even know how?

At five o'clock all the groups that had been working independently around the gym came together to practice speed jumping, just like we'd seen at the first practice we visited. It was kind of mesmerizing, watching those ropes whir in an endless circle, and I was starting to fall asleep. Then they stopped, coiled up their ropes carefully, put them in little bags, and then took out other bags and uncoiled ropes that looked exactly like the ones they'd just put away.

"Are they switching so the ropes don't wear out?" I asked one of the dads I'd just finished talking to. He was wearing a Pittsburgh Steelers jacket so I figured he might be less likely to socialize with the other parents, at least three of whom wore Ravens purple.

"They're doing power events now, doubles or triples," he explained. "They use a longer rope for that."

"Why?" It seemed to me that if a rope was long enough to get over a jumper's head, it didn't matter how she was jumping over it. But apparently I was wrong.

"They jump higher on multiples—doubles and

triples," he continued. "If the rope's too short, they miss."

"Then why don't they just use long ropes for everything?"

"They can go faster with a shorter rope. But if it's too short, they'll be likely to miss. The rope has to be adjusted just right."

"Ah. Thanks."

The jumpers were getting ready to start now, so I moved over near Hayley to watch her. The yellow handles of her rope perfectly matched her yellow tie-dyed shorts with the word "jump" emblazoned on the back. Her jumps were high and seemed slow in comparison with the others. I counted 47 before she stopped. While the others were still jumping, she walked over to her bag, took out a black band, and fastened it around her leg underneath her knee

I went back to the dad in the Steelers jacket. "What are those things they're wearing under their knees?" I pointed to Hayley and another girl with a similar band.

"Oh, I think that's to help support their knees. Triples are very hard on their legs. Most jumpers don't practice them a lot."

"Okay, thanks." I assumed that was why I saw Hayley spend so much of her time running. Repeated high jumping would be hard to practice over and over.

When they had all finished, I expected Hayley to give me the evil eye for standing close to her. Instead, she smiled and came even closer. "I saw you talking to Rachel a little while ago," she said in a tone so hushed it was almost a whisper. "About going through the bags. She and Morgan are good friends, and Morgan beat me in the qualifier."

"Does that mean something to you?"

"I'm just saying…" She walked off with an enigmatic smile.

So now she *wanted* me to find a culprit. Or, rather, she wanted me to conclude that Morgan was the culprit. What happened?

I got home, found nothing burning or even remotely smoky smelling, and felt like maybe on the scale of motherhood, I was successfully edging my way down from a 10 to a nine on the overprotective end of the spectrum. As I was getting a casserole out of the freezer, I heard a familiar loud thump against the wall.

"Evan," I called, "take the soccer ball outside if you want to practice."

"I just want to see the end of this," he called back. "It's really funny."

How funny can it be if you already know what happens? I shrugged and started pulling off the pieces of cheese that stuck to the foil when I took it off of the chicken and noodles.

I heard another thump and an "uh-oh."

"Nothing broke!" Evan yelled defensively as I set down the foil and headed for the living room. Ray Lewis was grimacing at me sideways from a plastic cereal bowl tipped over on the floor. A river of brown milk carried chunks of chocolate cereal toward the area rug in a raging torrent.

Outside the dog barked and flung herself against the door, bewailing the opportunity to eat up the soggy cereal.

"Clean it up!" I yelled, looking in vain for a towel. I wondered if I should pull off his t shirt to use to stop the milk before it reached the light blue rug.

"I am." He ran to the kitchen and returned with

impressive speed. Carrying one paper towel.

"That's not going to be nearly enough. Why did you do this? I told you not to set drinks on the floor. And I told you not to play soccer in the house."

"I wasn't playing soccer."

I held up my hand. "Don't talk. Just grab the biggest towel you can find from the bathroom."

Chocolate milk didn't stain as badly as other brown stuff, did it? But spilled milk smelled horrible if it didn't get cleaned up very thoroughly. We spent the better part of an hour wiping, scrubbing and rinsing the rug, with me repeatedly asking him why he'd violated my rules and him repeatedly saying he didn't know.

I forgot to put dinner in the oven so we had to microwave it and it came out rubbery. Dinner was pretty dismal.

At least it was Thursday and that meant tomorrow was Friday.

And that meant the weekend.

But that also meant that I had only three more days to find out if Morgan had damaged Hayley's rope, so that she could lodge a complaint by the registration deadline.

When I hit the snooze alarm the next morning, I knocked a scrap of paper off the nightstand, but I didn't bother to pick it up until I was getting ready to leave. It was something I'd taken out of my pocket the night before. "WV" was scratched into the paper.

Something about West Virginia…didn't ring any bells. Must have stood for something else. I flipped the paper the other way—maybe it was "NM." The "n" obviously stood for "not." But "not" what?

I stuck it in my pocket and left for work.

On my way to work, I decided I would park on Church Street to see if the sight of the Flager house would somehow make everything clear for me.

I found a space near the house, and after I'd parked I just sat in the van and stared at the front porch for a minute or two. Clarity continued to elude me. With a sigh, I climbed out and started walking down toward Main Street.

Then I heard footsteps behind me. They weren't ominous footsteps exactly—they were the footsteps of someone with squeaky shoes. When I turned around to look, I saw two older men bundled in fur-lined winter coats. They were probably just out for a morning walk. I smiled and waved.

Neither of them waved back. In fact, they almost growled at me. Their fur hoods and fierce expressions made me think of bears forced out of hibernation.

Guess I didn't look like I could afford to live on this street. They probably got tired of people parking here to avoid the meters on Main Street. Oh, well. I continued on and the squeaking continued behind me. As I turned the corner, I glanced back. The men had stopped, but they were still watching me.

One of them was wearing bedroom slippers. Maybe he was just frowning because his feet were frozen. Lucky for me I had crazier things to worry about as I headed into work.

17

All day I watched the caller ID on the phone hoping I wouldn't get a call from either Gina or Doreen. Fortunately since Dave was out in the morning, I didn't worry about him pestering me to finish up my cases. I got out two clean sheets of paper to list what I knew about each one so I could see just how close I was to making the case.

The sheets were depressingly empty and white. I decided to finish up reviewing client reports and invoices so I wouldn't be worrying about those and could focus all my attention on those cases.

I also decided to go out to lunch instead eating the ham sandwich I'd brought from home. I'd feed it to the dog later.

1:30 and still no Dave. The guilt was starting to press on me, though. It was almost a relief when Doreen's number finally showed up on the caller ID.

"Karen?" she asked after I answered.

"Yeah, it's me."

"Oh, good." Relief sounded in her voice. "I was afraid you'd changed the number. But I must have just dialed wrong last time.

I anticipated her question and started in with my answer that wasn't really an answer. "Hey, um, I still haven't conclusively determined whether that sunroom was in use when the roof collapsed. I got nothing from the neighbors. The Flaglers gave me a photo showing the room in use with Christmas decorations, so I guess that's the closest I can get."

"Sounds pretty good to me."

"But they could have faked that picture. You can put up Christmas decorations any time of the year."

"True."

"I have no proof that they did, though. And even if they did, the bird was in the picture, so if it was after Christmas, the bird was still alive."

"Okay, it sounds like they've proved their claim." Doreen sounded confident and relieved.

I was not. "But something bothers me."

"What?"

I hesitated. "I don't know."

"Something mysterious, then."

"Yeah." I started to spin around in my chair like Brittany does, but since I was talking on a phone with a cord, this turned out to be a terrible idea. "I know," I said as I unwound the phone cord from around my neck, "there's got to be a way to find out when that room was finished. I haven't thought of it and it bugs me. I've seen receipts for the replacement furniture, but they don't have the receipts for the originals they bought so I couldn't check those."

"Hmmm." She thought for a moment. "Well, the last thing people usually do before moving in furniture is paint and finish the floors."

"So if we can find out when the carpeting went in, that would give us a good indication."

"It would."

"But the Flaglers own the carpet company. They could easily forge a receipt with any date they wanted on it."

"So we shouldn't get it from them," Doreen agreed.

If this were a detective agency on TV, I'd have someone on staff who could hack into their computer and get the receipt. I almost asked whether Doreen had someone. Maybe Brittany...ah, no. If she had those kinds of skills, I didn't want to know.

"I'm so sorry," I admitted. "I can't think of anything." I felt awful giving up, but at the same time, I felt a tremendous burden lifting off my shoulders. I really had done my best, and gotten an answer that seemed to satisfy the client. And it might even be the right answer.

"How much was that parrot worth again?" she asked.

"About fifteen grand."

She paused. "Why don't you think about it over the weekend?"

Wham! The weight hit my shoulders as if God himself had dropped it from the heavens.

"Oh, okay," I said slowly."Uh, have a great weekend." Maybe I should have thanked her for giving me more time. But I didn't feel very grateful.

When I tried to hang up the phone, I missed. There was a stapler where the switchboard base used to be. The base had been moved about a foot to the right. Rodney was standing next to my desk with a tape measure and a frown.

"We need to move the filing cabinets," he said once I'd managed to replace the receiver in the base.

"We've discussed this before," I said with a sigh. "We can't move them. They are located over support beams so they won't fall through the floor."

"But they are blocking the emergency escape route in the Emergency Action Plan I created for compliance with OSHA regulations."

"What?"

"And I assigned you the job of carrying the mobile emergency immediate medical assistance administration station."

"What?" I repeated again, trying to understand why Rodney wanted our file cabinets to fall through the floor.

"That's the first aid kit. We'll keep it in your bottom drawer." He held up a mammoth plastic box with a big red cross on the front.

"You will not." I moved protectively in front of my desk drawer.

"But the Occupational Safety and Health Administration requires that these supplies be readily available."

I shook my head. "No way. I know government is out of control sometimes, but they do not have regulations requiring you to fill up my desk with rubber gloves and gauze tape. Put that thing in the kitchen."

"But the OSHA recommendation is that the supplies be centrally located, and the kitchen is—"

I held up my hand. "Slow down. What is this all about? Why do we need to worry about OSHA regs?"

"If one of the employees were to suffer an injury and file a worker's compensation claim, our worker's comp insurance would not cover the amount if we were found to be out of compliance with OSHA regulations. Therefore, I have arranged for an OSHA inspector to come out next week to certify our compliance."

"I'm not going suffer grievous harm if I have to walk to the kitchen to get a Band-Aid," I assured him as I reached for my coffee cup. "And if I did, I would be way too embarrassed to file a worker's comp claim."

"Profess whatever you wish now, when the time came and medical bills pile up, you might feel very different."

I just looked at him for a moment. "You sound like a commercial. Did you ever work for a personal injury law firm?"

He shook his head and didn't seem nearly as insulted as I would have expected. "No, but I did spend a summer as an intern at OSHA headquarters."

"Really?" It all made sense now. That officious sense of self-righteousness he wore like an undershirt. I should have recognized it as governmentitis right away.

He considered for a moment. "Well, just half the summer. Our family always spent the month of August at—"

I held up my hand again to interrupt. "You've just given me a great idea. I need you to be an OSHA inspector for me."

Though he opened his mouth, I stopped him before he could voice his objection. "Just on the phone." I continued. "We need a copy of a receipt, and I need a reason for the company to give it to us."

He crossed his arms in front of his chest. "And I need a reason why you think I would commit the felony of impersonating a federal agent."

"I need you to use your expertise. Remember, you said we all need to do the jobs for which we've been trained. You know how OSHA works."

His forehead creased in puzzlement. "What does that have to do with a receipt?"

"I need a receipt for carpet installation. The customer who received the installation also happens to own the company. So if I ask her for the receipt, she can make up one that may not be accurate. I need to know when carpet was installed." I moved away from my chair and urged him to sit down in my place. "So we'll just call the main number for Flagler Flooring and tell whoever answers the phone that you're investigating an injury to a guy who installed carpet at 3775 Church Street and you need them to fax you a receipt for the installation showing the date and names of the men who did the work."

"But I don't know if OSHA would investigate that type of incident."

"Well, let's pretend. They probably don't know either." I shoved the phone receiver into his hands.

"That sounds simple enough," he allowed as I reached around him to type the company name into the search engine to get the phone number. "But it's still not worth the risk. It is a federal crime to impersonate—"

"So say your're a state agent. Or a county agent. Or make up an agency."

"Oh," his expression brightened. "I could do that. But why can't you do it?"

"I would not be nearly as believable as you." And it was true. He had a voice that rang with genuine bureaucratic solidity. "If you do this for me," I proposed, "I will tell Dave that you're indispensable to the company."

He blinked. "You would?"

"Yeah."

"Really? Because my probationary period is almost over. This could make a big difference whether I keep my job." He looked at me thoughtfully for a moment. "I was pretty sure you wanted him to let me go."

"Oh, uh, well…" I had assumed that when Dave renewed his contract with Rodney's uncle, he agreed to keep on the nephew indefinitely. Smart guy, putting the probationary period in the contract. I hoped I hadn't blown it. "Whatever's in the best interest of the firm," I said, quoting back one of Rodney's own favorite mantras. "Now," I waved toward the computer "here's the phone number of their headquarters. You want the installation receipt for 3775 Church Street in December of last year. Got that?"

"Yes." He nodded. Before dialing the number he mouthed the information over a few times, and his shoulders were hunched forward, giving the impression that he was as nervous as a box of chocolate in a room full of women on a diet. But to his credit, all this changed once he started talking on the phone.

"I need accounts," he said in that officious tone I knew so well. "Yes, this is Barney Magpie with the Occupational Health and Safety Bureau," he said, emphasizing the last word.

Barney Magpie? Really? I suppressed a shudder.

He cleared his throat. "I am investigating an incident involving a worker purportedly injured while installing carpet for your company and I need to see a copy of the receipt showing that he performed the installation on the date he claims."

And what was that date? I was sure they would ask. We didn't know it. That was the whole purpose of this call. How would Rodney admit that we didn't know?

"No," he said sternly. "I can't give you the date. You might falsify the record."

I was impressed.

"I can't give you the name of the injured party either," he continued, "for the same reason. That should be obvious."

Okay, he was doing pretty well.

"I can give you address of the customer," he explained, "and you should look it up from that. I can tell you it was in December of last year. Yes, I'll hold," he sighed with officious reluctance.

I held my breath as he waited. It took less time than I expected.

"Very good," he announced. "And the date?" He typed something into his phone. "And the name of the installation crew members?" His thumbs moved furiously as he typed in more information.

"Get a copy!" I urged.

"Can you fax me a copy? The number is…."

I looked over his shoulder at the date he'd written down. December 18. Well before the date of the roof collapse. Before Christmas even. Well, that settled it. I didn't even need the fax. The carpet had been installed early enough that the room must have been finished by Christmas. The picture was genuine.

But I waited by the fax machine anyway, just in case Rodney had written it down wrong.

Flagler Flooring, December 18, 3:53 p.m. I even read the names of the installers, as if it made a difference. The date was good. The room should have been in use. It was covered with 170 square feet of Stanton Shaggy Plush, which means virtually everything else in the room had to be finished.

I almost crumpled up the fax, but then I realized I should add it to the file I would send Doreen. I'd send her everything—I didn't want to keep any remnant of this failure around to haunt me.

Why did I feel like I was a failure? I'd proved that the claim was genuine. I'd satisfied the insurance company.

"Was that what you needed?" Rodney asked with

the hopeful expression of a young puppy.

"Oh, yeah, absolutely." I had proof that—

Why did that name "Stanton Shaggy Plush" seem so odd? Mrs. Flagler had mentioned it. But then she'd corrected herself. The carpet I remembered in the room wasn't plush at all. It was hard and matted, like a blanket saturated with glue. I sat down at the computer and opened up the picture of the room with the parrot cage.

The carpet was just as I remembered it—dense and hard, a carpeting made for outdoor use. I did a search on Stanton Shaggy Plush and found that it was made by a company that claimed to manufacture the most richly textured wool carpets in the world. The fibers were long and plush. That plush carpet was apparently what had been installed on December 18. It was not the carpet in the sunroom now. And it was not the carpet in the picture, either.

The picture with the parrot had been taken later than December 18. The picture had been taken after the plush carpet was ruined in the ceiling collapse. They had staged the picture later, after the ceiling had been repaired and new carpet installed.

Dave's voice boomed over my shoulder. "Oh no, not the bloody parrot again."

"You shouldn't say 'bloody.'" I recited, repeating something I'd heard the other night. "It's a curse word in England." How could I distract him so I could finish this in peace?

"It isn't a curse word here."

"Well it should be. It stands for Christ's blood." I clicked on another window to block out the parrot picture and replace it with a giant invoice.

"When did you get so religious?"

"I'm not. I learned it from a lady who was teaching me how to crochet." I spun around to face him. "I made you a potholder. I was going to save it for Christmas, but I can give it to you now if you want."

He glanced at my computer. "I know you're still wasting time on that nothing case for the nobody at the insurance agency."

"She's not a nobody. And right now I'm collecting accounts due for the firm. I'm waiting for information from you, as a matter of fact, before I can send out these invoices. Are you caught up on your paperwork?"

He growled something I probably didn't want to hear and stalked off to his office.

I had held him off this time, but I couldn't continue indefinitely if I ever wanted him to give me any more casework.

I needed to look at the parrot picture. But it would have to wait.

Instead, I picked up the blank sheet of paper I had pulled out for the Callaghan case.

It was very empty.

I was cold. I put on my sweater.

The paper was still empty.

There was a brown spot on the sleeve of my sweater. Chocolate milk from last night? Had I been wearing my cardigan last night? I sniffed it to see if it smelled like sour chocolate.

The paper was still empty.

I could write the names again. Or there were those initials. Were they "NM" or "WV"?

Maybe it stood for "Not milk?" Maybe I wrote a note about the spot on my sleeve.

It really looked more like an "WV." White vehicle? Wear velvet? Went voting? Nothing made sense. I glanced at my watch, hoping it might be time to leave. Then I could look at the parrot picture again at home. I flipped my wrist and looked at it again.

Watch.

Aha! WV meant "Watch video." But I already had watched the jump rope video, or at least the beginning of it. It was a show so it wouldn't tell me much about what had happened at a competition. Then I remembered—Hayley had volunteered to do a power demonstration at a show. I was going to watch the video to see if she'd done a power demonstration at the previous show also. The moms had said most of the team was there.

I found the video again, and went for coffee while YouTube showed a commercial for something they thought would appeal to teens. Then I enjoyed my caffeine while I watched jumpers of all ages and abilities demonstrate their tricks. They had music on for most of it that was so loud I couldn't hear what the coach was saying on the microphone. But at one point the jumpers jumped with no music while the coach walked around with a microphone. I turned up the volume to hear what she was saying.

"The jumpers see how many jumps they can complete in one minute," the coach was telling the audience. "For most of these guys, the rope is going over their head 4-5 times each second." The audience oohed appreciatively. A new set of jumpers came out. "Another competitive event focuses on power jumping, completing multiple revolutions between each jump. The younger jumpers do double-unders." Most of the jumpers who'd walked out started to bounce quickly on two feet. It looked like regular jumps. I was glad I didn't have to judge any of this since it all looked the same to me. "And the older jumpers," the coach continued, "have to do triple-unders. The rope goes under their feet three times between each jump." Hayley was the only one demonstrating this skill, and the audience again oohed and ahhed with appreciation. She looked just like she had at practice, except she was wearing a blue uniform instead of those yellow "jump" shorts. And the handles on her rope weren't yellow either. They were blue. Did that mean anything?

The demo ended. Music came back on, and the jumpers brought out a bunch of long ropes that they crossed on top of each other and then turned at the same time. It looked like a giant mushroom. Kids jumped in, and it was one big blob of jumping and turning. And then it was over.

I called Gina to ask what the different colored rope handles meant.

"They use different lengths for different events," she explained. "The shortest lengths are for short speed events. They stand up taller for longer events and use longer ropes."

"Do the colors refer to the length of the rope?"

"It can. It's whatever color the jumper chooses."

"Does it for Hayley? Does she use different colors for different events."

"I think so."

"What color does she use for jumping triples?"

She laughed "I have no idea."

"Would the coach know?"

"I have no idea about that, either. I doubt it. There'd be no way for her to remember all that for each jumper."

"Okay thanks." I hung up before she could remind me how soon she needed an answer.

She called back—I saw her number on the caller ID—but I let it ring.

Rodney buzzed me a minute later. "I have a Mrs. Callaghan on the line. She says she needs to speak to you urgently."

"Tell her I'm in a meeting."

"But you're not."

"I'm meeting with you right now."

"Not really."

"Close enough. Ask if you can find out what this is in reference to. If she has any useful info to add, she'll tell you. If not, then I need more time before I'm ready to talk to her again."

He sighed. "That's not very professional."

I played my trump card. "Do you want me to tell Dave you're 'value added' for this office or not?"

He sighed and went back to the phone. "I'm sorry, Mrs. Callaghan," he said smoothly. "She's just gone into a meeting. If you can give me a detailed message, I will hand it to her as soon as she comes out. Oh, no, I couldn't possibly interrupt her. We value our client confidentiality as a sacred trust."

Score another one for Rodney.

18

The brown spot on the sleeve of my sweater was chocolate milk, and it wasn't coming out. I poured half the bottle of dish detergent from the office kitchen on it and the stain still wouldn't come out. Why wouldn't Evan listen when I told him not to play with the ball in the house? I should make him buy me a new sweater with his allowance. He needed to learn that there were consequences for refusing to listen.

One consequence was that he'd have to go to jump rope again with me. I had planned to give him the option of staying at home, since no one seemed to think it odd for me to be there yesterday by myself. But he seemed happy enough to go and said he was learning to do a frog and a toad. As long as he didn't bring any of the amphibians home with him, I was okay with that.

Other than the corner where Evan's class met, the rest of the gym space didn't look very organized. Jumpers were talking, Hayley and Juno were jogging with a few others, and Lindsey and a couple of other girls were practicing tricks. I decided to sit near some parents and "read" a magazine while I eavesdropped on their conversation. They were discussing hotel reservations for the National competition.

"So," I butted in after a few minutes, "it sounds like there are a lot of kids from the team going."

One of the moms who'd been holding an array of

crayons for her young daughter turned to me and nodded. "All of the older jumpers are going, I think."

"Well," I said in a low voice, leaning closer, "I heard that one of the girls who was expected to make it didn't qualify."

"Really?" she seemed surprised. "Who was that?"

"Hayley." A man looked up from his iPad. I assumed he was the father of one of the jumpers since he was wearing a jacket with the team logo embroidered on the front. "Had a rope break."

The mom shook her head, dropping a crayon. She reached down under the bleacher to feel around for it. "But they get a re-jump for that."

I spotted the runaway crayon and bent down to pick it up. It was labeled "vomit orange" so I hoped the thing wasn't scented.

"It was triples," the dad replied. "Guess she was too tired. Should have taken her first score."

"What does that mean?" I asked as I handed back the crayon.

"When a rope breaks," the dad explained, "the jumper has the option of re-jumping the event. But they also have the option to keep the score. If they re-jump and the score is worse, they have to use it."

"Maybe her first score wasn't high enough to qualify." The mom suggested, waving a blue crayon.

The dad shrugged. "Hard to guess. Might not have been."

"Were you on that station?" The crayon mom asked.

"Yeah." He nodded. "We called the coach over and the head judge explained the situation. Hayley seemed pretty upset. She had enough jumps to meet the minimum, but probably not enough to make the top four. As it turns out, though, that first score was probably high enough. No one did real well that day."

I closed my mouth, once I realized it had been hanging open. I'd had no mention of this from either Hayley or Gina.

Gina wasn't in the room. Bonnie was sitting hunched over her tablet, apparently watching a movie. Since the parents had stopped talking, I decided to grab Hayley the next time she jogged by. But she didn't jog by again because the coach called them all forward for a rope check. I moved closer to watch.

Coach Nan asked to see their one minute speed, three minute speed, power and freestyle ropes, expecting them to have two of each. Any kids who were missing a rope or had a rope with a possible weakness were told to see her son, who had a big box of what looked like fishing tackle. When Hayley's turn came, she held up two red handled ropes for short speed events, two blue handled ropes for the longer speed event, two yellow handled ropes for power, and two ropes with long black handles for freestyle. They were all apparently in satisfactory condition.

But I'd seen her jump power in the video with blue handled rope. It would be shorter, which one of the moms told me would enable her to jump faster. But it would increase her likelihood of missing. At an earlier practice, the coach told her she needed a longer rope. Why would she deliberately go against her coach's advice? Had she done that on the morning of the competition? Was that why her rope broke—it was too short? Was this whole thing Hayley's fault after all? I wrote "WDV ("watch different video) on my hand to remind me to watch the video of the competition again to see whether she was using the blue handled rope like she had in the power demonstration.

To my surprise, Hayley followed me as I walked back toward the bleachers. "Did you find out anything else about Morgan or Rachel?" she asked.

"No." I studied her face closely. What did she expect me to find? Why did she care now when earlier she wanted me to go away?

"I did find out that you had a chance to take a higher score," I pointed out. "And you didn't tell me about it. If you'd taken your first score, you would have qualified."

A look of pain flashed across her face but she erased it quickly. "Normally that score wouldn't have been enough. I had to take another attempt. But I wouldn't have needed it if I could have continued with my first jump. If someone hadn't loosened the screws on my rope so it would come apart."

"How do you know that's what happened?"

"I always check my ropes before the start of the tournament. The coach makes us do it. Someone must have loosened the screws after the rope check."

I veered away from the bleachers to see if she would follow. She did, showing that she definitely wanted to talk to me now. I stopped and turned to her. "Can I ask you a question? If you were using a rope that was too short, would that make it more likely to break?"

She blinked, but recovered her composure very quickly. "No. I don't see why it would. Unless you stepped on it. And that didn't happen in my case. The rope just came apart."

I would watch that, too, when I watched the video, to see whether the rope caught on her shoe.

"Someone messed with my rope," she insisted with

a scowl that made her look older and very much like her mother. "And I think it was Rachel doing it to help Morgan. She probably needed Morgan to pay for the hotel bill for her. She lives off of Morgan's leftovers."

"What does that mean?"

She shook her head dismissively. "Never mind. But Lindsey saw Rachel by my bag. It would have been so easy for her to take a screwdriver from the repair box and loosen the screw just enough to jar it out when I was about half way through my jump."

I looked at her for a moment, trying to size her up. "You seem to know exactly what had to happen."

She sighed and glanced toward the practice floor where jumpers were working or chatting at their own pace. "I've had a lot of time to think about it. This is my last year, you know. This was my last chance." She turned back to me with a new light of determination shining in her blue eyes. "This *is* my last chance. I don't want to lose it."

Either her mom had convinced her to fight for this or something else had.

I decided to play along and feigned an agreement I didn't feel. "Okay, but I need to make this logical. Why do you think Rachel would sabotage your rope to help Morgan qualify? Your mom told me Morgan qualified in freestyle. She was already going."

"Well," Hayley scoffed, "there was no guarantee of that. After she dropped her rope."

"Would lower her score a lot?"

She laughed. "Oh, yeah. She dropped her rope halfway through and it took her a long time to recover. Probably lost a quarter of her points." Sympathy was not exactly oozing from every pore. In fact, she looked entirely too pleased, as if it were one of her favorite memories.

I decided to take her down a peg. "But she was still good enough to beat you in freestyle, right?"

She shrugged. "She was still good enough to beat several as it turned out. Lots of jumpers had misses."

"Including you?"

This seemed to finally get to her. She looked away from me and up toward the lights set like stars in the ceiling overhead. "I wasn't competing in freestyle."

"But you have freestyle ropes."

With a sigh, she faced me again. "I was an alternate. Only the top five from our team in that age division were allowed compete in freestyle."

"There's not a limit of five in other events, though, is there?"

"No. Freestyle takes a big panel of judges. They have to limit the field to keep the tournament from running long."

"That means Morgan outranked you in freestyle."

She shrugged again, this time with so much exaggeration it seemed she was trying to convince herself as much as me. "It's not really my thing. I'm not the cheerleader type."

"So," I paused for a moment and glanced at Morgan and Rachel as they flicked their ropes around in a matching pattern. "You think after Morgan botched her freestyle that she had Rachel loosen the screws on your rope so it would break halfway through your expected jump and you'd be too tired to jump properly the second time. Is that right?"

"Yes."

"Do you have any proof at all?"

"Rachel was seen going through—"

I waved away her argument. "Yes, besides that."

"I told you," her eyes narrowed and her voice hardened. "It couldn't have been an accident. I checked my ropes at the start."

"Okay. If it was a deliberate act, and I'm not saying it was, it could have been someone else. Someone like Juno or Gwen. Or the parent of one of your competitors."

She shook her head. "No, Juno had already qualified. She had a 162 in speed which automatically qualifies. And Gwen was automatically qualified with team show—our group routine."

"Why didn't you qualify with the group routine?"

She shrugged again and I had to figure her shoulders were getting tired of all of her *I don't care* posturing. "I didn't like the choreography and didn't want to spend all year working on it, being bossed around by the cheerleader types like Rachel."

"Was Morgan in it?" Then she, too, would have automatically qualified.

"No, she wasn't." She shook her head. "So she had to do something to ensure that she'd qualify so she could be with her girls."

I glanced over to where the trio stood talking and swinging their ropes. "So what do you want me to do? I don't have enough proof to make any kind of legal case. Do you want me to confront them and see if they'll confess?"

She shook her head. "No, they have no shame. Mom says you should file a complaint with the tournament manager and submit a statement saying you've found proof that Morgan cheated in order to qualify."

"But I haven't found proof."

"You've found circumstantial evidence. Use that to

build your case."

This girl had obviously spent some time watching movies or TV shows about lawyers.

I took a deep breath. "Let me ask you—what changed your mind?"

"Me?"

"Yes." My gaze roamed the gym again and then came to rest on her. "When I first came here, you wanted me to leave and you did not want the matter investigated. It was your mother who was the driving force behind this. And now—something's different. Now you want me to find a culprit. A specific culprit."

She tried to lighten her tone. "I just want to go to Nationals for my last year. And someone destroyed my chance. I don't think it's fair for her to be rewarded for it. Do you?"

"Okay. I'll draft my statement and submit it to your mom on Monday." I didn't know if it would be what she had in mind. But didn't Dave always emphasize that we needed to follow the money? If the money wanted a statement, I could write up something implying what they wanted without deliberating lying.

She flashed me a million dollar smile which reminded me of the cheerleaders she seemed to disdain. "Thanks. I knew I could count on you."

I nearly bumped into Lindsey as I turned and walked away deep in thought. She gave me a nervous smile.

"Hey," I held up a hand to stop her. "Can I talk to you for a minute?"

"Sure." She would have looked more enthused if I'd asked permission to pull half her teeth.

I nodded for her to walk with me over to the side. "I want to hear again about what you saw the morning of the competition. You said you saw someone going through jumpers' bags."

"Yes."

"Did you see someone open your sister's bag in particular?"

She paused, avoiding my gaze. "Yes."

"Who was it?"

She paused again. "Does it matter? I think the whole thing was an accident."

"Your sister doesn't."

Her grey eyes widened in surprise as she shifted her gaze to me. "She doesn't? But—but—what does she...say happened?"

I lowered my voice still further. "She thinks Rachel loosened the screws on her power rope so that the rope would break when she was far enough into her jump to be too tired to score well on a re-jump."

"She thinks Rachel did that? Why?"

"To help Morgan qualify."

She shrank inward. "Oh."

"What do you think?"

"Well, um…" her gaze dropped to the floor." I don't know. If Hayley thinks that Rachel would have—"

Though I interrupted her, I tried to keep my tone gentle. "I didn't ask what Hayley thought. I asked what *you* thought."

Her voice grew very small and her gaze remained riveted to the floor. "I don't know. I didn't see anything."

"I thought you saw Rachel going through jumpers' bags."

"Oh, yeah," she admitted dully. "I saw that."

"But you couldn't tell if she went through your

sister's bag?"

She shook her head. "No."

"You said you saw someone going through Hayley's bag. So if it wasn't Rachel, who was it?"

Finally she looked up at me, her eyes glassy with tears. "I don't know. It-it was someone in a blue jacket, but our whole team has blue jackets."

"Could you tell anything else? Whether it was male or female?"

"Female." She gave tight-lipped nod. "That much I can say."

"Did you notice anything else?"

She shook her head, but the guilt and pain in her eyes said otherwise.

I pulled out a card and scribbled my cell number on it. "This is my personal number. If you remember anything else, please call me."

"Okay." She took the card, stared at the card for a moment, then clutched it in her fist.

I stepped a little closer. "Are you sure you didn't notice anything else? Any color besides the blue jacket? Any detail?"

She stepped back a bit, closed her eyes and shook her head slightly as if trying to get away from a cloud of gnats. "Just a flash of hair."

"Hair? What did you notice about it?"

Her forehead creased with pain and for a moment she glanced away. Then she turned to face me, her lip curled in disgust. "It was streaked, okay? I noticed it because the color stood out."

She turned and ran toward the restroom before I could say anything else.

I stared after her in shock for a moment.

Bonnie. It had to be.

I didn't realize I was pacing back and forth until I ran into another parent and had to apologize.

To say this was driving me crazy was a bit of an understatement. Lindsey had essentially admitted she'd seen Bonnie go into her sister's rope bag, and that meant she was probably the one who loosened the screw on the rope. How could I get that girl to admit it?

Did I need to?

To keep from running into anyone else, I moved over closer to the wall in front of a bulletin board listing upcoming sports programs. Registration was now underway for toddler mini-golf and adult dodge ball. Then I saw a flyer that nearly made me choke. On the "Community News" section of the board, a flyer headline screamed "HAVE YOU SEEN THIS WOMAN?" A blurry photo showed a woman with short dark hair and sunglasses getting out of her van, and a second photo showed her walking. The Neighborhood Watch of Old Ellicott City warned people that the woman had been stalking residents with possible nefarious intentions.

The Neighborhood Watch was after me.

That was the last thing I needed. After checking to make sure no one was watching, I pried the staples out with my fingernails and removed the flyer. Where else had they posted this thing? Was it online anywhere? Fortunately, the pictures were grainy and my van was pretty nondescript. I hoped the only person who realized it was me, was me. But if Mr. Burkstead saw it, he might cancel his surveillance contract. Before I could figure out what to do about being listed as Public Enemy Number One on the paranoid-neighbor-circuit, Evan ran up to me. "Watch this!" He threw his rope handle on the floor, then yanked it up and caught it with his other hand. "See what I learned to do?"

"Yeah, cool."

"Oh, and I almost got a toad, too."

I eyed him suspiciously. "Where? You don't have any frogs or salamanders in your pockets do you?"

He laughed. "Frogs and toads, mom, not salawhatevers."

"Okay, what's a toad?"

"It's this." He jumped the rope, then lifted one leg and crossed his arms under the raised leg. The rope got tangled on the back of his neck before he could bring it around to jump again. "Well, I can't do it yet."

"It looks pretty hard."

"It is. And a frog is even harder. But Coach Dan says jumpers are tough. He said one boy on the team fell on his face and knocked out all his braces and didn't even cry."

"Okay, don't show me that one."

"I don't have braces yet."

"I know. You might knock out all your teeth instead."

He pulled me toward the door. "Can we go? I'm starving."

I glanced wistfully over at Lindsey. Pressing her wouldn't get me any more information, at least not at the moment. But there had to be some way to get her to tell me what she knew   .

"Yeah," I agreed, turning away. "We can go. For now."

19

That night the rug still looked dirty where the milk had soaked into it, but at least it smelled more like dog hair than sour milk. Finally, the dog was serving a useful purpose. Evan and Alicia's dad had picked them up not long after we returned from the gym, so at least there would be no further incidents with soccer balls in the house for the evening. I sprayed carpet shampoo everywhere and then cleaned upstairs while it dried and supposedly soaked up stains and smells. Brian would be over later, after basketball. So that meant that in theory at least I had time to fold and put away laundry, vacuum all the rooms upstairs, clean the bathrooms, empty the scary things out of the refrigerator and vacuum up the carpet cleaner spray before he arrived.

In actuality, of course, I only had time to do about a third of that. I didn't want Brian to come into a house covered in carpet shampoo, so I vacuumed up all the dried foam and then bent down to sniff the rug. Now it smelled like cheap dryer sheets, which was a definite improvement.

"Do I want to know what you're doing?" Brian asked dubiously as he came in.

I sat up. "Oh, hi, didn't hear you come in. I was, uh, smelling the rug."

He raised one eyebrow, displaying that skeptical look just like the one his mom had used on him at dinner. "Uh-huh."

"Evan spilled chocolate milk on it."

"You know, if you wanted some that badly I could have picked up a whole bottle for you."

"Very funny." I stood up and brushed the lint off my knees. "I cleaned the carpet to get the smell out and I was checking to see if it worked."

"Did it?"

"I guess. It now smells like the candle section at the dollar store."

"Could be a lot worse." He sat down on the couch and waved for me to come join him.

"Yeah, I know." I started toward him, but then stopped as cast one final glance at the spill site. "Ugh. It still looks brown, at least from this angle. Brown stains are never good. All because Evan was playing with the soccer ball in the house again."

"Hmm." Brian beckoned me closer. "Why didn't you make *him* smell the rug?"

"I made him scrub it for about an hour last night." I glanced from the carpet to Brian and decided that between the two, Brian was much better to look at. I plopped down next to him on the sofa.

"That's all you can do, then." He pulled me closer next to him and put his arm around my shoulder. "Repeat the instructions, wait for the kids to ignore them, then make sure they have to deal with the consequences. Repeat daily."

I sighed. "So you have that problem, too."

"Oh, yeah."

"But your kids love you." I turned to look at him "And they don't have to live with you. I figured they'd listen better."

"Ah." He assumed a serious face and spoke in a

pedantic tone, as if he were giving a lecture. "It's part of the developing teen brain, they don't give full weight to possible consequences." He grinned. "I learned that in a training class."

"And teens ignore instructions from authority figures?"

"Well, we both already knew that."

"Yeah." I sat back, trying to fight off dejection. Despite the fact that it was Friday night and Brian was there, I couldn't let go of work and kids. And it wasn't just my kids. I thought of that gym full of teens ignoring their coach. Using cellphones when they were supposed to be turned off. Jumping with a shorter rope because it might make them faster, even if it made them more likely to miss.

I sat up straight. "Do you mind if I check something on the computer?"

"No, of course not." But he let me go with obvious reluctance.

"It's work related," I apologized as I stood and headed over to the counter under the opening to the kitchen to pick up the computer.

He sighed, but then laughed. "You have to deal with so much of my 'work' every time we meet. It certainly won't kill me to put up with yours for a change."

The battery on the laptop was down to almost nothing, so I had to plug it in and stand by the outlet under the counter to watch the video of the jump rope tournament.

And Molly, who'd been banished outside when I started cleaning the rug, could see me where I was standing and started barking and throwing herself against the door to get my attention.

"Is it okay if I let the dog in?" I set down the computer and was actually half way to the door by the time I finished asking, so obviously I assumed he would not mind.

But his smile faltered a bit and there was a slight hesitation before he said (rather unconvincingly) "Sure."

I paused with my hand on the door handle. "It's not that cold out. She'll be fine staying outside."

He waved toward the now-whining mass of brown, white and black fur plastered to the glass door. "I don't think she would agree."

"Her opinion won't become relevant until she starts paying rent."

"Oh, come on. Let her in."

"Are you allergic?" I remembered something his dad had said about keeping the dog in the yard. And the first time he'd been over she'd growled and treated him like a cat burglar who smelled too much like cat.

"No."

"Then what is it?"

"Nothing."

I just looked at him.

"Okay, I, uh." He glanced down at his hands, which were now clasped in his lap. "I get nervous around dogs."

I left the door and came toward him. "I'm sorry, I had no idea. But you know Molly wouldn't hurt a fly. She's too dumb to figure out how to hurt a fly." She had sensed his unease though.

He looked up. "I believe you. And I'm not afraid she's going to hurt me."

"Then what are you afraid of?"

"I'm not afraid of anything," he protested sharply. A little too sharply.

I crossed my hands in front of my chest. "Are too."

"Okay," he admitted with a sigh. "I'm afraid she's going to make a mess."

"A mess?"

" Dogs throw up when they're around me. It's okay outside but inside…" He grimaced.

"Yeah, dog vomit is pretty nasty," I agreed. "However, Molly's got a pretty tough stomach." I headed back to the door. Brian was clearly imagining this problem, and I would prove it to him. "I think we're safe." I pulled open the door and the dog darted into the room. Halfway across the living room, she stopped, lowered her head and growled.

"See?" Brian pointed to the inhospitable house pet with a righteous sense of triumph. "I'm making her nauseous."

"No. She's probably just annoyed that you didn't bring her dinner." While I discounted his theory about dog digestive problems, I had no doubt that his wariness around her was making her uncomfortable in return. One of them would have to go.

Of the two, he had much better breath. So I headed into the kitchen. She followed me, her great feathery tail wagging fiercely as she watched me take out a box of rawhide treats. I had no trouble at all luring her to the basement door. "There's more in it for you later if you can keep the growling down," I promised as I patted her on the head.

She took the treat from my fingers and scampered down to her favorite bean bag chair in the basement. I closed the door and turned back to my slightly dog-phobic houseguest.

"You should have told me sooner. I had no idea she bothered you."

"Yeah, well, somehow dog vomit never seemed to come up in conversation."

"Hmmn. What were we talking about anyway?"

"I don't know." He nodded toward the counter with the computer. "You had to look up something for work. It's either jump rope or parrots at the moment, right?"

"Uh, yeah." I would bet I was the only investigator in history ever plagued with this combination of embarrassing cases. But it would be over soon.

Hopefully.

I found the tournament video, and after I fast-forwarded to Hayley's first power jump, I paused the action. There was no way to zoom in, but I didn't really need to. I could see that she was using her yellow-handled rope, just like she was supposed to. But I noticed something else—a blue streak in her hair. Bonnie wasn't the only one with streaked hair that day.

"I don't believe it," I murmured. She must have colored over the blue, because her hair looked pretty natural when I'd seen it. But on the day of the tournament, there was no doubt it was streaked. But why should it be suspicious for Hayley to go through her own bag? There would be no reason for Lindsey to tell me about it.

"What?" Brian asked from the sofa.

"I think it's...I don't know." In the frozen camera shot, with Hayley holding yellow handles and revealing a blue streak of hair, I noticed another color. The judge standing nearest to her was wearing a navy blue zip up hoodie over her white shirt. In fact, several of the judges wore jackets, some of them white and some blue.

But none of the jumpers were wearing jackets. It

would have been too hot or cumbersome to jump in a jacket. And Hayley's uniform shirt was mostly yellow.

So it was not Hayley her sister had seen going through her rope bag. It was probably a judge in a blue jacket. One of the parents. One of the parents with streaked hair.

I hit "play" and watched the rest of the jump. It didn't look like Hayley stepped on her rope or did anything that would cause it to come apart.

Next, I fast forwarded to watch Morgan's freestyle. Was it bad enough to inspire her mother to take desperate action to make sure her girl would qualify in the last event?

She started in a pose exuding extreme confidence with her back over-arched like a gymnast. Then she burst into a series of high jumps with her rope tucked under her legs in various poses. She danced across the floor with the sparkling smile of a beauty pageant contestant, kicking and flinging her rope like a lariat. I think some of the moves were like the frogs that Evan had tried to show me. But where his efforts were awkward and slow—as well as unsuccessful—Morgan glided from one move to another as if it were a simple walk across the room, never once stopping the rope in its smooth orbit around her body. I couldn't imagine anyone doing more. But about half way through her routine, her rope got wrapped around her leg and she dropped both handles. It took her a long time to recover and untangle her rope. After that, she continued to jump but seemed in a daze—her movements were slow and much less complex than before. After bowing for the judges, she left the floor in tears. Even though I found her obnoxious and her mother unethical and crude, I couldn't help but feel for her.

I could very easily imagine that after that, she or her mom might think she was unlikely to qualify. But would they go so far as to try to take out another opponent?

"Wow," Brian breathed over my shoulder. "So that's the kind of stuff Evan's learning to do?"

I turned to him. "Yeah, for this week, at least. When I finish the case he won't have to go any more."

"Do you expect to finish soon?"

I sighed and turned back to the screen. "I have to. Everyone wanted me done by now."

"Except Evan. I think he's having fun with it."

I looked up again. "Really?"

"Speaking of fun, how's the knitting club?"

"Oh, uh, great." My gaze went right back to the computer. "I made a wonderful…"

"What?"

"Potholder." Setting the computer aside with a sigh, I decided it was finally time to stop pretending. I turned, leaned against the counter and crossed my hands against my chest. "I uh, don't really remember how to knit. So the knitting club is kind of a disaster. But I just didn't want to stay in the mom's group. The women in there were all so perfect with perfect lives and perfect families. And I'm so *not*." He saw that kind of perfect every week in church. Heck, he'd been married to it. I'm sure if he and Chloe had had children they would have raised perfect little junior U.N. Ambassadors or something.

"Ha," Brian scoffed as he stood and walked over to me. "They're not perfect, at least not the moms I know. And you should see their kids!" He laughed, but then took my hand and squeezed it, looking into my eyes. His eyes were such a deep, rich blue they were almost pretty and seemed wasted on a guy. All of a sudden, he looked very serious. "But you're closer to perfect than any of them."

I tried to lighten the mood with a laugh. "That sounds like a really bad pick up line."

"Just the truth, the way I see it. You try, Karen. All the time. I love that about you." He pulled me closer and his voice rumbled low in his chest. "I love a lot of things about you."

It should have been a really sweet moment. Or really sexy. I don't know, it all seemed like something straight out of romance novel and heaven knows Brian certainly looked like the hero. I should have melted into his arms. Instead, my insides were squirming and it was all I could do to keep from pulling away.

"Okay." His voice grew flat. "I was wrong. Now you've stopped trying. "What's wrong?"

"Nothing."

He narrowed those blue eyes at me. "Lying is not one of your better skill sets."

I squeezed his hand and released it, like somehow it would be easier to explain myself with a little distance. Then I clasped my hands together, but it didn't feel right. I wasn't sure what to do with my hands. They seemed superfluous all of a sudden. I looked up into Brian's face. His eyes were almost the same color as Hayley's though his hair was much darker. Why was I comparing this big burley blacksmith with a teenaged girl? Why was I even thinking about her at all? I was supposed to be concentrating on Brian. But I didn't want to. Well really I did, but I couldn't. Something wasn't right.

I put my hands behind my back and leaned against the wall. "I'm not comfortable with getting serious," I admitted. "About us. It's too soon."

"Fair enough." He leaned back against the counter next to me. "I'm sorry. I guess I'm just a serious guy."

I forced a smile. "Well, just pretend not to be. For a while, at least."

He nodded slowly. "Okay, if I'm not serious, can I be curious?"

"Maybe."

"What scares you about serious?"

"I didn't say I was scared."

"Your body language did—and by the way, that was from another seminar."

"Okay, okay." I paced away from the counter, needing time to come up with an answer. I hadn't thought of myself as scared, but once he said it, I knew he was right. I was scared to pieces. Why? What scared me about "serious?" I paced a few more steps and turned around.

"Okay." I took a deep breath. "Serious in a relationship is marriage. And I failed at that. Badly. But I figure I can't fail at 'Just Seeing Someone.'"

His forehead wrinkled as he considered that for a moment. "Well, yeah, it can be done."

"Maybe so, but I think I can get that far without screwing up. But doing more is—more than I'm ready for." *And then there's Chloe.* But I was too scared to even bring up that subject now.

He put up his hands. "Hey that's fine. There's nothing wrong with that. For now. But understand— marriage is the natural progression eventually."

I nodded. "At the end."

"No." He walked toward me slowly. "It's really a new beginning. Between two people who are in love."

I fought the urge to step back. "But we're not in

love yet, are we?"

"I know I am." He pulled me close, and this time I did melt into his arms, into a kiss that probably lasted most of the weekend. I began to understand the desire for more. I wouldn't think of it as serious. It was "Seeing Someone Plus."

He pulled away slightly, his breath a little ragged, his long dark hair all askew around his face. "So are you?"

I blinked. "Am I what?"

"In love?"

This time I was the one who pulled him close. "I'll have to research that a little further."

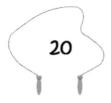

20

Brian couldn't stay over—it would look promiscuous to the teens he worked with even if he slept downstairs on the sofa. But he promised to be back early the next morning and said that he had taken the day off from the 1776 House and that the whole weekend was mine.

I was ecstatic for about three seconds, before I realized his weekend wasn't mine to accept. I had work to do. I still had to figure out whether the Flaglers were trying to scam the insurance company and how to get Lindsey Callaghan to tell me whether it was Bonnie she had seen going through her sister's rope bag. And it all had to be done by Monday or Dave would never again trust me with anything more interesting than a billing statement.

So before Brian arrived for coffee the next morning, I plopped down on the sofa with the laptop, pulled up the parrot picture, magnified it as much as I could, and stared into its depths, willing the pixels to give up their secrets. Then I think I fell back asleep.

"I didn't know you liked birds. There's a special indoor exhibit at the zoo. Wanna go?"

A cup of coffee hovered in front of my face, its heavenly aroma suddenly recalling me to consciousness. "I forgot to turn on the coffee pot, didn't I?" I reached out to accept the warm mug from Brian's hands, which were just as pleasantly warm. "Thanks."

"You forgot to put in water, too, but I figured that out."

"Hey, at least I left two clean cups out for you to find."

"No spoons, though."

"Spoons are for babies."

He flung himself down on the sofa next to me. "So what's with the close-up of the parrot?"

"I'm investigating its demise."

"A murder investigation?" He reached over to pick up his mug from the coffee table. In his hands, the sizeable hand-thrown clay mug looked like a tiny teacup.

"My client does not suspect foul play."

"Nice pun."

It took me a minute. Then I smiled and drank down at least a third of the oversized mug of coffee. "Actually, my client does suspect foul play of a sort. I'm supposed to figure out whether the bird was in the owner's new sunroom when the roof collapsed. The insurance agent thinks the homeowners may be trying to con them into paying for replacement of an expensive parrot that died of other causes."

His eyes widened with excitement. "Like murder?"

"Like Death by Something Not Covered Under their Policy."

"And what did the autopsy report reveal?"

"The vet reported that the parrot was, indeed, dead at the time it was examined."

He blinked. "That's it?"

"Pretty much. Cause of death, as near as I could tell, was that it ceased to be alive."

"Not very helpful." He grinned over the rim of his

coffee mug.

I sighed and inhaled another sizeable quantity of coffee. "The parrot had no marks on it so it probably had a heart attack or something, but whether that was caused by the roof collapsing or by being forced to view endless carpet samples, I have no idea."

"Carpet samples?" His grin was now lopsided with curiousity.

"Yeah, the owners have their own carpet business. And now they have me listed as a suspcious character with the Neighborhood Watch."

"No way."

"Yeah, I even have my own 'Wanted' poster."

"I'm jealous."

I sighed. "Actually, I need to find out where else they posted that thing and take it down before someone sees it. At least it doesn't have my name on it."

"What does it have?"

"Some bad pictures of me getting out of my car. Probably taken the last time I parked on Church Street." I remembered the frowning old men who'd followed me down the street. The Neighborhood Watch in action. Maybe I should have been worried, but suddenly I really didn't care. I gave Brian a smile. "If I tell you any more, I'll have to kill you."

"By making me view endless carpet samples."

I considered for a moment. "Or there's always Mrs. Peacock in the ballroom with the candlestick."

He sat up with so much alacrity I thought he must be one of those Clue fanatics. But instead it was the birds that caught his attention. "Peacocks – hey, that's part of the special exhibit I was telling you about. We got a flyer about it at church. There's a session on birds of prey, a session on birds of the rich and famous and a big aviary where you feed the birds and have them land on you."

"The birds of prey?"

"No, I think that's in a separate section, and they're on a leash."

"Doesn't give them much of a chance, does it?"

"So do you want to go?" His voice and face suddenly bore this childlike hopeful expression. "It's a little chilly, but not windy. And the sun's out. Almost like spring."

I couldn't imagine going to the zoo without my kids. And yet, why not? They were too old to be excited by it and not old enough to admit to curiosity or feel any sense of nostalgia.

"I thought the zoo was closed in the winter."

"Parts of it are. Not much fun to watch animals hibernate, I guess. But the polar bears should be out. This is like summer to them. So what do you think?"

I couldn't bring myself to disappoint that pleading little boy look in his eyes. And maybe going to a bird exhibit could even help me make the case. Maybe someone at the zoo could tell me whether those rare blue parrots were susceptible to heart attacks. So I agreed and was rewarded with a kiss and a lemon jelly donut.

When we got to the zoo, I hurried past white painted Victorian entrance buildings that always made me think of frosted gingerbread and headed for the long curved road that led to the zoo habitats. My route was blocked by a chain of small children bundled in layers of fleece holding mittened hands as they waited for the zoo tram. I figured by the time the tram arrived and over-stuffed preschoolers climbed onboard, half the day would be over. So I sidestepped the chain and began to powerwalk down the trail.

"We aren't taking the tram?" Brian sounded sincerely disappointed, but I shook my head.

"I need the exercise." I didn't mention that I was anxious to talk to a bird handler and get my questions answered and work out of the way, but Brian could have probably guessed that.

The Baltimore zoo is pretty old, and parts of it are closed now. When my kids were little, we would come and see animals in hundred-year-old iron cages. It probably wasn't much fun for the little monkeys and really boring for the big animals like snow leopards to be stuck in those small cages. But the kids loved it because the animals were so close. In the newer, more natural exhibits, the kids would press their faces up to the glass to view an African savannah with lots of waving grass and a few camouflaged animals barely visible in the distance. So they were sad when the zoo went humane and closed the section with the old cages. Or maybe they were just sad because I made them walk down the long new path instead of taking the tram.

At least it was downhill. Even in the leafless gray of January, there was a peaceful sense of space around us as we followed the animal footprints painted along the road. We enjoyed that sense of quiet peace for almost five minutes before a tram full of screeching pre-schoolers nearly mowed us down.

When we reached the end of the road, I could see a big balloon-like enclosure off in the distance to the right of the Africa section. That must have been the traveling aviary. But before I could even start toward it, Brian grabbed my arm.

A handler with the birds of prey was set up with a

small outside display to our left. So we learned about the sharp eyesight of hawks and saw cute little owls that tore the heads off chipmunks.

Then after that we had to visit the polar bears, and the raven (he looks much bigger on TV at football games), and climb inside the Arctic tram (which is just a bus with big tires) and finally I stopped Brian when he started to pull me toward the train at the edge of the Children's Zoo.

"You must have had a deprived childhood," I surmised.

"Sorry." He grinned. "I'm just having a good time doing whatever I want. I spend so much time being a chaperone and negotiating what we do next that it's fun just to be random for a while."

"Hmm." I looked up into big blue eyes almost too bright with excitement. "I think I may have opened Pandora's box when I said you needed to be more spontaneous. You now have the attention span of a toddler."

"I promise not to scream if I don't get my way."

"That's good because—"

"I will scream if we don't stop for French fries, though." He grabbed my arm and pulled me toward the concession stand.

"You only get French fries," I said between panting breaths, "if you're good when we go to see the tent with the birds."

He pulled up short at the counter. "I don't think they'll have any dead ones there. You're investigating a dead parrot, right?"

"You are less help than a toddler. And not even as cute."

He made a sad face which seemed to upset the

young girl behind the counter.

"Well," I conceded, "at least you don't have any food on your face and you know how to blow your own nose."

The girl behind the counter began to back away. But she did take our order and delivered a cup of relatively warm French fries without too much delay.

As we munched on the limp strips of fried potato, I steered Brian toward the tent with the bird exhibit. But as we drew closer and the enclosure filled more of my field of vision, I felt less and less anxious to step inside. I think I realized just how much hope I'd placed on this visit. In the back of my mind I thought that somehow talking to an expert was going to make everything crystal clear for me.

And what if it didn't?

I wished for luck as we neared the door. But that seemed pretty lame. Wishes were so flimsy and luck was totally random.

I could pray for success.

Where had that idea come from?

It sounded like something Brian would say. But he wasn't talking to me. In fact, he wasn't even near the door. He was several feet away in front of a portable tank staring face to face with an enormous lizard bathed in the demonic red glow of an industrial-sized heat lamp.

This didn't seem like the ideal setting for a prayer, but once the idea had taken hold, I didn't want to let go of it. *Okay God.* I glanced over at the red glowing lizard tank, and then back to the door of the aviary. *I know I've kind of ignored you lately. But if there's something dishonest about this dead parrot thing, please help me figure it out.*

I didn't put in an "Amen" or any kind of closing.

That seemed too formal for the zoo.

Suddenly I felt the oddest sensation of lightness, as if a weight had been lifted off my shoulders. I had been so busy trying to figure out how to fit in at church that I'd ignored God. And now, even though I was just using him to get help with a very worldly problem, I didn't feel guilty, I felt better. Like I'd set something straight that had been knocked over. I felt right.

Brian would understand. I walked over to him.

"Hey, honey."I wrapped my arm around his waist. "I just had this revelation."

He turned to me with a look of pure delight. "Did you know that komodo dragons have so much bacteria in their mouths that their bite is deadly even though they're not venomous?"

"Um, no. I had no idea." My urge to share vanished.

Brian was focused on reptiles so I returned my focus to the birds. "I'm going in here. You can stay out here and commune with your lizard if you want."

"No, I want to help." He opened the door for me and then immediately disappeared, just like a toddler would. But at least I didn't have to worry about a stranger trying to abduct a six foot tall burly blacksmith.

The sound in the aviary was nearly deafening. It was not deep and booming like an explosion, but a cacophony of calls, whistles and chirps in every frequency the human ear could register. And it was all undercut by a rustling hum, as if thousands of unseen birds were fluffing their feathers and gossiping in small clusters.

But while I could hear a variety of the winged creatures, I couldn't see very many at all and none that resembled the bird in question. There was one blue bird up on a high fake tree limb, but it was way too small to be a parrot. I finally had to find a uniformed attendant and ask if they had any parrots.

"There's an Amazon right there." She pointed to a big green bird on a branch right in front of me."

"Oh, yeah. Do you have any of the blue-mutated variety?"

Her smile almost developed into a laugh. "No, those are almost nonexistent in the wild. Breeders try to create them because they're so expensive. But of course, the more they breed, the less valuable they will become."

I stepped closer to her, glad I found someone who knew about parrots and hoping she could hear me over the screech of feathered friends all around us. "I'm trying to find out more about them. Like if they're more fragile than other parrots. Can you tell me anything about this one?" I opened up the picture file on my phone and held it out for her to look it.

"Can you zoom in more?"

"Maybe." I wished one of my kids was there to help. Fortunately, the zoo attendant was young enough that she understood how to use my phone. She zoomed right in on the bird better than I'd been able to do even on my computer at home.

"Hmmn." She frowned at the screen. She turned the phone sideways. She turned it back upright. "Well. Really?"

"What can you tell about it?"

She handed the phone back to me. "That is not a happy bird."

I looked at the close-up. "Is it agitated? Upset?"

"It's sick. See how it's leaning back? Birds don't do that." She frowned and looked closer. "In fact, they can't do that. No bird could keep its balance with its weight shifted that far back."

"So it's extremely sick?"

She peered at the screen for a few moments longer and then looked up at me. "It's dead."

"What?"

"Probably. See there around the right foot?" She pointed to the screen. "It's held on the perch with wire."

"It is?"

"Yeah, gold wire, like they use to make jewelry. And all those fake plants?" She shook her head. "Any self-respecting parrot would shred that stuff to bits in two minutes. Any *live* self-respecting parrot."

I suddenly remembered that receipt we'd found. Craft supplies. Artificial greens and jewelry wire. I thought the Flaglers had been making Christmas wreaths. But what they were really doing was decorating the cage with so much greenery that it would be hard to see the bird clearly. It would be hard to realize it was already dead when they staged the picture in the rebuilt sunroom with flat carpet that was different than the plush variety they had originally installed.

"That is a blue mutated yellow-napped Amazon, isn't it?" I asked.

"Yeah." She chuckled. "At least it was."

21

I was so ecstatic about having learned something definitive that I didn't mind that it took me 20 minutes to find Brian. He was in some kind of booth watching a video about the aerodynamics of diving hawks. I'd walked by it about seven times before I realized he was in there. I didn't care. I could tell Doreen that the clients had used a fake photo to try to prove the bird was alive when the room was in use. They would be too embarrassed to press their claim after that—if they did sue, the resulting publicity would destroy their business. Finally, I'd made the case. Dave wouldn't care since he considered the favor over after only a cursory investigation. But I had higher standards, at least for myself. And it felt good to fulfill them.

Even though we'd just had French fries, Brian wanted popcorn so we got a bucket and fed most of it to the squirrels and pigeons. And then we saw the penguins and giraffes and elephants and a herd of some animals with antlers. We even took a ride on the train at the edge of Children's Zoo. The day was sunny, Brian held my hand, life was wonderful.

And then . . .

My phone rang.

The phone should not be able to ring when you're riding a train in the zoo and you might be in love and everything is going so well, for once.

A glance at the screen told me that at least it wasn't Jeff calling to tell me the kids had been killed in a horrible accident. The number wasn't someone in my family, so nothing bad had happened to my mom, or my brother, or any family or friends.

It was just Gina Callaghan calling to tell me I was useless. Her attitude was apparent from the first irate syllable she uttered. "Lindsey said you'd given her your cell phone number. That was totally inappropriate." Her voice was brittle and taut, like strings breaking on a violin. "You should have given *me* this number. You don't go making private arrangements with a 14-year-old without informing her parents. And she told me what she'd told you. You haven't done any investigation at all. *At all.*" By this time, she was practically screaming. "Everything you've learned you heard from my own daughter. I could have done as much without charging myself hundreds of dollars. You are worse than useless and I'm filing a complaint with the—the—whoever you file complaints with about you people." Finally she paused for breath.

Brian tugged at my arm. "They want us to get off the train. The ride's over. The next group needs to get on."

I waved him away.

He held up a twenty dollar bill to the conductor. "We want to ride again."

"Nope." The conductor shook his head. "You have to get off and get back on."

Brian crossed his rather substantial arms in front of his chest. "Make me."

The conductor took the money and moved on.

"Did you hang up on me?" Gina's voice demanded in my ear.

"No." I couldn't decide whether to defend myself or not. A lot of what she said was true. I hadn't learned much of anything that she couldn't have learned from her own daughter.

"I want my money back," she demanded in a shrill screech that was probably audible throughout the entire Baltimore metropolitan area."You didn't even deliver a written plan of action, which I specifically asked for at our first meeting."

A written plan of action. Yes, she had asked for it. Why hadn't I given her one? I struggled to recall that conversation. I remembered that I didn't have a plan of action. And she wanted me to start right away, so we dropped it. "But you told me to go ahead without one." I answered finally.

"I did not."

Did too, I wanted to say. *And I have it recorded, because we always record initial interviews with new clients.*

But that day I forgot to turn on the recorder.

I stared at the phone stupidly, tears beginning to blur my vision. I was useless. I'd disappointed her and would soon disappoint Dave.

Brian grabbed the phone. "This is Karen Maxwell's personal assistant. Please call back during business hours or we will need to bill you at our premium weekend rates." He pushed the end call button and threw the phone in his jacket pocket.

Hot tears spilled over onto my cheeks. "This is a stupid thing to cry over."

"You're right." Brian put his arm around me and pulled me close. "But go ahead anyway. Get over it so we can get on with our weekend."

I think we probably rode the train for another 45

minutes while I went through bouts of self doubt and "I'm okay now—no not really." What finally did stop my crying fit was the fact that I'd run out of Kleenex. Brian very valiantly offered me his sleeve, but I had some pride left.

Brian handed the conductor another twenty on the way out. "Thanks."

The man said gruffly, "I couldn't have let you do that if there was a line, you know. Good thing it's January."

Brian reached out to offer a handshake. "We appreciate it."

The conductor stepped closer to take Brian's hand and spoke in a much lower voice. "Is she okay?"

"Yeah." I answered him even though he wasn't speaking to me. "I'm okay."

Somehow, some way, I was going to learn the whole truth about this. And then Gina Callaghan was going to learn the whole truth. Whether she paid for it or not.

I looked at my watch. There might be just enough time to catch them. "Can we go now?"

"Yeah." Brian nodded. "You getting cold? Or just tired of animals?"

"Neither. I want to go to a health fair."

He gave me a quizzical grin. "Feeling the need for a blood pressure check?"

"I want to lower it. And I have an idea how." I started to walk faster, dragging him along with me.

"Wait. I thought you were not going to think about work for the rest of the weekend."

"What makes you think this is work?" I reached into his pocket, pulled out my phone and pulled up the Jumptastics website to get the address of the show.

"We're going to a church."

He shook his head. "After that we're going to a movie. I need something a little more realistic in my day."

Forty minutes later we pulled up to a large, yellow, cinderblock building that had been attached to the side of an old stone church. As we walked inside, a woman at a table surrounded by balloons directed us to the social hall at the end of the corridor. We passed several bulletin boards on our way down the hall and I tried to scan each one quickly to make sure I wasn't featured on any of them. As we got close to the social hall, I could hear an announcer thanking the Jumptastics for their great demonstration and asking for another round of applause. We'd missed the show, but the team was still in the building. I would only have a couple of minutes to find Lindsey and isolate her from her mother and sister, all while remaining out of her mother's sight.

I turned to Brian and stopped him just before we entered the auditorium. "Okay, I need you to find this girl." I held up a picture of Hayley I'd taken with my phone at practice. "Ask her how to do something with a jump rope. "

"Something?"

"Get her to show you the difference between a double and a triple. Ask lots of questions. And try to get her to show you in a corner somewhere."

"Won't that look suspicious?"

"Ask a couple of them to demonstrate at the same time. Say you want to tell your youth group about it. Anything. Just keep her busy for a few minutes."

"Okay."

Now for her mom. When I stepped into the room

jammed with display tables, I could see her standing with her daughters in an open area in the back as they packed up ropes and put on their warm up suits. I quickly ducked back out into the hallway. If Gina saw me, I'd never get a chance to talk to Lindsey. I found a tall muscular black man with a red "volunteer" shirt on.

"Excuse me?" I stepped sideways so that the man would block me from being fully visible to Gina. "I, uh, want to get that group to perform at my church health fair. And I heard that Gina Callaghan arranges that sort of thing, but I don't know who she is. Could you have her paged?"

He looked surprised, but nodded anyway. "Uh, yeah, I guess."

"Tell her to meet me here by the door. Just outside the door."

"And who are you?" He asked kindly.

"Uh, my name's Doreen. Doreen Carpet."

I cringed. Doreen Parrot would have been better.

"Meet Doreen by the door," the volunteer repeated, not giving a sign that he didn't believe my family had been named after a floor covering.

"Uh, yeah."

As soon as the volunteer man headed for the microphone, I turned to hide behind a display of healthy foods.

"Would you like to try some jicama?" An older woman with a toothy grin held up a paper cup of diced white cubes.

"Um, no thanks." I peered between panels talking about the dangers of trans fats.

"Margarine is the enemy," the toothy woman said, still trying to get me to take the cup of jicama.

"Huh?"

She waved toward the panel in front of me. "See? It kills your body 12 ways."

I pretended to read, but really I was looking for Lindsey. I saw that Brian had cornered her sister and two boys not far from where they had been when we arrived. But I couldn't see Lindsey or her mom.

A voice sounded over the loud speaker. "Paging Mrs. Gina Callaghan. Please meet Doreen Carpet at the auditorium door."

To my relief, Gina soon appeared in my field of vision, following the summons quite promptly. Unfortunately, her younger daughter was right behind her.

I hadn't planned on that.

I grabbed the cup of jicama from the woman in front of me and picked up a flyer about the dangers of margarine and dashed out onto the main floor. Approaching Lindsey from the side, I waved the margarine flyer in front of my face in a desperate attempt to make myself invisible to her mom. "Oh, your jumping was amazing. Here, try some jicama." I shoved the cup into her hand, forcing her to stop. "Margarine is the enemy you know."

With all the booths and background noise, Gina didn't seem to notice that I'd pulled her daughter away. Maybe she hadn't even realized that Lindsey was following her.

"I need to talk to you," I said in an urgent undertone to Lindsey as recognition dawned in her eyes.

She glanced toward her mom, who was now several paces away. The space between rapidly filled with kids in heavy coats balancing plates of grapes and granola bars. Then she turned to me. "I don't think I should talk to you. Mom's pretty angry with you."

"Well she should be angry with *you*."

"Me?" Her eyes widened with surprise.

"You're holding back something. I think you know who was responsible for your sister's rope break. And you're the only one who can give me proof."

"N-no." She took a step back. "That's not true. Someone else knows."

"Well nobody is willing to talk. And an innocent girl is going to be accused of cheating." *Was she innocent if her mom was at fault?* I pushed that thought out of my mind.

Lindsey clamped her lips together, but I could see they were trembling. "I don't think it will bother her. And she's going to the competition anyway."

"No." I shook my head. "Not if the officials think she cheated. I'm sure they'll disqualify her from competing in any event. She might be disqualified for life."

Her forehead creased into a look of pain. "I hadn't thought of that."

"So," I stepped closer and lowered my voice. "Will you tell me who it was?"

She glanced toward the doorway where her mother had disappeared, and I grew hopeful. Now that she realized her mother couldn't overhear, she'd finally speak up.

"I can't." She shook her head. "I just can't."

She pushed the cup of jicama back in my hands and ran away.

Brian was completely red in the face and out of breath when I found him later in a corner with a jump rope in his hands. Damp strands of loose dark hair framed his face.

"I think if I'd just had a little more time," he paused for breath, "I could get the double. But the triple?" He shook his head. "I don't know how they do it." Then he shook his head more vigorously and droplets of sweat sprayed out in all directions. "Did you get what you needed?"

I tried not to sound as dejected as I felt. "No."

"I'm sorry." He leaned against the cinderblock wall and pushed his hair back out of his eyes.

I leaned back next to him. "Me too. I think she knows something, and she'd feel better if she confessed."

He nodded slowly. "Guilt can be a good thing. But sometimes it takes a while to work."

Too restless to remain next to Brian, I huffed with impatience and pushed away from the wall. "We don't have a while. Her mom's going to file a formal complaint on Monday and accuse a girl of doing something I'm almost sure she didn't do."

"Well, you've done all you can to prevent that, haven't you?"

I nodded.

"You can always show up and argue in the girl's defense, if you think she didn't do it."

I considered that possibility as I looked for the best path out of the room jammed with families collecting free samples of everything from dental floss to dried dragonfruit.

Should she be penalized if her mother was at fault? I decided my kids shouldn't be held liable for the stupid things I'd done, so Morgan should not be penalized either, even if her mother sabotaged the rope. "I guess I could argue on her behalf. I'd be going against my own client, but then she said she wants a refund so…"

He pushed back from the wall. "So her interests are no longer your interests."

"I guess not." We threaded our way out of the room and didn't speak again until we'd passed out of the crowded space into the hallway, which was at least 10 degrees cooler.

Brian turned to me. "Can we go to a movie now?"

"You sound like my son."

"All this thinking is making my head hurt. I need a good car chase. Or a fight scene with zombies."

"How about zombies driving fast cars with lots of explosives in the trunk?" I suggested.

"Oh, yeah."

"Fine." I held open the door for him. "I'll drop you off at the movie theatre and go have dinner. You can text me to pick you up when it's over."

He pouted. "You're no fun."

"I'm just different fun. And you have to admit, I have never once made you sit through a musical or even a romantic comedy."

He strode toward his truck with purpose, but then stopped and turned to me. "How about a musical with singing zombies in fast cars that blow up a lot?"

"Listen. I could have said I wanted to go to watch ice skating. Or dragged you to Vera Bradley bingo. I think dinner is a good compromise."

"Yeah okay. Can we go to a restaurant where things blow up?"

I shook my head wondering if an alien had somehow invaded Brian's body and taken over. "I kind of think I liked you better in chaperone mode."

"Not happening. It's my day off." He crouched and got ready to run. "Race you to the car."

"Okay," I agreed as I took off at a much more

leisurely pace. "Winner has to buy dinner."

I think he was half way to his truck before he realized what he was going to "win" if he got there first.

The next morning in church I recognized a lot more faces, some from the MOMs group and some from the knitting group. They seemed to recognize me, too, and they smiled and no one blamed me for dropping out of their group or for being listed as a suspicious character with the Neighborhood Watch. Of course, they didn't know I had dropped out of their groups yet. And they might not yet have seen the flyers. They'd figure it out. And if they blamed me, it would be their problem, not mine. Brian didn't blame me. He knew I'd tried.

And I knew that in the course of trying to find my niche in church, I'd lost God. I had to start building that relationship first. Then I could worry about joining committees and remembering people's names. For a few moments during the worship service, I think I actually paid attention to the words I was saying and the songs I was singing, instead of thinking about what I needed to be doing for work or whose schedule overlapped this week. I walked out feeling refreshed, at least until we got as far as the table full of doughnuts and coffeecake. The marble cake was really good. And it's hard to pass up doughnuts. So then I just felt like a pig. A slightly more spiritual pig.

As we walked out of the building, the bright sunlight made me wince. It was all light and no heat, though. I wished I'd worn a heavier jacket.

"Are we going out for lunch?" Brian asked hopefully.

"To a salad bar, maybe. I've already ingested a

week's worth of calories. Wait a minute." I stopped as I realized what he had just suggested. "Don't you have a youth bowling trip or paintball or handbell practice or Bible dodgeball or something like that?"

"Nope. Nothing. Well, there is a laser tag trip later, but I didn't promise to go."

"Oh. Wow." I suddenly felt almost faint. He really did mean the whole weekend. I hadn't thought it was possible. "In that case, maybe we can see a movie with a car chase. Especially since nothing exploded at the restaurant last night."

"Today I need more than a car chase. Aliens maybe. Superpowers. And loud music."

I pulled out my phone and shielded the screen with my hands. "Let's see what's playing at the mall." Before I could open the browser I noticed that I had a text message from a number I didn't recognize. My kids are about the only people who text me, other than a shoe store where I once entered a text promotion to get a free pair of socks.

Curiosity made me open the message.

"This is Lindsey. I hav something 2 tell u. Can u come 2 practice 2day at 2? Meet u out in back."

The jump rope team even practiced on Sundays? "Yeesh."

Brian grew serious at once. "Is something wrong?"

"No, not really." I looked up from the phone and smiled. "Actually this is good. I think. But the movie will have to wait."

"Bird or rope?"

"Rope."

He waved toward his truck. "Let's go then."

We started across the parking lot. "You don't have to come with me and give up your whole weekend to my work."

"My whole weekend is with you. And really, I don't care where that is, as long as we're together."

That was sweet. Unbelievable, but sweet. I gave him a skeptical look. "You don't really mean that."

"I do."

"If I wanted to spend the weekend shopping for oven mitts, you would care."

"Yeah, okay," he agreed with a nod, "but I know you hate to shop so it was never a real danger."

As we reached the truck, I glanced at the phone again while I waited for Brian to unlock the door. "We have a little time before Lindsey wants me to meet her, so let's go find some exploding lunch first."

"You know, if you want to shop for exploding oven mitts…" He held the door open for me and I stepped into cab of the truck heated by the warmth of the sun that I had been unable to detect just a few minutes before.

We arrived at the athletic center a little early. I assumed Lindsey had suggested a time when she planned to slip outside without being noticed, so I just stayed in the truck to wait.

"You're supposed to meet her out in back?" Brian asked as he turned off the ignition.

"Yeah."

"There's nothing back there but the dumpsters. This is sounding like a gangster movie."

I grinned. "You're afraid a gang of vigilant soccer moms is going to jump me back there?"

"I'm going to cover you, just in case."

"Cover me?" I shook my head in disbelief. "With what? A Supersoaker?"

"I was thinking Nerf darts, but you're right, the water gun has better range. Let's see if I have one back there." He climbed out and started rummaging through the truck bed.

While he was still looking, I saw Lindsey walk out the door and around the side of the building.

"I'm off," I called over my shoulder as I jumped out of the truck cab and pushed the door closed.

"Hey, I couldn't find a water gun, but I have this to shoot if necessary." He snapped a rubber band on his wrist.

"I feel safer already." I stepped toward the back of

the truck and lowered my voice. "Actually, please stay here, and if you see Lindsey's mom come out, distract her so she doesn't go around back."

"What does Lindsey's mom look like?"

"Hmm." How could I describe her in a way that made sense to a guy? "Don't let *any* mom go around back. Or any female, for that matter."

"I only have one rubber band."

"You'll think of something." I smiled reassuringly and then hurried after Lindsey.

Gravel shifted under my feet, sending waves of cold up my legs as I rounded the corner of the white block building. Only one car was parked on the side of the complex and the baseball fields stretched out in bleak winter emptyness all around, When I turned the corner to the back of the building, I was surprised to see no sign of Lindsey. Had her mother had come out a fire exit and pulled her inside? But a moment later I saw her on the far side of the green dumpsters, leaning against the white blocks of the building. She looked small and fragile huddled with her hands in the pockets of her thin warm-up jacket with a rope draped over her shoulders like a totally ineffectual scarf.

I smiled when she looked over at me.

"I'm not sure I should tell you anything else," she said before I had the chance to even attempt to exchange pleasantries. She paced a few steps away from me, her feet crunching in the gravel.

"You don't have to." That's what I said aloud. *But I want you to!* My brain screamed. *I can't tell you how much.*

As she turned back toward me I could see that she was chewing her lower lip. "I'm not sure I should not tell you, either. I thought by now I would have made up my mind. If I wasn't going to tell you, I wasn't going to come out. But I came out so I must have decided, but I still don't think I have." She sighed. "Even though I came out here." She turned away again and took several steps away, twisting her rope around her fingers as she walked.

I wandered a few steps in the opposite direction, unsure what to say to keep her from running away.

In the charged silence, we acted like prisoners pacing in the yard of a penitentiary and I would have offered her a cigarette if either of us smoked. Even gum would have been good.

I felt around in my jacket pocket. "Want a mint?" I had a couple of those cheap red and white peppermints from the restaurant where we'd had lunch. At least I hoped they were from that restaurant. Knowing my pockets, they could have come from lunch anywhere in the last 5-10 years.

She took the mint, tore the wrapper with nervous ferocity, and shoved it into her mouth.

I ate one too, just to show solidarity. And so that if I had given her some kind of poisonously stale candy, she wouldn't have to die alone.

We sucked on the mints in silence for a moment.

"Hayley messed up her own rope." She looked at me sideways after she'd said it.

I crunched through the rest of my mint in surprise, a sudden burst of peppermint making my eyes water. "Hayley? Why?" Yes, she had streaked hair, but what would she gain by "messing up" her own rope?

"I think she wanted the chance to re-jump with a shorter rope," she said slowly. "I saw her doing something to her triples rope before the power heats started. Maybe she was loosening it so it would come apart so she could use her shorter speed rope on the re-jump, or maybe she was shortening it before the event started and she just didn't get it tightened all the way. She always said she did better with a shorter rope, but the coach wouldn't let her use one. Either way, she was the only one I saw touching anything out of that bag."

"But she's willing to let someone else take the blame for it now."

She looked me full in the face for the first time. "You have to talk to *her* about that. And you can't tell my mom I told you."

I almost laughed, even though it wasn't a funny moment at all. "I have to. You're the only proof I have. Your mom won't believe me if I just tell her I think Hayley sabotaged her own rope. She's so certain that Bonnie did it. In fact, I was, too. When you told me you saw someone with streaked hair…"

She grimaced and turned to the wall. "I just saw glimpses, you know? I didn't want to admit it was Hayley—either to you or to myself." Then she turned back to me. "I was angry that you forced it out of me. But I guess now that was a good thing."

"So will you tell your mom what you saw?"

Her face settled into an ugly frown. "She won't believe me either. She would never believe her precious Hayley would go against her coach's orders. She'll just say I'm jealous."

"Are you?" I immediately wished I hadn't asked the question.

She looked away again, this time toward the vast expanse of dead grass beyond the parking lot that was probably full of soccer players during the other three seasons of the year. "Yeah," she admitted in a soft voice laced with disgust. Then she turned back to me and her voice grew stronger. "But she's my sister. I

won't lie for her. That's why I had to tell you. If I
didn't, it would be like a lie. And it wouldn't help her.
She'd feel guilty in the end."

"No," another voice said behind us. "I wouldn't."

We turned in surprise. Neither of us had heard
Hayley come around the side of the building , but now
she stood in the parking lot just a few feet away. In the
distance I could see Brian at the corner of the building
taking aim with his rubber band, just in case.

And then I laughed, which was terrible because this
was still not a moment for laughter.

Hayley scowled. "Which one of us do you think is
funny?"

"I'm, uh, laughing at my boyfriend. He followed
you out to protect me, I guess. He watches too many
movies."

Hayley ran her hand over her slicked back hair,
tucking a few loose strands back into her ponytail.
"Morgan Doddridge is a lying, cheating sorry excuse for
a human. She posted on Facebook that I had a sore that
looked like Herpes. I made her take it down, but
everyone saw it. Alex dumped me. I don't know
whether he was afraid of catching it or if he just
couldn't be seen with me. Either way, it was her fault."

I grimaced. "No guy is worth lying over like this."

"You're right." Hayley nodded as if she were
agreeing, but there was a gleam of defiance in her eyes.
"But seeing Alex with Morgan in the gym reminded me
that somebody needed a taste of her own medicine."

"And she'll get it, someday," I pointed out. "But
not this day. Not this time. Accusing Morgan would
have been a lie, and you know it."

She sighed and raked her hands forward through
her hair, pulling it loose from the ponytail. Then she

yanked the rubber band out of her hair and shook it loose. "I'm ready to be done with all this, you know. To start college, leave this place behind, never look at another stupid jump rope again. I talked to the cross country coach at the school where I'll be going next year. I'm not that fast, but if I train more, maybe I could be."

I studied her face for a moment, seeing the fatigue, some disgust, and readiness for change. "Your mom wanted this for you?" I guessed. "The chance to make the Worlds team?"

She shrugged. "Yeah, probably."

Lindsey cleared her throat. "Mom wants Hayley to be a star. Like Mom was a star in high school. We both sucked at cheerleading, so she put us in jump rope. Our gym teacher said Hayley had a lot of talent."

I turned to Lindsey. "But I'm guessing she doesn't like it as much as you do."

She shook her head. "Oh no, I don't think so." She glanced at her sister. "Do you?"

Hayley blinked in surprise. "I didn't think *either* of us liked it that much. It's good community service doing shows and stuff, and it's great exercise, but it's not really a sport."

"Yes it is!" For a moment I thought Lindsey was going to breathe fire in her sister's face as she lunged forward as if to challenge her to a duel with the handle of her rope. "It's the greatest sport."

"So you really like it?" Hayley's surprise softened into a smile. "You can be the star for mom. She'd love that."

"No." Lindsey shook her head, visibly sinking into herself. Even her voice grew small. "I'm not as good as you."

Hayley patted her awkwardly on the shoulder. "You're three years younger. You'll get there."

Lindsey shook her head with more vehemence this time, her ponytail echoing the denial as it shook back and forth. "No, I won't. Your speed scores were better when you were in 7th grade than mine are now. No matter how hard I try I'll never be as good as you. And it sucks." Her eyes grew glassy with unshed tears.

I remembered what Brian said about trying and attempted to encourage her as he had encouraged me. "Listen, Lindsey. Trying hard doesn't always get results, you're right. But it gets noticed. And in the end, it is worth it." The words seemed pretty lame coming from me. I don't think I helped at all.

But Hayley wrapped her arm around her sister's shoulders in an embrace of genuine affection, and that seemed to make all the difference. "*I* will notice," she said to her sister. "And I will be your biggest fan."

Lindsey started to cry, and the sisters hugged, and I now felt like I was intruding on a long overdue family moment. I wasn't quite sure how I was going to write this up in a client report. But I felt pretty sure I wasn't going to have to come to Morgan's defense. Gina Callaghan would be a fool to go after her now.

"Two cases solved," Brian said with satisfaction as we pulled up in front of my townhouse.

"One weekend lost," I countered.

"Not at all. I had fun."

I sighed as looked at the dark, cold panes of my front windows. "I don't want to work every weekend."

"That's part of having a career, though, isn't it? Instead of just a job."

I turned to him. "So you're back in counselor

mode? But I guess you're probably right. Which do you have?"

"It's a lot easier to figure out for someone else than yourself." He opened his door and started to get out, putting a quick end to that line of questioning.

I laughed. "I'll get you on that later, then. Besides, with all your church stuff, you don't have time for another career."

I joined him outside the truck and bent down to pick up the seemingly ever-present pile of unwanted free periodicals and phone books on the sidewalk.

"You do feel like you accomplished something, don't you?" Brian asked as he held the screen door open for me.

"Yeah." I pushed stuff around in my purse in a vain search for my keys. "I miss my kids, though."

"You would have missed them more if you hadn't been working."

"True. I hope their sleezeball of a father isn't late bringing them home."

As if on cue, I heard the familiar roar of undermufflerized horsepower as Jeff's convertible rounded the corner and screeched to a halt across the street. Alicia immediately jumped out and yanked her bag from the back seat.

"I hate you!" she yelled at her father. "You've totally ruined my life."

"So I'm not the only woman to say that to him," I murmured.

Brian laughed.

"And I'm not the only person to hear that from Alicia, either," I mused as I watched my daughter stalk toward the house.

Evan stayed in the car a little longer talking to his

dad and nodding occasionally. Then he, too, got out and carried his duffle bag to the front door.

Both kids stood there waiting for me.

"You have a key, don't you?" I asked as I dove back into the purse to fumble for the keys.

Evan shrugged. "Yeah, somewhere."

It was nice to know they needed me for something still, even if it was just to open the front door. "Did you have a good weekend?" I turned the key in the lock and leaned on the door. It opened with a welcoming whoosh. I held the screen door open for the others.

"It was okay," Evan answered as he staggered inside with his duffel bag.

Alicia pushed past me and threw her backpack against the wall. "It totally sucked. Dad like totally ruined my Facebook page." She shrugged off her fleece hoodie and let it drop to the floor.

"He like, totally ruined your vocabulary, too." I pointed to the hoodie with a nod telling her to pick it up. "And I thought we agreed you weren't going to use your Facebook page until you really turned 13."

"Well…" her face reddened. "*We* agreed that but I didn't agree to it with Dad, so I figured it was okay to use it at his house."

"*Hmmm.*" Despite my parental outrage, I had to smother a laugh at her clever if diabolical logic. "I don't think that's how agreements work."

She sighed as she dropped her hoodie on a hook by the door. "It doesn't matter anyway because I can never go on Facebook again ever. Ever ever."

"It does matter," I pointed out, "because it's important that we be able to trust each other even when we're apart. If you're not sure whether a rule I give you applies when you're at your dad's, you need to ask."

"Okay. Whatever." I was sure she rolled her eyes, but in the dark foyer all I could see was a profile blocked by flyaway hair, so if there was any facial expression for my benefit, it had no effect.

"Now…" I rubbed my hands together in anticipation as I went into the living room and reached over to the counter where I'd left the laptop. "Let's see this ruined page."

"No!" She was at my side in a second. "You can't."

"Oh yes I can." I typed in her user name and password. "Wow, look at all those pictures from when you were little. They're adorable."

"Mom, I'm wearing a toilet seat around my neck."

"You thought it was funny."

"Yeah, when I was like seven."

"And look at that one." I pointed toward the screen. "You had such bad allergies that year you carried a box of Kleenex with you everywhere you went."

"I have crusted snot all over my face." Agony resonated in her voice.

Through the opening into the kitchen I could see Evan snickering as he poured a glass of milk.

I turned back to the screen. "And your dance recital pictures!"

"I was so awful. How could you let me get on stage and make a fool of myself like that?"

"But you loved it."

"I didn't know any better." Her voice rose to a frantic wail.

As much as I enjoyed this moment of torture, I knew she'd had enough. It was time to help her to see that this mess could be cleaned up, just like any other mess. "If you don't like these pictures, can't you take them down?"

"No," she moaned with despair. "Facebook froze my account because of something Dad did when he put all these pictures up. He said he wanted to make sure any boys who looked at my site saw the real me. Now I'll never be able to show my face in public again."

I finally began to feel a little sympathy and stepped over to put my arm around my little girl's shoulders. "Facebook isn't the same as real life."

"Yeah," she sniffed as she pulled away. "It's bigger than real life."

"No." I leaned closer to look her in the eyes. "It's a little picture on a computer screen. You will get over this and life will go on." I glanced at the laptop. "But you'll probably want to stay off Facebook for a while, which is okay since you're not supposed to be on it anyway." I noticed a picture on the screen I hadn't seen before. "Hey, what's this one?"

She looked at me strangely. "One of my friends sent me the link. That's you, isn't it?"

As I clicked on it, a video began to play showing a woman who appeared to be trying to hide behind her hand as if she were a celebrity caught on a police camera. She took a plastic bag out of her pocket and put it over her head. Then she took off and ran down the street looking like a total dork. The woman's movements were set to music, and after it played once, it went in reverse and then stop-action and fast forward. Or I should say *I* went in reverse and then fast-forward. Because it was definitely me. Looking utterly ridiculous.

"What the..." I stopped myself before I could use any word that I would not want Evan repeating.

He had come out of the kitchen and now stepped up from behind me to hit the "replay" button. "What is this?"

I groaned. "One of the Flaglers must have made that video. I knew I saw someone looking at me through the window." A hot sensation started to burn in the pit of my stomach. "I'm going to kill that woman."

Alicia leaned closer and smirked. "Didn't you just say it's only a little picture on a computer screen? Now you know how I feel."

"What were you doing?" Evan asked in a voice choked with disbelief.

"Trying to prove they were cheating their insurance company. And they are. Oh, I'm going to get even with them for that." I turned to Evan. "If I give you a picture of a dead parrot, can you make a video for me?"

Brian put a hand on my shoulder. For a moment, I'd forgotten he was still with us. "Are you sure you want to go down that road? Revenge never works out quite the way you plan. And I know someone who can do it much better than you."

"Is he expensive?"

Brian chuckled. "In a way. It's God."

"I'm going to hire God to get revenge on the carpet queen?"

"Vengeance is mine, sayeth the Lord," he quoted, sounding like an old-time preacher. Except that he was grinning.

"How does that work?" I was pretty sure God was not going to post a damning video on social media for me.

"You just do your job," Brian explained, "and God will set retribution in motion. For starters, I understand it's hard to get insurance once your company drops you for fraud." He grinned again.

"Oh, I see." I nodded slowly. "And I can get Facebook to take down the video if I tell them it's unauthorized, right?"

He reached for the computer. "Let's do that right now."

"Keep a copy, though," Alicia insisted. "I want to learn the dance move."

I waved for Brian to keep going. "It's not a dance move. It was me being ridiculous."

Alicia snorted. "It's not fair that you can take down your embarrassing picture and I can't."

"If you'd followed my rule about using Facebook," I reminded her, "the embarrassing pictures would never have gotten up there. I'm sure we can close the account and take it all down if we need to. But in the meantime, you made the mistake, now you live with the consequences."

"I'm going to die." She stalked out of a room.

"Yes, you will," I called after her. "Eventually. Probably not any time soon, though." I turned to Brian. "Well, that should take care of my concerns about her seeing the mysterious Darrell or any other boys. She's right – no one will even look at her after seeing that picture during allergy season."

"Oh, I wouldn't get too comfortable." Brian clicked something on the computer and then looked up at me. "Alicia's pretty, and boys will be interested in her. You can't keep her a snot-faced little girl forever."

"Eew, that's disgusting," Evan said as he leaned over to take control of the mouse.

"I'm sure," I warned him, "that your dad's got an equally embarrassing set of photos for you, too, so watch out." I stepped away from the counter to let Evan have the computer all to himself. "Who knew Facebook could be such a double-edged sword? And my ex actually did something helpful, too." I mulled over the extreme improbability of it all as I drifted toward the sofa with Brian at my side. "Is the end of the world scheduled for any time soon?"

Brian smiled. "None of us knows. But if it is, I know this is right where I want to be."

He pulled me close, and this time I was able to look him in the eyes without cringing.

23

On Monday morning I walked into work with a warm glow that was barely dimmed by the parking difficulties and the blizzard of Styrofoam packing material that blew out of the overflowing dumpster to attack me just before I reached the door to our building. After brushing loose pieces out of my hair, I zipped through voicemail and email and started in on my reports.

Then I heard Dave whine in an unusually plaintive voice. "Where'd my car go?"

I glanced out the window. "Parked in your usual space."

"No, I mean the car on my screen. My screensaver. It's just words now."

My gaze turned to my own computer monitor and I also saw words scrolling across the screen. *"The strength of the team is each individual member. The strength of each member is the team."*

Rodney stepped over to my desk. "I'm now delivering the 'Message of the Day' via screensaver, so that we won't interrupt any important thought processes with a verbal announcement."

"It's a form of brain washing, isn't it?" I murmured, my eyes watching the words repeat over and over. It was kind of soothing in a way, especially when the words morphed into different fonts and changed colors.

Dave came over and clapped a hand on Rodney's back. "I have a great idea. Why don't you collect all your messages and put them in a nice book. Then you can give a copy to each of us for Christmas."

Rodney's forehead creased in consternation, and the hairs on his head looked as if they might consider moving out of place just a little. "But I got all the messages out of a book," he objected.

"Great." Dave grinned. "Just give us each a copy of the book, and we're good to go." He turned away from Rodney dismissively and stepped over to my desk. "Okay, Karen, please tell me you're finally finished with the dead bird and the weird sport case you were working on."

I smiled in triumph. "I am actually, though I do have to do the final reports for the clients. I can tell Doreen that her clients were, in fact, trying to fraudulently collect on their policy." I paused, not sure how much to tell him about Gina Callaghan's unfavorable opinion of my work. "The jump rope client won't like her results as much."

"Oh?" Dave stepped even closer, one eyebrow raised. He was either interested in what I had to say or scoping my desk out to see if I had brought any cookies today.

"Her daughter was the culprit," I explained. "If there is such a thing in this case."

"And you have proof?" He sat down on the edge of my desk and pulled open the top drawer.

"I have her confession, more or less." I took a deep breath while deciding how much to reveal. But since, as Brian pointed out, lying is not in my skill set, I decided to spill the whole ugly truth while Dave was rummaging through my drawer looking for snacks. "Before I had the full truth, the client called me on Saturday to say that since I'd learned nothing other than what her own daughter told me, we didn't earn our fee and she wanted a refund."

He shook his head. "That's not gonna happen."

I sighed. "What do you say when people get like that?"

"Listen." He looked up and slammed the desk drawer. "They hired us to investigate, to research the facts of a situation. Sometimes we spend much more of our time finding out what didn't happen rather than what did. It's the nature of the game. It's still information. It's still research. We still did our job, and we still deserve to be paid for it. I'm guessing that you learned that there were some people who could have, er…" He stopped and suddenly looked very confused. "Could have done whatever it was your client thought was done, and some that, er, could not possibly have done it. Whatever it was."

"Yes." I nodded.

"And some that might have but probably didn't."

"Yes."

He flashed me a sarcastic smile. "And I'm also guessing she had a scapegoat in mind that she wanted you to find guilty."

"Also yes."

"So, if you'd stopped when she told you she wanted a refund, would she have been happy with the result?"

I thought about that for a moment. "Maybe. Probably. But at least one of her daughters would have felt guilty and possibly confessed what she knew. You see, what she saw could have been interpreted as—"

He held up his hand to interrupt. "I don't need to

know. This was your case. It was always your case and I trust you to make sense of it. Give me a copy of the final report, but I'll probably never read it."

"What would you do—what will you do if the client demands a refund?" I wasn't sure I wanted to hear his answer, but I had to ask. "Will you back me up?"

"Oh, yeah." He nodded with more force than I'd expected. "Once we've put in the hours, we've done the work. We've earned our fee."

"But what if we've done the work and the job still isn't done?"

He shrugged. "Clients can't always afford to pay us to work until every job is done. Sometimes the answers just aren't there. They'd be paying us indefinitely."

"Okay." I sighed, feeling reassured but not as confident as I'd hoped. "I'm still not real anxious to talk to her."

To my surprise, Dave nodded in sympathy. "I don't blame you. She reminds me of Mom, and that's enough right there to ruin anyone's day."

I laughed.

"But it's okay." He stood taller and assumed the tone of Wise Brother Offering Advice. "You did your work on this one. Get yourself a cup of coffee and maybe a Pop-Tart with frosting and sprinkles. Sit down, lean back, and put your feet up on the desk. Then call her."

"Good idea on the coffee," I agreed. "But I don't eat Pop-Tarts, and if I put my feet on the desk, people can see up my skirt."

He shrugged and started toward his office. "Suit yourself. Doughnuts are good too, but I didn't bring any in today."

Rodney stepped over to us with a clipboard

clutched in his hands. "Have either of you coughed in the last three weeks?"

Dave stopped and shrugged again. "Yeah, probably."

I had no idea. "Hmmn, I'm sure I've at least cleared my throat. Does that count?"

Rodney scribbled something on his clipboard. "I'll make it count."

"Uh, that's great." Dave headed toward his office. "If anyone wants to go get doughnuts, I'll buy. And I want Boston Cream."

"Ooh," Brittany said from the doorway as she unwound her voluminous pink scarf. "I want the doughnuts with little ridges that look like truck tires."

"Well," Dave glanced over at her, "how would you like to go out and get some, since you just got here and you've still got your coat—er scarf on?"

She shrugged. "Sure. They're more like tractor tires, actually, but they're not dark. That might be kind of gross. If they were dark they'd look like mud." She re-wrapped the scarf around her neck. "Anyone want coffee?"

"No need." Rodney smiled magnanimously. "Our cappuccino maker is back in perfect working order. I apologize for neglecting it so shamefully earlier."

"Stop talking and go get the doughnuts so Karen can make her phone call," Dave insisted, waving Brittany toward the door.

But I didn't need sugar, or caffeine. I was a professional and I could face this woman and tell her that, well, her own daughter had set her up. I just wouldn't put it quite like that.

Maybe I did at least need the caffeine.

No. I picked up the phone and dialed. "Mrs.

Callaghan? This is Karen Maxwell. I will be submitting a final report to you with the results of the investigation, but I felt that I should inform you about—"

She cut me off with a strained voice. "Hayley told me everything."

"Everything?"

"More than I wanted to know, really. Herpes?" For a moment it almost sounded like she physically gagged. "We'll never live that down."

I didn't know what to say. *Sorry that you goaded your older daughter into blaming someone else for her mistake? Sorry that you can't appreciate the skills of your younger daughter because she's not good enough in your eyes?* I cleared my throat. "Our final statement will describe the investigative work done during the hours we billed. The amount left from what you've paid, if any, will be refunded."

Would she dare complain? I think I held my breath.

"I understand." She said after only a slight hesitation. "And thank you for your discretion. I don't think anyone on the team realized what we suspected. You played your part well."

"Thank you." The unexpected compliment gave me a warm glow. I almost didn't need the coffee now.

"Of course it wasn't really much of a stretch was it?" Her tone grew increasingly bitter. "You pretended to be a helicopter mom, having no life of her own and wanting to be intimately involved in every moment of her children's life. It's what we all are, really, aren't we?"

"Um, yeah, I guess." Was I as bad as that? Something to think about, definitely. But for now I was anxious to get as far away from this woman as possible. "I enjoyed meeting your daughters. Please give Hayley my best wishes for college. And I will look for Lindsey in a jump rope show sometime. It's obvious how much she loves the sport."

I hoped she'd think about that. Trying hard should count for something.

"Thank you, Mrs. Maxwell." Her voice began to recover its customary polite poise. "Goodbye."

I let out a deep breath as I hung up the phone. And then I turned to find Rodney standing by my desk with a cup of cappuccino on a silver tray. I reached for it with both hands. "Thank you."

"You're quite welcome." He lowered his voice. "Thank you for not telling Mr. Sarkesian that I ruined the original milk wand and you had to order a replacement."

"It wasn't all your fault. We should have taken turns cleaning it. Instead, we just let you do it all the time. So if it didn't get done, the blame should be spread equally."

"Thank you just the same." He smiled and looked less annoying than usual as he walked away.

I didn't put my feet up (I would have been afraid of tipping the chair over anyway) but I sat back and closed my eyes and just savored the coffee for about three seconds before the phone rang.

From the caller ID I could see it was Doreen. At least now I could reach for the phone with confidence.

"Hey Doreen, I have good news. Well, it's not all that good, but it is news."

"The sunroom wasn't finished?"

"I don't think it was. The picture the Flaglers gave me was faked to look like the room was in use at Christmas with the bird in its cage. But the bird was actually dead at the time the photo was taken. If you zoom in, you can see that he is wired onto his perch with craft wire. An expert told me the bird could not perch like that on his own."

I could hear her scribbling notes. "And that proves he's dead?"

"What self respecting bird is going to let himself be wired to a perch while he's still alive?" I asked.

"Okay, yeah."

"Anyway, that revelation alone should be enough to embarrass the Flaglers into dropping the claim. But if it's not, there's always the threat of being exposed on Facebook as animal abusers. Wouldn't be so good for their flooring business."

"Yeah, you're right. Thanks Karen. I owe you one."

"I think you owe me at least two. And tell them to take down all the posters they put up with the Neighborhood Watch."

"Posters?"

"They were really just flyers. But they had me labeled as a suspicious character. I want them all gone by the end of the day today."

She laughed. "Yeah, okay."

The other phone line rang, and I glanced at the caller ID. "Ugh. It's the landlord. I gotta go."

"No problem. Thanks again."

"Hey," Rodney waved his arms to get my attention as he ran to his desk. "That's for me. He's returning my call."

"Okay, then." I waved toward the phone. "It's all yours."

"Good morning, Mr. Hagland," Rodney intoned in his most officious voice. "Thank you for returning my phone call after only 38 minutes. Oh, wait, I called you yesterday. So that was a delay of 24 hours and 38 minutes."

I snickered and reached for my coffee, grateful to find that it was still warm.

"I'm back," Brittany announced as she flung open the door. "They didn't have any of the doughnuts that looked like tires so I got some that looked like—"

I held my finger up to my lips. "Shhh. I'm trying to eavesdrop on this conversation with the landlord."

"—volcanoes." She finished in a forlorn whisper. "But there's no lava or anything." She held out the box to me."

"Thanks," I whispered back.

"...very serious situation which requires your immediate attention," Rodney was saying. "The delay in waste removal during the month of January has resulted in a possible toxic mold contamination. Employees are suffering from bronchial irritation requiring a serious consideration of future medical treatment. We're prepared for an onslaught of worker's compensation claims, of course, but I'm concerned about the allegations of gross negligence in environmental management. Lawyers are jumping on those class action claims in a big way."

I had to bite my lip to keep from laughing aloud.

"Oh, I'm aware that this is a small office, Mr. Hagland." Rodney continued in a solicitous voice. "Would that such circumstances could insulate us from liability. But mold grows; it spreads; it travels through the air. Half of Ellicott City could be filing claims by the time this is over."

"What's he talking about?" Brittany whispered.

"I'm not really sure," I whispered back. "I don't think the landlord is either. I want to see where he's going with this."

Dave stepped out of his office and headed for the kitchen but I waved him over. "You've got to listen to Rodney," I whispered. "He's terrorizing the landlord!"

He grinned like the Cheshire cat. "Excellent."

"I think it very likely is too late," Rodney continued, "to take the kind of remedial action that will prevent this catastrophic liabilitical disaster."

Liabilitical?" I looked at Dave quizzically. "Is that even a word?"

"But," Rodney continued dramatically, "we can try. Once the trash is removed, all feasible nonporous surfaces should be primed with an ammonia based commercial grade primer and painted to tenant specifications. Floors must be sanded and refinished with spar grade polyurethane. Lighting fixtures replaced with antimicrobial antiglare fixtures. Oh, and of course installation of the Stratosphere air purifying system. The 4000 model has the highest EPA rating on the neutralization of airborne toxins."

Dave nodded toward Rodney. "Isn't that the air filter he tried to charge us for last month?"

"I think this is an even more expensive model," I whispered back.

Rodney stood and his voice grew stronger. "I think that if you take those ameliorating actions as soon as possible as a gesture of good will, we can hold off the lawsuits, or make a plausible argument that the responsible party acted with due diligence as soon as apprised of the dire seriousity of the situation."

"Seriousity?" Dave mouthed at me.

I smothered a laugh.

"Of course," Rodney continued, his confidence building with each sentence, "since these measures are made as a gesture of good will, the responsible party cannot pass these costs along to the tenants. That would counteract the ameliorating effect."

Dave shook his head in amazement. "Did he sleep on a dictionary or something?"

It was obvious that Rodney was now building to his crescendo. His voice radiated power and he seemed to stand about six inches taller than he had just a few minutes before.

"To override the detrimental effect of your egregious 24.5 hour delay in responding to my urgent summons," he warned, "you need to issue an immediate statement to all affected tenants listing the ameliorating actions you will take and assuring them that such benefits will be issued with no increase in tenant expenditures."

There was a pause for the landlord to answer, but he seemed speechless for once.

"Well," Rodney concluded, "I won't keep you from your work then. I'll look for your statement this afternoon. Goodbye, Mr. Hagland." He set down the receiver with a decisive *thunk*.

Then he stepped over and reached for a doughnut.

"Wow." Brittany showered him with a look of glowing admiration.

"Don't take this wrong," I told him, "but you should be a lawyer."

He smiled bashfully as he picked up a napkin. "I might go to law school someday. But I've always been afraid of the idea of standing up and arguing in court."

"You don't need to stand up and argue in court," I pointed out, "if you can sit down and argue on the phone like that."

"Law school?" Dave said with a shake of his head. "I'm not so sure this firm isn't actually the best place

for you. What you said just now was all a bluff—
exaggeration, imaginary ailments, dangers blown up like
soap bubbles, ready to pop with the slightest touch. Just
enough illusion to get your point across."

He grinned. "Well, yeah."

"You fit our team. We're all smoke and mirrors."

It sounded to me like Dave was getting ready to
offer Rodney investigative work. That might mean less
for me. But maybe that wasn't so bad after all. Unlike
case work, I never had to take invoices home over the
weekend.

Sharing the workload all around might not be a bad
idea. And if it was, it was Dave's idea, so I could blame
him if I wasn't happy with it later.

I opened the box of doughnuts and found that
Brittany had picked up two apple-filled with crumb
topping without me even telling her what I wanted.

Working with people with powers of observation
had its good points.

I grabbed a doughnut and went back to watch the
Message of the Day march across my computer screen
in rainbow colors.

Author's
Notes

Competitive Jump Rope

My daughter was in second grade when she saw the Kangaroo Kids Precision Jump Rope Team perform at a college basketball halftime show. She came home, pulled out a jump rope and imediately started trying to jump rope while bouncing on a ball – in the living room. I sent her outside and insisted that she learn to jump rope without the ball first.

Following suggestions on the team's website, she taught herself to jump well enough to try out for the team in the spring. And that began a ten-year odyssey for both of us. She made the lowest level of the team and worked her way up over the years with extra practice at camps and workshops. Along the way I became a coach and learned at a much slower pace than the kids I taught. Gradually my daughter improved to the point where she was one of the ones performing at halftime shows, doing jump rope tricks on a hoppity hop just like she'd always wanted to do.

This story was born during her early years on the team when we were learning about the sport and had never seen any competitions. It was accepted by my editor at Heartsong Presents Mysteries, but then the publisher cancelled the series before I had written more than the first three chapters.

So during many of our years working with the jump rope team, *Roped In* lay dormant in a neglected directory on my computer.

When an agent proposed re-releasing the mystery series in ebook format, I considered going back to finish the third book. By that time, my daughter had started coaching and competing on the team, and I wrote the end of the first draft of the book during the 2013 USA Jump Rope National Championship in Long Beach, California. Coincidentally, my daughter's best event turned out to be the power event, triple unders. Back when I first outlined the story, I had no idea that this event would be a part of our lives at all.

For my own storytelling purposes, I have changed a number of things about the competitions and have done the jumpers a bit of an injustice. In *Roped In*, jumpers struggle to qualify for the national competition in one or two events. But in actuality, many of these athletes are so versatile that they qualify in as many as 13 different events, ranging from individual skills such as power jumping to team events like speed relays and double dutch and even large group routines incorporating multiple skills in one event. That jumpers can achieve a high level of competence in so many different events is truly amazing. If you ever get a chance to watch competitive or performing jumpers in action, I urge you to take a look. You won't be sorry.

To increase the tension and decrease the confusion in my story, I altered a few details about competitions. For example, five jumpers in each age group qualify for nationals, not four as in my story, and the process of qualifying to represent the U.S. at the world competitions is completely separate from the USA Jump Rope national competition. Does that make sense? It doesn't have to. It's real life. Only in fiction do we question whether events make sense.

If you'd like to learn more about competitive jump rope, check out these sites for information: USA Jump Rope (http://www.usajumprope.org) AAU Jump Rope (http://www.aaujumprope.org), World Jump Rope Federation (http://wjrweb.azurewebsites.net), International Rope Skipping Federation (http://www.fisac-irsf.org). You can also learn more by visiting the sites of individual teams such as the Kangaroo Kids (http://www.kangarookids.org).

About the Cover

The cover of *Roped In* depicts a high school girl jumping a "swish-over-the-head-triple-under." This particular jump is different from the triple unders that Hayley would have completed as part of the power competition. A basic triple under doesn't look much different than a single jump, albeit a pretty high one. In fact, judges use sound more than sight in determining whether jumps are single, double or triple—they are that fast.

This cover was designed and created by Meg Weidman using vector graphics to enhance a photograph of herself jumping. I can't thank her enough for all the work she put into creating such a dynamic image that captures the action and whimsy of the story.

Thank You

I'd like to thank everyone who helped me improve this book. In particular, I owe a special debt of gratitude to my editors, Candice Speare Prentice and Jim Weidman, for their careful attention to the story, as well as to my critique partners Christie Kelley, Janet Mullany, Kate Poole and Kathy Love. Most of all, I'd like to thank my daughter, Meg Weidman for her input on the story, her beautiful cover art, and for inspiring me with her tireless work ethic and boundless enthusiasm for the sport of jump rope.

OTHER BOOKS BY
K.D. HAYS/KATE DOLAN

The name K.D. Hays is a pseudonym I started using when I created my first contemporary story, since the voice I used differed so greatly from the style of my earlier historical novels.

As K.D. Hays, I've written the Karen Maxwell contemporary Christian mystery series and also a young adult/middle grade children's book.

GEORGE WASHINGTON STEPPED HERE
(Karen Maxwell Mystery #1)

Soccer mom Karen Maxwell gets her first "undercover" assignment—as a soccer mom. Her mission? Discover who stole the historical society's most treasured artifact.

WORTH ITS WEIGHT IN OLD (Karen Maxwell Mystery #2)

Someone's destroying art in an Ellicott City gallery. Karen has to find out who and fast or she'll be stuck back in the office with Rodney the "Office Maximizer."

TOTO'S TALE by K.D. Hays and Meg Weidman

What really happened in Oz? Find out from the one character who saw the whole thing from the ground up.

AVERY'S TREASURE by Kate Dolan

Pirate Henry Avery disappeared with one of the largest fortunes ever taken on the high seas, but he's afraid to spend it for fear of attracting too much attention. Tired of living like a pauper, his daughter sets sail with Captain Charles Vane to follow a "map" to the hidden treasure. This story follows the accounts of real pirates including Avery, Vane, Calico Jack Rackham and even Blackbeard.

LANGLEY'S CHOICE by Kate Dolan
A betrothed couple in colonial Maryland must grow up before they can grow together. The adventure takes them from the plantations near Elkridge Landing, to the high seas at the dawning of the age of piracy, to the frontier town of Charles Town, South Carolina, and then back to Maryland for the circus atmosphere of "court days."

A CERTAIN WANT OF REASON (Love & Lunacy #1) by Kate Dolan
A farcical romp through London in 1816, from the drawing rooms to Bedlam: A young woman who has devoted her life to caring for her eccentric siblings meets a lord feigning insanity in a desperate attempt to avoid an unwanted marriage.

THE APPEARANCE OF IMPROPRIETY (Love & Lunacy #2) by Kate Dolan
When Sophie Bayles inadvertently ruins a young man's chance for employment, she sets out to find him a new position. Even though he doesn't want her to.

DECEPTIVE BEHAVIOR (Love & Lunacy #3) by Kate Dolan
When it comes to men, Geni Bayles has made so many mistakes that she can't trust herself. But just as she agrees to settle for an arranged marriage, she falls in love—with a man who thinks she's somebody else.

DINNERS WITH MR. DANVILLE (Love & Lunacy #4) by Kate Dolan

Helen has seen first hand what the illogical emotion of love can do to people. So when her sister has the nerve to suggest that Helen has fallen in love with their neighbor, she sets out to prove her wrong. But she's not ready for the truth—and neither is Mr. Danville.

CHANGE OF ADDRESS by Kate Dolan

Moving away from their ancestral home just before Christmas, Amanda and her unconventional mother and sister meet their new neighbors under the worst of circumstances.

SENSE OF THE SEASON by Kate Dolan

When William Fletcher wakes up on the floor of the almshouse staring into the eyes of the local bully who had terrorized him during his teen years, he knows he's in trouble. Fortunately, she doesn't recognize him—at least, not at first....

RESTITUTION by Kate Dolan

Maryland 1774—A peddler paid to deliver potentially treasonous correspondence entices a Moravian widow and her sons to move to Annapolis. She becomes entranced with the refinements of English civilization while he grows committed to the patriot cause.

Thanks for reading! Please visit my website **katedolan.com** for the lastest news and to read my blog, Living History.

—Kate Dolan/K.D. Hays